Diary of a Confused Feminist

MUST DO BETTER

for anyone who needs courage – you're far braver than you think.

HODDER CHILDREN'S BOOKS

First published in Great Britain in 2022 by Hodder & Stoughton

1 3 5 7 9 10 8 6 4 2

Text copyright © Kate Weston, 2022
Images copyright © Shutterstock.com

The moral rights of the author have been asserted.

All characters and events in this publication, other than those clearly in the public domain, are fictitious and any resemblance to real persons, living or dead, is purely coincidental.

A CIP catalogue record for this book is available from the British Library.

ISBN 978 1 444 95506 4

Typeset in Franklin Gothic

Printed and bound by Clays Ltd, Elcograf S.p.A.

The paper and board used in this book are made from wood from responsible sources.

MIX
Paper from
responsible sources
FSC® C104740

Hodder Children's Books
An imprint of Hachette Children's Group
Part of Hodder & Stoughton Limited
Carmelite House
50 Victoria Embankment
London EC4Y 0DZ

An Hachette UK Company
www.hachette.co.uk

www.hachettechildrens.co.uk

Diary of a Confused Feminist

MUST DO BETTER

Kate Weston

Hodder
Children's
Books

Previously

On the Shit Show Formally Known as my 'Life'

1. Me and my two BFFs Sam and Millie became feminists (being a feminist means you believe in equality for EVERYONE and also SMASHING THE PATRIARCHY), and with some selfless and brave activism (think the Suffragettes with Snapchat) we attempted to educate the whole school. Sadly, this didn't *always* go to plan.

2. Our first bit of activism was cruelly cut short by Mr Clarke (headteacher/patriarchy personified) stopping us midway through writing #TimesUp on the playground in red paint (to symbolise menstrual blood), resulting in us accidentally immortalising the school creep #Tim instead.

3. When Sam and Millie got boyfriends, I thusly decided, in a perhaps not *entirely* feminist manner, that it was time to pursue my crush on Hot Josh – ASOS model, sex god and feminist ally (or so I thought . . .) And although my attempts to seduce him went *somewhat* rogue, he proved he wasn't bothered by me throwing a menstrual cup at his feet (you had to be there), when he ASKED ME OUT and KISSED ME ON THE HEAD.

4. BUT THEN: Hot Josh turned out to be Shit Josh and I was completely humiliated when I found out that he'd just been

using me to make my arch nemesis Terrible Trudy jealous and the two of them started going out. (And yes, I know it's not feminist to be down on another woman but trust me, Trudy is no member of the Sisterhood. She calls her crew The Bitches. Which is NOT COOL OR FEMINIST.)

5. I've always worried a lot and sometimes my worries take over a bit. After Hot/Shit Josh's rejection, I started to feel really down. Everyone else seemed like fully formed, grown-up adults, with boyfriends and *sex lives*, and I was just a kid, still wearing the M&S multipack knickers my mum buys for me and pining over a stupid boy. Not good enough, not feminist enough, not *enough*, full stop.

6. Things started to get even trickier in my head and I was diagnosed with depression and anxiety. I thought my life was over, but it turns out that loads of people suffer from the same thing, even celebrities like Emma Stone and Jennifer Lawrence, which TBH made me feel much better. I also started seeing a therapist called Sarah once a week. I still see her, and it's a really long journey, but I feel like she's really helping.

7. Back at school and feeling stronger – with a lot of help from my friends and family – I started Feminist Friday, a weekly post on the school blog about feminism. Henceforthly, taking the first steps in my future career as a feminist journalist and writer extraordinaire!

8. Meanwhile Shit Josh turned out to be Even-Shitter-Josh when we found out he was not only cheating on Trudy but also sending dick pics to literally all and sundry (I don't know what that expression means either).

9. We clubbed together as good feminists should, helped Terrible Trudy get rid of Shitty Josh and made sure he got his reckoning. Something which she will have no doubt completely forgotten about when we start back at school and her and The Bitches resume making our lives a misery again. Sometimes being a feminist is a thankless task.

10. In a final burst of activism, we launched the Feminist Society at the school play by making it rain tampons! (Again, you probably had to be there, but it was *majestic*.) And now we're ready for our first meeting on the first day of term, TOMORROW!

Monday 6th January

Kat Evans, reporting for feminist duty!

This is it! The start of a new year, a new term, and THIS term I am absolutely NOT going to make a tit of myself.

I'm also going to try and be as positive and upbeat as I can about everything, as I've read that it will bring light and joy into my life, apparently.

With that said, though . . . WHY must we go back to school? WHYYY? It's cold, dark and miserable. An atrocity. WHERE IS THE HUMANITY?

Vulva Vulva Vulva
Sam, Millie, Me

Me: Did you guys know that in Greek mythology there was an elderly woman called Baubo, who cheered people up by flashing them her vulva? Xxx

Sam: Oh god, Millie, she's started already and we're not even at school yet xxx

Millie: Kat, no. It's too early for vulvas, it's not even 7am. Xxxx

Me: So, you don't want me to show you my vulva when you're feeling sad to be back at school today then? Xxx

4

Sam: NO.

Millie: NO.

So ungrateful.

8.45 a.m.

The outside looking in
Staring out into the cold, hard, grey abyss of the playground and our prison-esque school beyond

Sam, Millie and I are standing on the precipice of re-entering school, AKA Hell. Hades. The Lake of Fire.

Thick black coats cover our maroon uniforms, black sunglasses protect our eyes from the harsh winter glare (or lack of it – to be honest we're just wearing them to give the world a sort of blurry haze), and black fingerless gloves prevent . . . nothing, least of all the tips of our fingers from getting frostbite, but they DO look quite arty and tortured, which is how we feel today.

The joy has been stripped from our cold, red faces, as we pass one single cup of bitter black coffee between us at the gate. All three of us know that the moment we walk through it all freedom and fun is over.

Some may think our state of mourning at the end of the Christmas holidays is over dramatic. Those people are wrong, mostly around the age of forty-five and are the very people responsible for shipping us all back here this morning.

This time yesterday I was still happily burrito-ed in bed, with my dog Bea and a copy of *The Second Sex* – a MONSTER of a feminist book which, over the holiday, I have more than once dropped upon my face after falling asleep, nearly causing black eyes and a broken nose. (Now I think of it, my nose does feel a little squishier than it did before.) Honestly, the peril I put myself in for feminism may not quite be what Pussy Riot went through, but it's up there.

I take a sip of black coffee and pass the cup on, preparing to put my best foot forward. Which is a rubbish saying, by the way, NO ONE has a best foot. All feet are disgusting. The hooves of Satan.

I'm aware I'm doing a lot of hell chat this morning, but Christmas is *over*, and after the tinsel and Santa hats come eternal damnation, fiery hell pits and the return to school.

'Right, then,' Sam says, wagging the empty cup.

'Right, then,' Millie says.

'Nope,' I say.

We traipse forwards into the playground, and I feel like a new and unsuspecting lamb, taking its first shaky steps into a brave new world. Whatever – positivity! I can do this!

Today also marks the start of the Feminist Society, the shining light in a dark day! It's set to be the greatest achievement of my life so far, and I feel genuinely positive about it. I've got my shit together this term. I'm going to prove myself to be a strong, intelligent, patriarchy-smashing femini—

WHAT. THE. FUCK?

Almost as if she's been waiting, poised by the gate, Terrible Trudy appears without warning and swings the BIGGEST HANDBAG I HAVE EVER SEEN at us, as soon as we set foot on school soil. I'm knocked off my feet with a whoosh, rendered legless by the weapon of mass hand-baggage smacking me in the face. The three of us go down like dominoes. I become a cartoon character as I fall into Millie, frantically clutching her for stability, who in turn falls into Sam, until the three of us land on the cold hard ground, a pile of limbs and embarrassment.

I feel like roadkill. The familiar sensation of gravel in my face and shame in my soul has brought me right back to earth and it's no surprise that I look up to see Trudy and the huge, black Chanel bag, looming over us like a chic wrecking ball.

'Ooops!' she says, putting her hand over her mouth with faux embarrassment. 'My mistake.'

As my absolute nemesis, the worst person in the school and head of her little crew The Bitches, Trudy never does anything by accident. I should imagine she's been practising that bag swing for maximum devastation since New Year.

Trudy's smiling down at us smugly, the world's most fashionable weapon back on her arm and The Bitches forming their protective barrier around her.

There are five Bitches in total:

Trudy: Head Bitch. Constantly on the lookout for new and inventive ways to Ruin. My. Life.

Amelie: Second Bitch in Command/Deputy Bitch/Vice Principal Bitch

Tiffany: Third Bitch in Command. Always with an eye on the deputy prize

Nia: Fourth Bitch in Command. Usually found stuck in Amelie and Tiffany's shadows, not to mention Trudy's

Tia: Just happy to be included

Trudy is the only person I know who can make the word 'feminist' sound on par with syphilis. It's been her mission to ruin my life since preschool when I made an enemy of her by not simply handing over my favourite cuddly bunny when she tried to steal it. She reigns only by terror.

'Already scrabbling around on the floor, I see. New year, same losers,' she quips, peering over her massive designer sunglasses.

I want to retaliate and say something witty, cutting and superior, but my mind is blank. Why does this always happen? I'll be sitting on the loo later and think of the most victorious comeback, with only the loo roll to tell, and the loo roll never appreciates my wit.

'Do Chanel know you're using their bags as violent weapons?' Sam questions.

'Probably not, since that's CLEARLY a fake,' Millie responds, brushing her knees and offering me a hand as she gets up.

'You know Chanel only has one n. Two and it's Channel,' I say, proud of myself for finally saying something witty in the moment. No one needs to know that I only know this because I've been burned before.

'Christmas present? Was it filled with coal?' Millie asks, shaking gravel from her coat.

We're not normally this mean, but this is a girl who's tortured us since the age of four. And it would seem she is indeed suffering selective memory loss about the way we rescued her from Shit Josh last year.

'Like any of you could tell what was real and what was fake,' she says, tossing her hair. 'Anyway, welcome back, LOSERS. Come on, Bitches.'

With that Trudy and her crew flounce off towards school.

And so it begins. We stumble towards form room dusting each other off.

Strength and positivity left on the tarmac.

8.50 a.m.

Matt: Ouch! Saw you guys falling victim to Trudy from the common room. Happy return to hell-day! Xxx

Matt: P.S. That bag is minging. If it's actually Chanel I will eat my own toenails.

Matt's my other BFF, he's in the year above and way, way cooler than me. He moved next door with his mum Sandra when his dad ran off with his PA. His mum went through a tricky period – painting all the walls in their house red was a real statement, he said it felt very womb-like – and Matt spent a lot of time hanging out at ours. We've been really close ever since. I was the person Matt came out to first, and he was the first of my friends I spoke to after my diagnosis last term.

Pretty livid he didn't rescue me from the bag of doom after all we've been through, to be honest.

9 a.m.
Form room

The familiar smell of musty trainers left in lockers hits me as we walk into form room, and I see everyone there just the same as before, doing the same things and probably having the same conversations. Happy New Groundhog Day.

Comedy Krish (the school comedian) and Polly (thrower of MIGHTY parties) are trying to ignore something that creepy Tim Matthews – he of accidental legendary #Tim fame – is saying to them. Knowing him, it's probably some elaborate lie about how many girls he got off with over Christmas when we all know that he's got no game.

Trudy's somehow made it here before us, probably propelled by glee after the playground handbagging, and is sitting on Tia and Nia's desk, clasping her vicious weapon. Amelie and Tiffany are buzzing around behind her even though the three of them aren't even in this form room.

Sam and Millie take their seats next to me and we try to avoid #Tim's gaze as he stares at us while rummaging noisily in his bag. I officially do not want *anything* to do with whatever's going on there.

'I'm SO missing Trinidad right now,' Sam says unwrapping herself from her huge, thick scarf.

'I bet. It's so bloody cold here,' Millie says rubbing her hands together.

Sam got back from Trinidad two days ago, after her annual trip to see her family there. Her parents grew up and fell in love in Trinidad but moved to the UK before they had Sam. I for one could never understand leaving Trinidad to come and live . . . here.

'Nan's practically invited Dave to come stay with us next Christmas. It was mortifying. We were on a video call, she butted in and started telling him how handsome he is. I COULD HAVE DIED.'

'Speaking of embarrassing,' Millie says, 'have you seen Issy and Freddie together lately, Kat?'

Freddie is my disgusting little brother in the year below, who is SOMEHOW going out with Millie's angelic, beautiful little sister. It's a relationship which really hammers home my own spinster, single status.

'I try not to,' I say.

'They're just so gross, always touching each other.'

'Ewww. I still can't believe that child has a girlfriend. You know Mum and I caught him and Dad using our menstrual cups as pretend ear trumpets over Christmas?'

'Oh my god!' Sam looks mortified on my behalf. 'Please tell me you won't be using them again?'

'Don't worry, we got new ones. No one wants a waxy vagina. You should have seen Freddie's face when he realised what they were. He was in the shower so long afterwards I thought he'd come out part seal.'

'Dad loves him,' Millie says. 'Especially since he gave him that old phone when Mum rage-stuffed his on Christmas Day.'

I feel bad that when Millie phoned on Christmas Day saying her mum had stuffed her dad's phone up the turkey's butt during an argument I snorted with laughter and had to pretend I was choking on a festive nut.

'Honestly, I still don't even know what they were fighting about. They were like a pair of rowing toddlers.'

I can kind of understand the motive to stuff a phone in a turkey. When Freddie and I were toddlers, we'd stuff each other's toys down the loo. I still think if Barbie was a more realistic shape, we'd never have lost her to that U-bend.

'I hope they go back to normal soon. It's starting to get a bit miserable,' Millie says.

'Would you like me to cheer you up by flashing you my—'

'NO!' Sam and Millie both shout at once.

'How about pictures of topless Harry Styles and a puppy?' Sam offers her phone.

Millie nods enthusiastically so I decide now is not the right time to point out that that's objectification and not good feminism as we all huddle happily round Sam's phone.

9.05 a.m.

We must have all been too deep down a topless Harry Styles hole to notice him coming, but suddenly a smell akin to the leftover Christmas cheeseboard at my nan's house is wafting sinisterly over our perving joy. I look up from Harry Styles to find #Tim, close enough to lick my eyeball and holding a mysterious box in his sweaty hands. I have an uneasy feeling in the pit of my uterus.

'KAT!' he says loud enough for everyone in form room to turn around and stare at me with a mix of pity and intrigue. 'HAPPY NEW YEAR!'

I'm staring at him, frozen in fear. WHY ME? My fingers have started tingling. It's possible that I may actually be dying from embarrassment, or might suffer from imminent spontaneous human combustion, because my once-cold face is now burning up like a furnace.

I can feel Millie and Sam shuffling away from me at speed, sideways, like little worker crabs with a job to do. I'll remember this.

'I've had time to reflect over the holidays and feel that last term I may have made some poor decisions. I shouldn't have taken Josh's side. I should have stuck with my old friends. The ones I've had since Reception, who have stuck by me through thick and thin. Like you.' He seems to be shaking a fist, like he's making some kind of impassioned speech, the ominous box still clasped in his other clammy paw.

WHEN HAVE WE EVER BEEN FRIENDS?

The only time I speak to him is to either tell him not to harass me any more or to point out that 'the more you feel them the bigger they get' is NOT scientific. I have certainly never stood by him through thick OR thin. I feel trapped at this desk and unable to escape the horror.

'I'm sorry for my actions last term and I will do everything I can to redeem myself. I hope that one day you can forgive me but, in the meantime, I got you this moisturiser. My mum said that a good place to start with apologies for girls is with something that they can . . . pamper . . . themselves with.' He opens the box and thrusts it towards me, a grim smirk crossing his lips.

It takes me a while to fully register what I'm looking at and when I do, I feel like I'm going through varying stages of disgust and mortification.

It is moisturiser all right . . . for vaginal dryness.

'Oh, man,' Krish whistles as the whole class looks on at my horrified face. 'Less facial, more vajacial. That's for a hoohoo!'

#Tim looks proud while the room erupts into laughter and I can hear Trudy behind me muttering something about it being the most action I'll ever get. I know I should correct Krish and say it's a vulva not a hoohoo, but I'm too far down this shame spiral to form any kind of sentence.

For the love of Mary Wollstonecraft, get it together, Kat!

Sam and Millie have slid so far down in their chairs that they're nearly under the table laughing. I'm just staring at him in complete disbelief.

'Come on, time to sit down, perv,' Krish says, pushing #Tim away from us after what seems like a year.

The room finally starts to descend into chatter again as #Tim whistles off back to his seat with his tube of lube.

I turn to thank Krish but he's distracted by something over by the door. I follow his gaze and see an incredibly beautiful girl, who I've never seen before, walking across the room. She's got long, glossy, dark hair, dark eyes, and a tan, but the subtle kind, the kind that the celebs have on Insta, not the ones that you try and do at home only to find that you've made yourself into a walking Wotsit.

She's wearing our school uniform but somehow she looks like a woman in it, rather than the three-year-old I revert to as soon as I put mine on. I'm also one hundred per cent sure that her skirt is NOT regulation length.

She walks across the room and sits down at an empty desk towards the back, the whole room still and watching. She keeps her head down, puts her bag on the desk, a kind of cool black tote thing, and pulls out her phone. She's clearly trying to pretend she hasn't noticed that everyone's staring at her, despite the fact that we're all creepily gripped. Who IS she?

She's coping well under pressure, whoever she is. With this many people staring at me I'd probably have fallen over, shown everyone my pants, and accidentally flung a menstrual-related item out of my bag and across the room.

'Who *is* that?' Sam asks.

'No idea,' I say.

'She's hot,' Krish says, appearing next to us and closer to the new girl.

The three of us turn our heads and glare at him but he doesn't notice. Eventually Millie breaks her stare and shrugs.

'Agreed,' she says as Sam and I both give in and nod too.

I see #Tim out of the corner of my eye. He's putting his gross gift back into its box while staring at her. I worry he might be considering re-gifting it to her.

'Whoever she is, we should probably protect her from *that*,' I say watching #Tim getting up from his seat and starting to move towards her, feminine moisturiser in hand.

'Oh god no.' Sam puts her hands over her face.

'Morning! Hope you all had a nice holiday.' Just in the nick of time, Miss Mills, our form tutor has entered the room, giving the new girl a lucky escape.

Miss Mills is my favourite teacher. She teaches English and supported me to start the Feminist Friday blog posts and the Feminist Society.

The whole form spins to face the front of the class, Trudy, Amelie and Tiffany scuttle out and #Tim sits down so abruptly that he misses his chair and lands on the floor. Still staring at new girl. Still holding his grubby gift.

'Hope you all had an enjoyable Christmas. You'll notice we've got a new face this term,' Miss Mills says, ignoring #Tim and heading over to where new girl is sitting. 'This is Sienna. She'll be joining us for the rest of the year.'

Sienna looks like she wants the ground to swallow her up, her cheeks reddening, until Miss Mills walks away again, and she bows her head back down to look at her desk.

I feel a bit bad for her. It must be hard starting a new school at this point in the year. Also, weird, though – who moves schools the term before GCSEs? I wonder why she's moved?

Maybe I'll invite her to the Feminist Society later. See if we can make her feel welcome . . . or find out what the deal is.

9.15 a.m.

'Hey, I'm Kat,' I say, approaching Sienna's desk as everyone preps to go to class.

'Oh, hey,' she says, barely looking up.

'I'm head of the Feminist Society, and we're having our first meeting today,' I say, gesturing to where Sam and Millie are waiting for me. 'We just wanted to invite you along. It's 12.30 in Room 404.'

'Oh. Thanks,' she says, still looking down.

'Cool! Maybe see you there?' I say and she nods.

She seems either shy or aloof and I can't quite work out which.

'I wonder how come she's changed schools so close to exams?' Millie asks applying a slick of gel to her ever-growing brows. They were one of her Christmas projects and they seem to have flourished. I'm pretty impressed. The only personal growth I managed was yet more pubic hair.

Millie's other Christmas project was trying to find a local drama group so that she can work towards her lifelong goal of becoming an actress one day. Unfortunately, that didn't go as well as the brows because it turns out this town's AmDram group consists of a single eighty-year-old woman who will only perform one-woman monologues about spiders.

'I know. How do you make friends at this stage? We should be super nice to her,' I say.

'Of course,' says Sam grabbing the brow gel from Millie and inspecting it.

'Did you hear the latest on Shit Josh by the way?' Sam says, her eyes lighting up.

'I have not, nor do I want to hear anything about him. I am above that,' I say, head held high. 'He's inconsequential to me now and besides I'm way too mature for idle gossip. We should talk about something worthier of our time, like the Feminist Society.'

'Oh, OK,' Sam says, looking over to Millie.

'Was it about the nuns?' Millie whispers, giving me a side-eye.

What? Now she's piqued my interest and I'm livid.

'Yes! Hilarious,' says Sam. 'And what about the thing about him and the army camp in Scotland?' They both fall about laughing.

Oh, FFS.

'You've basically told me half the story now, so I'm going to need you to finish it and tell me the whole thing even though I SAID I was happy not knowing. Thank you very much,' I say, still trying to maintain my dignity and be above it all, while Sam and Millie grin at me. They knew *full well* that I would crack eventually. It's very unfeminist of them actually.

'WELL, since you asked . . .' says Sam. 'His mum sent him to an army camp on one of those remote Scottish islands over Christmas to reform him. He was with lots of other wrong-doers who had been sent by their parents. Then when he came back, they got him a place at a boarding school in Switzerland, run by nuns, for the sexually depraved. He'll finish school there and hopefully never come back.' Wow, that IS good gossip. Worth losing the moral high ground for.

'There's another rumour that he got thrown off the island after three days because he was found wanking a stray sheep, but no one actually believes that,' Millie adds.

'I heard it was a goat,' Sam argues.

'Either way, only God can save him now,' I say in a faux serious tone, clasping my hands in prayer.

Deep down, even though I know that thing with the sheep

probably didn't happen, I'm still thinking, *If it did happen, that means he found a sheep sexier than me.* That really is quite the achievement. Kat Evans, the sexiest thing in the room, unless there happen to be farm animals about.

'ANYWAY,' I say, trying to steer my brain towards more feminist matters, 'I think we've spent quite enough time talking about this rubbish. How's the Feminist Society banner looking?'

'All done!' Sam says patting her bag.

'SHOW US!' Millie and I say excitedly.

'OK!' Sam takes her bulging bag off her shoulder and starts pulling out a never-ending banner, like a magician pulling bunting out of a hat.

Sam doesn't realise how talented she is. She's currently waiting to find out if she got a scholarship to an art summer camp. It's one that her sister Jas used to get every year, and Millie and I know she'll get it but she's not sure. I think she feels like she's in Jas's shadow a bit, especially since she started at London College of Fashion.

The banner's finally out and laid across the counter by the sinks and, OH WOW, it's beautiful – all sparkly and covered in hot pink leopard print and drawings of prominent feminists like Emmeline Pankhurst, Beyoncé and Michelle Obama.

'Oh, Sam . . .' I say, lost for words.

'It's AMAZING, Sam!' Millie says, giving her a hug.

'Well, that's it, then,' I say. 'I guess we're all set.'

'Aye, aye, captain,' Sam says, saluting.

'So what do you think you'll say?' Millie asks.

'I think as it's a first meeting, I'll just ask everyone why they've come, and what feminism means to them, and take it from there,' I say.

I mean, what could possibly go wrong?

Last term when I learned about feminism, I thought it would give me confidence and help me feel a bit more womanly. I guess I always felt like I wasn't quite good enough as a woman or as a person. But then I worried that I wasn't even *feminist enough* to be a feminist, as if it was an exclusive club I couldn't be part of because I wasn't clever enough or womanly enough or because I liked make-up and fancied boys. Also, because I have tiny boobs and I'd never done the thing where you put a mirror between your legs and stare your actual vulva in the eye.

But since then I've learned the most important thing about being a feminist, which is that *anyone can be one*. You just have to believe that everyone should have equal rights. And try not to waste time worrying about whether or not you are more sexually attractive than a sheep.

11 a.m.
History

It's the last class before lunch and the Feminist Society meeting, and I am trying to concentrate and NOT get distracted by the rumour I just heard that we might be going on a school trip to our French exchange school. The one where Sexy Sébastien goes, who I met when the exchangers came over here last year.

Last term I felt bad that literally EVERYONE except me had a boyfriend, but this term I'm above that. I'm busy with the Feminist Society and I'm definitely not going to bow down to social pressures and become obsessed with being in a relationship. Nope. Not me. Even if we are going to France . . . even if Sexy Sébastien walked in here right now in just his pants and asked for my consent to snog my face off, I would simply say 'NO, SIR-EEE! I am too busy campaigning for equality and smashing the patriarchy.'

Anyway, he's *not* here and Millie and Sam are already going out with the only acceptable guys in our school. Sam's boyfriend Dave is captain of the school football team and Millie's boyfriend Nick is in Sixth Form. They got together last term when she played Juliet in the school production of *Romeo and Juliet* and he played Romeo. She's been in love with him since Reception. The way she talks about their relationship you'd think they were Gigi and Zayn.

As I said, though, I'm totally fine on my own. I have definitely not spent a single minute of this class daydreaming about Sexy Sébastien, the *only* person that I've ever really got in any way sexy with (hence the name).

On the last night of the French exchange in Year Ten there was a party. After an ill-advised dalliance with the punch, I decided that my French, and in particular my French accent, was very good, maybe even seductive? So, I went over to Sexy Sébastien and his friends, who were looking nonchalant and cool with their skateboards, and made my very slinky approach.

Or so I thought. Millie and Sam told me afterwards I looked like I was performing a tiptoe mime, but I am pretty sure they were just winding me up.

After what felt like hours but apparently was only twenty minutes, in which I slipped back into English but kept my very bad French accent, dribbled slightly, drank more punch, and became very slurry, we proceeded to go off to a more secluded area of the garden (fine, it was a bush, OK? We went into a bush) and after some snogging (I believe that if I was quite salivary before, I may have been a LAKE of saliva here) Sébastien nonchalantly (he did *everything* nonchalantly – so sexy) grabbed my sweaty hand and put it into his pants. Unfortunately, I had NO idea what to do, freaked out, and said 'awww', patted his penis like you would a dog's head, and came running out of the bush again.

According to the girls, afterwards I apparently just kept repeating 'I pat' and 'good dog' over and over again. It took about half an hour for them to realise that I had greeted my first experience with a penis in the same way you would a cute cockapoo.

I didn't really see Sébastien again after that. I tried not to. But now that it's possible we might actually be going to his school in France, I may just have to sneak a peek at his Instagram.

I obviously WON'T let it distract me from the Feminist Society and smashing the patriarchy. I'm only thinking about it now because I'm bored. I mean, it's not my fault this class isn't relatable enough. No one does needlework any more – why would I give a shit about a French tapestry?

I SHOULD be thinking about the Feminist Society meeting, though. I'm actually a bit nervous about it. I really hope I don't make a twat of myself in front of loads of people, again.

I know Mr Clarke wasn't happy about the way that we advertised the first meeting, because we did slightly hijack the school play: in his words 'throwing personal products at parents is not how we broach important political debate'. The fact he called them 'personal products' says everything you need to know about Mr 'Prude' Clarke. They're period products, sir. Period.

With him as head teacher, and the fact that Freddie told me over Christmas there's a group of boys in his year who've started cat-calling girls, the school needs feminism more than ever. This meeting is going to be the start of something really great, I can feel it in my fallopian tubes.

12.30 p.m.

Room 404
The first meeting of the Feminist Society

The banner is up, we've set out as many seats as we can cram into this teeny tiny room, and . . . there is no one here.

Not a soul.

I've started to wonder what's worse: making a fool of myself in front of loads of people, or no one being here for me to make a fool of myself in front of?

Matt and Nick have to work on an English project, and Dave has football practice. Who else would come? Why didn't I think about this?

'Of course, people will come. It's bang on 12.30. Give it a minute,' Sam says, rubbing my tense shoulders.

'Yeah, I'm sure Issy's coming,' Millie says, getting her phone out and raising an eyebrow at it. 'Oh. She's got gymnastics practice.'

No one's coming. It's just going to be the three of us in a tiny grim room. Made to feel even grimmer by the ten thousand empty chairs we've laid out that are now staring back at us.

I feel like Mr Clarke assigned us this room on purpose, to keep us oppressed. The walls probably used to be white but are kind of yellow now, the carpet is a filthy grey with (fortunately) unidentifiable staining and there's only one single tiny window which we've needed to open on account of the fact it smells so bad in here. The three of us are shivering in our coats and scarves but the cold is preferable to the smell of gone-off milk that was here when we arrived.

12.35 p.m.

There are five people here now. Not quite the crowd I was expecting, but given my earlier panic, I'm a confusing mixture of comforted and disappointed.

There are two girls from Sixth Form and three from Year

Seven, so at least we've got quite the spectrum, even if it's sparse.

'We'll just wait a few minutes and see if anyone else is coming before we start,' I say with more confidence than I feel.

12.40 p.m.
Confidence level: currently zero

We waited five agonising minutes to see if anyone else is coming but I don't think they are. I swear I saw Sienna walk past at one point, and I thought she was coming in, but she didn't.

'So, maybe we should start before we all freeze our tits off, haha!' I say jovially, to no response, just five expectant faces staring at me as I feel my face burning, again. 'So, erm, maybe we'll start with why you guys came? Why do you think the school needs a Feminist Society? And what does feminism mean to you?'

I feel like I'm having an out-of-body experience. Five people staring at you with red noses and chattering teeth feels quite judgemental actually.

1.15 p.m.

I was worried that no one was going to say anything, but now I'm worried this one girl from Sixth Form called Jane won't stop. She's been talking for literally twenty minutes already about upskirting, slut-shaming, mansplaining and intersectionality. All these important terms and I barely even know what they mean. For most of them I can guess, but she uses them with such ease that I'm beginning to wonder if SHE should be running this group instead of me.

'So, I think that's why we need one, because until there is an equal society, it doesn't matter how smart we are, how well we do in our A Levels, we'll never lessen the gender pay gap so we're destined never to earn as much as men!'

Her monologue/TED Talk started with the first time she was oppressed by the patriarchy in nursery (being forced to play with a doll when she wanted to set up a pretend bank) and has finished with the gender pay gap. She knows so much more than me that I'm starting to feel like a complete fraud.

As Jane sits down to five-person applause, I find myself completely lost for words. Everyone's staring at me, my cheeks are burning yet again, and I can't think of a single thing to say. Luckily, I'm saved by a knock at the door and all of us turn to see a tiny Year Seven or Eight boy walk in looking slightly petrified and lost.

'Excuse me, miss,' he says. 'Are you my clitoris? Have you seen my labia?'

I'm staring at him. He's staring right back at me looking genuinely distressed, and then he turns and bolts out of the door.

For a moment, I'm too confused to say anything. Then I feel the rage boiling as I march to the door. I know exactly who's behind this, and it's confirmed when I look down the corridor in time to see the boy run up to Comedy Krish who hands him a fiver before running away himself.

'See, it's immaturity like that that we have to deal with on a daily basis!' says Jane, gesturing at the door angrily.

The worst thing is, I actually really want to laugh, and when I look over at Millie and Sam I can see they already are. They have their scarves over their mouths, their shoulders are shaking, and their eyes are watering.

Oh god, and now I have even less of an idea of what to say. I feel like whatever it is won't hold any weight against Jane's feminist speech anyway.

'OK,' I say with as much authority as I can possibly muster. 'Let's leave it here and pick this up again next week.'

At least that gives me a chance to research everything Jane was talking about.

Not quite the patriarchy-smashing start to the Feminist Society I was hoping for.

1.30 p.m.
Forlorn in form

Well, THAT was a disaster. Five people, and I bet none of them come back. Jane will probably set up her own Feminist Society because she thinks I'm so inept. I already felt like a big joke before Labia Boy's interruption. Comedy Krish and his buddy were just the final clitoris in the coffin, and after he was so kind earlier too. At least I can prepare better for next week now, I guess.

2.30 p.m.
Chemistry

I think Chemistry would sit better with me if they just called stuff what it actually was. It's so confusing to have to remember what all the letters mean and some of them aren't even the start of the word that they represent.

I can't concentrate anyway, though because I'm just re-living the shame and embarrassment I feel over my Feminist Society failure. I can't believe I ever thought that I would be good at running a society. I must have been high off all the Christmas cheese twists or something.

I'm trying really hard not to let my thoughts spiral, but I can't help worrying that the reason no one came to the meeting was because of me. Maybe if someone cooler was doing it more people would come?

If there was a Feminism Head Office they'd probably call me and say: 'Thank you for your good intentions, but actually you're ruining everything, please cease and desist using the words *feminist* or *feminism*. You are a deterrent.'

3.30 p.m.
The playground
Heading out on evening release from the prison

The three of us are shuffling through the playground, just glad to have made it through another day of Terrible Trudy, heinous

#Tim, and another feminist fail for me. So much for a fresh start.

'Might go home and work on this week's Feminist Friday,' I say. 'Maybe if I write a good one, I can get some more people to come to the meetings.' I'm also going to look up intersectionality, upskirting, mansplaining, slut-shaming, and all the other terms Jane used and I only pretended to understand. Like the feminist fraud I am.

'What you doing it on this week?' Sam asks.

'Not sure yet. I need to go home and get my research on, I think. What are you guys up to?'

'Going to hang out with Jas some more, before she heads back to uni next week.'

'Nick's coming over!' Millie says, joyful that she finally gets some time alone with him without her parents around.

I see Sienna up ahead standing on her own and in some kind of second wind I start feeling a bit bold. I'm going to try to do one last good thing today.

'Hey! Wanna join us?' I ask, walking up to her and giving her a big smile.

'No thanks,' she says bluntly, walking off towards the gates.

I feel like I've been slapped.

'Well, that was rude,' Millie says as she and Sam come and join me.

'At least we won't be wasting time trying to talk to her any more,' Sam reasons.

'Absolutely not,' Millie says.

'Agreed,' I say, still flustered from the insult.

I watch Sienna walk off, but something weird happening by the gates distracts me.

'What the hell?' asks Sam, as we all take in what's ahead of us.

There appears to be a whole dance troupe heading our way, and they've just started playing the loudest music I've ever heard. It's a stampede dressed in fluorescent pink and sequins.

'What's going on?' I shout over the music, looking towards the dayglo display in front of us.

As if by magic, Trudy appears in front of them, microphone in hand (what MONSTER gave her that?), and The Bitches at her side. The dancers freeze and the music stops.

'TRUDY HAS AN ANNOUNCEMENT! TRUDY HAS AN ANNOUNCEMENT!!' Tiffany and Amelie are screaming into microphones. I see Matt's amused little face pop out of the door to the Sixth Form block, with Nick's just behind.

'This'll be good,' Millie whispers, giving Nick a wave and blowing him a kiss.

I see Sienna's stopped against the gate, looking very interested for once, as Trudy's voice booms across the playground.

'You are all cordially invited to my sweet sixteenth birthday at The Den on Saturday 15th February,' Trudy shouts down the microphone. 'Please take a flyer, details of appropriate gifts and dress code can be found on the website. The theme is Prom, so bring a date or be a loser,' she finishes, looking pointedly at me.

She drops the mic with a thud and struts out of the school

gates and away from the crime scene she created. The music goes back on and the dancers dance out behind her.

I glance back to where Sienna was. She seems to have disappeared too.

'Take a flyer, take a flyer,' Tia and Nia are saying as they try and pass them around the playground.

Millie, Sam and I all stare at each other.

'That was . . . quite a lot,' Sam says.

Nick and Matt come and join us, and they're looking equally bemused.

'It sounds TERRIBLE. We're going, though, right?' Matt says as he takes a picture of the flyer, presumably to send to his boyfriend Si who doesn't go to our school.

They met at life-drawing class and bonded over their attempts at professionalism in the face of a naked penis.

'Oh, absolutely,' I say.

The Den is the only club within a 10,000-mile radius. It's supposed to be pretty grim there. I've heard stories of people getting pubic lice just from being in the toilets. Rumour has it the carpet is so riddled with semen that you can get chlamydia from direct contact with the floor. I'll wear two pairs of knickers that night, just in case.

3.50 p.m.
Walking home with Matt and Si

I'm going to be so happy to get home after today. How can one day feel like actual years? Might just get back into bed, pull the covers over my head and pretend none of it ever happened.

I'm about to say goodbye to Matt and Si, when our heads are turned by the sound of criminally loud music coming from my house.

'Is that . . . Michael Bublé?' Si asks.

'Babe, what day is it?' Matt asks as we all head towards the front door with trepidation.

I look at Matt, the realisation dawning.

'Oh crap . . .' I say, feeling the panic rise.

I turn my key gingerly in the lock, but as I push it open our worst fears are both confirmed and revealed.

Every year, on this same day, my mum asks my dad to clear away Christmas, something that would be a perfectly normal task for anyone else. Not Dad, though.

He gets sad that the presents, tree and Mariah Carey all have to go back in their boxes and so, ignoring his normal rules on day-drinking, he throws himself a 'post-Christmas-party' to keep himself perky during the process. Usually by the time we get back he's rolling around like a pissed Santa.

Dad 'works' from home, as a comedy writer. (He writes a sitcom about a single father and his teenage daughter . . . Nat. Guess what? Last year, Nat discovered menstrual cups for the first time. Can't think WHERE he got that idea from.) Hence it's him that's tasked with clearing away Christmas every year, even though he's the LEAST responsible member of the household.

33

'Kids!' Dad shouts over Bublé's 'Christmas Hits' when he clocks us.

'You OK there, Dad?' I ask, suspecting that he has drunk himself to the point where he thinks he can sing – a dangerous and psychologically damaging place to be. Our poor dog, Bea, is cowering in her bed.

'HOW WAS SCHOOOUUUUULL?' Yep, very drunk.

'It was good, Dad. How was your day? Busy?' I ask as Matt and Si sit at the counter, their chins resting in their hands, like they're watching a particularly gripping episode of *Hollyoaks*.

'Well, kids, Mum said she wanted NO TRACE of Christmas.' He makes a slashing movement with his hand and shakes his head, nearly taking out the five empty glasses sitting in front of him and making Matt and Si duck for cover. 'So, I may have drunk all of the leftover wine that we had open! AND THEN, I did finish the chocolate liqueurs, because they are Christmas, so I did eat it and them and the cheese that was in the shape of a Christmas tree because there must BRIE NO CHRISTMAS. And I said Port SALUT to all the Christmas cheese. And THEN, I danced with Bea, we did the most beautiful dance, and I did a sit down and now I am ready for a liiiiittle nap.' He makes a small pinching gesture with his fingers and starts singing while Matt and Si join in, egging him on, like the pair of little shits that they are.

No wonder poor Bea's in bed. She looks up at me with a pleading expression.

'So the tree's still up, then?' I ask.

'UP!' He says, raising his arms to the sky. 'Bea likes it. She is at one in her natural habitat with the wonder of nature.'

Bea waggles an eyebrow at me and hunkers down further in her bed.

'It's such a beautiful tree, isn't it?' Matt says encouragingly. 'Wouldn't you just like to dance with her?'

'But, Matthew! I am a married man! Although I'm sure one dance can't hurt . . .' Dad says, springing up and heading into the living room, Matt and Si hot on his heels. He takes a branch in each hand and attempts a tango. The tree sheds what needles are left, and Dad sheds his dignity, as he falls to the floor.

'Dad, I think you've reached the nap phase of Christmas clear-up,' I say.

'SSSSS a good idea,' he says, standing up unsteadily. 'I miss the baby Jesus. Everything was nice with the baby Jesus. And the mince pies. We should have MINCE PIES ALL YEAR ROUND.'

'I know, Dad, I know,' I say, ushering him up the stairs to his room so he can sleep it off, his yearly sacrifice for us all completed for another year.

I text Mum:

> **Me:** As predicted. He's drunk on liqueurs again. Fourth year running x

Mum: Perfect. No one eats them otherwise! X

Mum: Tree still up? X

We head upstairs with Bea, who seems eager to spend time with someone who won't breathe hot, chocolatey brandy over her.

4.30 p.m.
My bedroom

'What's this about a new girl?' Matt asks.

'This close to GCSEs?' Si says, sounding shocked.

'She's in my form, she's called Sienna. I tried to talk to her twice and the first time she barely said anything, the second time she was just RUDE. I thought she was shy, but I don't know. She outright rejected me the second time. I felt silly.'

'Don't feel silly! You were being kind! That's who you are! It's her loss,' Matt says.

'How peculiar. I wonder what her story is? Something fishy is afoot, I feel!' Si says making a fake monocle with his fingers.

'And how did the meeting go?' Matt asks, putting his legs over Si's lap as they languish on my bed and I sit on the floor. Don't worry about me, guys.

'Awful,' I say with my head in my hands.

'How so?' Si asks picking up Matt's foot and massaging it (the most amount of action that bed's ever seen).

'No one came.'

36

'No one?' Matt asks, raising an eyebrow with the knowledge that I can, at times, be one to catastrophise.

'Five people came.'

'Five's good!' Si says.

'Five plus you three makes eight! That's a good amount!' Matt says.

'It's just not . . . well, I just thought . . . maybe there'd be more. Like, there can't only be eight people in our whole school that agree that everyone should be equal? And deserve equal pay and opportunities?' I say. 'There must be loads more than that, and maybe it's just that they don't like me.'

'I was worried about this,' Matt says. 'You can't take these things personally. Honestly, I think it's a combination of things: the start of term, people forgetting AND people not really knowing or realising what feminism is and why we need the Feminist Society. I think a lot of people think feminism was just something that we needed in the past, to get women the vote. They don't realise it's more than that. The inequalities are happening now, here and around the world.'

He might have a point here. Maybe this week's blog can be a call to join the Feminist Society? I can remind people about it AND be more explicit about what it actually is and why we need it. I just need to make everyone realise how important it is.

'She's got that look about her,' Si says.

'She's already in the zone, plotting her post,' Matt says.

Before Matt and Si are even out the door, I'm already sitting down at my desk ready to get cracking with some key research.

'POWER TO THE FANNY!' Matt shouts as they leave.

He's trying to remind me of a mortifying day where I shouted that at Hot Josh while making a vagina with my fingers, but I'm too excited about the Feminist Society to engage with his childishness right now.

4.40 p.m.

If I'm going to make the Feminist Society the best that it can be I need to know exactly what all those things TED-Talk Jane was going on about earlier mean. So I'm going to do what all good, intrepid journalists do and get researching!

> Google: What is intersectional feminism?   🔍

> **Intersectional Feminism** is a term coined by Kimberlé Crenshaw in 1989. It recognises that barriers to equality can vary greatly depending on a person's race, age, class, religion, sexuality or gender identity.

So, while I may be discriminated against for being a woman, a Black woman, like Kimberlé Crenshaw, will be discriminated against for being Black as *well* as for being a woman. She comes up against more barriers to equality. And we need to work to make sure that these barriers are removed. It starts with me, I must do better, be more aware, especially of my own privilege.

Why have I NEVER heard of this term before? It feels so

important. Of course, different people experience different levels of discrimination. I guess I've only ever considered my own experience. I've just assumed that we're all going through the same thing, and we're not.

> **Google: What is upskirting?**   🔍

> The activist Gina Martin campaigned to get a bill passed
> making **Upskirting** – the act of taking a picture up a woman's
> skirt – illegal after it happened to her one day and she felt
> powerless to do anything about it.

WHHATTT? That people exist who would even do this blows my mind. And thank GOD – and Gina Martin – that it's illegal now and people can be prosecuted for it.

> **Google: What is slut-shaming?**   🔍

> Stigmatising a woman for engaging in behaviour judged to
> be promiscuous or sexually provocative.

> **Google: What is mansplaining?**   🔍

> A man explaining something, typically to a woman, in a way
> that is condescending.

Well, we've all had that happen to us, haven't we?

My brain is swimming with all these new terms and I feel like there's so much to read about, I don't think I'll ever be able to learn everything there is to know. But maybe I should be constantly learning?

Or maybe I should know all this stuff already? Maybe I was right in the first instance. Maybe I'm not a feminist after all?

I take a deep breath – try to stop the thoughts from spiralling – and begin writing the most exciting Feminist Society invitation possible, to go on this week's Feminist Friday blog.

6 p.m.
My bedroom, scribbling away

'KAT!' Ah! Mum's home!

Mum works as a scientist in the lab at the hospital. Mum and Sandra (Matt's mum) are the reason that I'm a feminist. They told me about it last year after a lot of wine and some gesturing with a carrot stick.

I shut my laptop and head downstairs. From what I can smell I think she's brought dinner home too.

Dad's sitting at the kitchen counter clutching his head, taking small delicate sips at a glass of water.

'How was your day, love?' Mum says, setting a Chinese takeaway down on the table.

'Meh,' I say. 'Hardly anyone came to the meeting and then Comedy Krish sent a small boy in to ask if I was his clitoris and if I'd seen his labia.'

Dad starts laughing and it fully dawns on me that I've just said 'clitoris' AND 'labia' to my parents. It just came out.

Freddie squirms in his seat. God, why did I do that? What's wrong with my filthy mouth?

'You'd be surprised how many grown men don't know where the clitoris is, Kitty Kat,' Mum says, giving Dad an evil eye.

Oh god. CAN WE NOT? I know I started it, but WHAT IS WRONG WITH PARENTS?

I would rather eat glass than hear either of my parents say clitoris again.

10.30 p.m.
My bed still, plotting for the Feminist Society

Vulva Vulva Vulva
Sam, Millie, Me

Me: Guys, do you think we need to name the Feminist Society something more imaginative?

Sam: Lunch and Labia

Millie:

Message: WhatsApp Group name changed by Millie:
Lunch and Labia

41

Millie: Fabulous fannies?

Sam: Tremendous Twats?

Sam: The Vaginettes?!

Millie: THE MUFFRAGETTES?!

Me: I wish I'd never asked.

Sam: Do you think that kid really didn't know what a clitoris is?

Sam: Show me a man who actually knows what one is and where to find one, though . . .

Millie: Nick does. 😊

Oh god, if Nick's found Millie's clitoris, does that mean that she's orgasming? Is everyone orgasming now apart from me? It's bad enough that everyone's got boyfriends apart from me but they're all ORGASMING NOW TOO?

I shouldn't be bitter, I should be pleased that my friends are having a nice time in their pants.

Lunch and Labia
Sam, Millie, Me

Sam: Can he show Dave where it's located please? I'm getting bored of trying to tell him that just shoving his hand in my knickers and leaving it there isn't going to get me off.

42

Millie: You should just give him a bit of gentle guidance until he gets the right spot. That's what I did with Nick.

Me: Is the whole world getting off apart from me?

Sam: And me

Millie: You don't need a man to get yourself off, Kat.

Sam: She has a point. And it's quicker and easier to get yourself off than it is to direct a man to do it. There should be some kind of tour guide down there waiting for them. 'Welcome, it's this way.'

Millie: They should teach it in biology, rather than making it all about semen.

Sam: Exactly, we're sixteen now, pretty soon everyone'll be doing it, we may as well know how to do it well.

Me: FREE THE CLITORIS!

Message: WhatsApp Group name changed by Kat: **Clitoris Liberation Crew**

Sam: Exactly. And treat yourself, Kat, have a little wank x

Millie: Seconded x

Sam: You know your little brother's probably crisping up his sheets every night.

Me: URGH SAM!!! x

Why am I always about twenty steps behind everyone else?

10.35 p.m.
In bed

Right before I go to sleep is one of my most anxious times and the fact that I now know the whole world is getting off apart from me isn't helping.

I worry about everything. I'm glad that I have Sarah now who I can share some of my worries with because before that it was just me, and I felt very alone. At least now I can start to reason with some of the monsters in my head.

The thing is that a lot of the stuff I worry about I don't feel like I can tell people. It doesn't feel normal to tell people that I worry about leaving my light on at night-time in case it gets too hot while I'm asleep and bursts into flames and then we all die.

So, years ago I started touching the light switch three times before I went to sleep. At first it was a thing I did to make sure that it was definitely off, then it became something that I HAD to do, and then it became something that if I didn't do, I would feel so stressed and worried that something bad was going to happen it made me feel ill. Now I have to do it every night before I sleep, and I can't tell people that.

The girls have been really good at helping with my anxiety (I haven't told them about the light switch, though). It's silly to think about now, but at first I was worried about telling them in case they didn't want to be friends with me any more. Sometimes I still worry that the two of them will ditch me. That they'll realise how abnormal I am and not want to hang out with me. Then I worry that everyone hates me, because I'm the worst person in the world and that I don't deserve any of the nice things that happen. Sometimes I just want to be somewhere where no one can see me and realise how weird I am, somewhere where I am safe.

I worry so much about my worries that I feel like I'm in a never-ending cycle. This is normally when the pains start. I get pains in my chest, feel dizzy, and the world goes a bit blurry, everything starts to feel far away, and I can't breathe. I found out last year when I was diagnosed that this is called a panic attack.

It's been happening much less since I started seeing Sarah and I'm able to talk things through and get things a bit clearer in my head.

One of the things I find most frustrating is when I get brain fog. My brain sort of overloads itself and I can't make sense of any of it. I can't focus, I can't read, I can't write and then I start to feel stupid, because what use is a writer who can't write? The frustration makes it worse, and then I get furious with myself and hate myself, and then we're back at panic attacks.

Whenever people have mental health issues in books and films, there always seems to be some defining moment where they realise what the problem is and why they feel crap and then everything gets brighter, the sun comes out and they skip off merrily to enjoy the rest of their life. It's not like that. I do feel a *bit* better, but I'm not *completely* better. I certainly haven't woken up one morning feeling cured.

Anyway – positivity! My therapist also says it's a good idea to try and end each day with three positive things, so here goes . . .

3 Positive Things:
1. Maybe Trudy's Chanel bag will come to life and eat her? Bit mean, sorry.
2. I have learned a LOT of new feminist terms today. Mostly thanks to Jane, who may or may not be better placed to head the Feminist Society, but I will NOT DWELL on that.
3. I have written the most exciting – and FANCY – post for Feminist Friday, calling on everyone to join the Feminist Society, and I now can't wait for next week's meeting.

Tuesday 7th January

9 a.m.

Mortified in form room

I was feeling good when I woke up this morning – ready to tackle the world of feminism again with everything new that I've learned – only to find Freddie had put Post-it notes around the house, saying things like 'Clitoris here?' 'Are you my clitoris?' etc. He thinks he's hilarious. *Eyeroll*

To make matters worse, I have just walked all the way to school, all the way through the playground, all the way to form room, to discover that upon my arse was a post-it note that reads in thick, black, marker pen – so as to be visible from the moon:

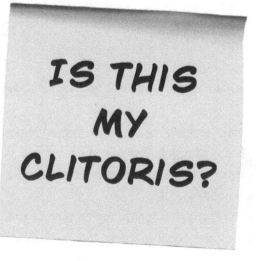

IS THIS MY CLITORIS?

10.30 a.m.
The playground

'I can help you find your clitoris!' one of the gross boys in Freddie's year shouts at me and all his mates fall about laughing.

Great, thanks, Freddie. Cementing another humiliating term for me.

I know all about those guys because he was telling me how they're constantly wolf-whistling girls in his year and making disgusting comments.

Well, the Feminist Society's going to sort them out. As soon as I've got over this latest EXTREME HUMILIATION.

4.30 p.m.
Under my duvet where I live now

I take back everything I said about this term being less mortifying than last term.

'Kat! It really isn't so bad!' Sam says.

'No one can tell it's actually you in all those pictures,' Millie says.

'And really it's only because you're tagged in them. We just need to keep un-tagging them as they come in,' Sam says, poised over her phone as I peek out of a small air hole I've made in the bedding.

'I am NEVER going to forgive my brother for this. NEVER!' I say, flinging off the floofy safety of the duvet for a moment to take a brave peek at the outside world.

'Knock knock!' I hear Matt saying from behind my bedroom door. 'Just walked past your Dad writing his latest sitcom episode. Lot of clit in it.'

'URGHHHH!' I throw the duvet back over me.

5.30 p.m.
Emerging from my duvet shell, like a tortoise from hibernation

'The rate of tagging does appear to be slowing,' Matt says like a scientist, as he monitors my Instagram. 'By dinner time we should only be seeing one or two taggings an hour.'

'And THAT is teamwork!' Sam says as the three of them high five.

They've all been logged into my Instagram account un-tagging me from every.single.meme for the last hour.

Honestly, you would think people didn't have GCSEs to revise for, the rate that they're being posted.

8 p.m.
The sofa

What's really all that shameful about having a Post-it note on my butt that says the word clitoris on it anyway? Is it really THAT bad? Really? I don't think so.

'Hey, heard you have a clitoris on your butt,' Freddie says, jumping on to the sofa.

Shithead.

10.30 p.m.

I tried to distract myself from my worries by staring at pictures of Sexy Sébastien, shutting my eyes and imagining what it would be like to see him again. He's super-hot in all his Instagram pics, especially one of him skateboarding with his top off.

I imagine the two of us meeting again if it turns out to be true about the French trip, and him saying: 'But, Kat, you are more beautiful than I remembered.'

And then I say: 'I'm so sorry I slapped your furry French thingy.'

And then he says: 'NO! I am sorry I scared you with my sexy schlong, please.' And he reaches his hand out to me, pulls me towards him and brushes a stray hair off my face (there's only ever ONE stray hair in these fantasies, though in reality, sadly, MOST of my hair is stray) and leans down to kiss me. Softly at first (it's always softly at first, but I think really I would launch at his face like a dog at an ice cream) and then we fall into each other . . . overcome with passion . . .

10.45 p.m.

. . . and then after weeks of sophisticated French sexing we will emerge in time for Trudy's party; he will fly back with me just so he can be my date, and as we walk in everything will sparkle, especially my non-virgin eyes and boobs (which will be bigger because I am no longer a virgin – I know this doesn't really happen but I don't want to ruin my fantasy with science and facts) and we will glide through Trudy's party, deem it tacky and beneath us, and leave to go somewhere more sophisticated.

11 p.m.

Still thinking about Sexbastien in my boudoir (trying to be sexier, is good no?)

When the girls were talking about me empowering myself to wank yesterday . . . does that mean that *they* do it? It's not like I'm not horny, I'm massively horny, I'm a teenage girl. But I've never really felt like I could do it. Like, my parents are literally *downstairs*. Maybe for all my chat about feminism and being loud and proud about being a woman, I'm actually a prude?

I CAN'T be a prude! That is NOT part of my BRAND. I need to sort this out. I MUST MASTURBATE! FOR FEMINISM!

I shut my eyes and try and think of Sexbastien in a more naked sort of way, but all I picture is penis-gate, over and over again.

How do people work the logistics of wanking when their parents are literally ALWAYS around? All I can hear is them downstairs watching *The Vicar of Dibley*.

I feel like wanking is a feminist issue. Whenever you watch films or TV about teenagers, there's always a wanking boy in it, watching porn and getting caught by their mum. Why are there never any wanking girls? We're just as horny. It's hormones.

Why is it only boys that are accepted by society as wankers?

51

And also, why do they get the term 'wanking' and girls always get the term 'masturbate'? I'm sticking to wanking. Wank, wank, wank. Masturbating sounds like you're kneading something. I'm not kneading my clitoris.

There should be more chat about women wankers.

And yet here I am, not wanking.

The patriarchy is literally in my pants.

3 Positive Things:

1. I've got 99 problems but a wank ain't one . . .

2. To wank or not to wank . . . that is the question.

3. I shall save a lot of money on make-up now that I must live as a hermit due to being tagged in approximately thousands of pictures of my Post-it-noted arse.

Oh god, none of these are positive, are they?

Wednesday 8th January

9 a.m.
Walking through the playground

I have checked my arse for Post-it notes more times than is appropriate today. I'm literally touching up my butt every five seconds with a frantic expression on my face.

People must think I've got worms.

11 a.m.
French class

OH MY FEMINIST GOD! Madame Rauche has confirmed the rumours – we're going to France! NEXT MONTH. To visit our French exchanges, our French exchanges who live in PARIS! It's to get another chance to practise our French as well, but whatever. I will see SEXY Sébastien again. And I WILL SEX HIM! And all of my fantasies will come true! This is FATE.

And who knows, maybe I will even bring him back for Trudy's party, and Trudy will regret saying everyone HAS to have dates for her party because mine will be SO HOT.

We'll be staying in a youth hostel, which I'll confess doesn't sound THAT glamorous, but who cares? Me and my two best friends will be in PARIS!

Just because the last time I saw him I was running away from his man sausage, doesn't mean that romance can't flourish. Unless I'm on the most wanted list for crimes against penis now, and I get stopped at the border and refused entry to France. But in my defence, it's really hard to know what to do when someone offers you their furry worm and you're not expecting it. I'll be ready for it the second time around.

'Kat! *À quoi penses-tu?*' Madame Rauche shouts at me. Which actually means, 'What are you thinking about?' But it sounds like she's said something about 'two penises' to me and I can feel my face going bright, bright red. Can she read my thoughts? Does she know what's going on in there?

'*Je ne pense à rien,*' I reply.

I definitely just said '*pense*' rather than 'penis', didn't I?

It feels like I said penis.

Oh god, did I just say '*je ne* penis?'

Millie and Sam are staring at me like I said 'penis', but that might just be because I have gone really very red from *pense-*ing so much about 'penis'.

Madame Rauche nods at me and moves on. Thank fuck for that. Now I shall continue to *pense* about penis.

11.10 a.m.
Still swooning in French

. . . and then when we are thirty we will have small, very chicly dressed French children and live in Paris, cycling around and eating at boulangeries.

54

I put my hand on my chin and let out a sigh.

Eek, was that an audible sigh? Millie and Sam have both turned to look at me. Yes, it was audible. And Madame Rauche is looking at me again too now.

OK, no more penis *pense*-ing. It's too dangerous. I sit up straight and hold my pen poised over my notebook. If I project an air of concentration, I might escape unscathed.

She's turned back to the board. Phew. Millie and Sam however are both still staring.

'What's wrong with you?' Sam mouths across the room.

Oops.

3.30 p.m.
The playground

'I wonder how Sébastien is these days,' I say casually as we walk towards the playground at the end of the day, as if I haven't been planning our wedding all day.

'Oh, THAT's why you were so excitable in French this morning? You were thinking about Sébastien's *saucisson*!' Sam chuckles to herself.

'I just thought maybe . . . as, you know, I've not been necessarily LUCKY in love lately, perhaps I could go back where I know I've been successful in the past? Back to the scene of the crime, so to speak . . . you know . . .' I make a patting action with my hand reminiscent of the one I made in his pants and both the girls laugh at me. At least my sexual encounters are funny, I suppose. Imagine how boring the story would be if I'd just given him a hand job.

Matt and Nick are heading towards us across the playground.

'Hey, vaginas!' Matt shouts. 'What we up to?'

'We just found out we're going to Paris!' I say excitedly. 'For our French exchange!'

'And now we're going for milkshakes,' says Millie. 'Wanna come?'

'That sounds fun!' Nick says, sliding an arm around Millie's shoulder.

'I'll just text Dave and tell him the plan,' says Sam. 'Anyone seen him?' We all shake our heads as Sam frowns at her phone. 'He's not responded to my last two text messages. Guess I'll just tell him where we're going, and he can come and find us.'

4 p.m.
Scoops

I wonder if Sébastien remembers me? Maybe he hates me? But everyone deserves a second chance at love. Don't they?

'What are you dreaming about over there?' Si asks, throwing a sugar sachet at me.

'Probably Sébastien . . .' Matt says, fluttering his lashes over at me.

'Ah yes, the French lover from the bush,' Si says.

'The bush, but not *her* bush. I believe she ran away before there was any rummaging.' Matt grabs my phone off me. 'Let's see if he's still single. A small Instagram reconnaissance mission is in order, I think!'

'STOP IT!' I try to grab my phone back but Millie and Sam stop me. I really don't want them seeing that Sébastien is already VERY MUCH in my recent searches. I may have looked at his profile a *few* times in the last forty-eight hours, possibly while listening to Taylor Swift's 'Love Story'.

'Surname, please . . .' Matt asks, holding the phone away from me. 'Oh, wait . . . Well, whaddaya know . . . no need for a surname, he's already in recent searches.'

'OoooOOOOOOOOOOOOooohhhhHHHHH!' literally everyone at the table screeches, except for Dave, who seems so distracted by his own phone that he may as well not have come.

For god's sake. Why is no one grown-up around here?

They're lucky I love them.

'He's a HOTTY!' Si says to me, getting up the half-naked skateboard pic that I have once or twice fallen asleep dreaming about. 'Why don't you just follow him? See if he follows you back?'

'NO!' I practically shout. 'I can't do that!'

'How come? You should follow him or stop perving, you know?' Sam says.

'It's true, no one likes an Insta lurker,' Si says.

I'm not an Insta lurker, am I?

5.30 p.m.
Home

I keep catching myself going off into daydreams, thinking about the sexpedition to France as I have now named it (obviously just in my own head, never to be said out loud). I nearly got run over twice on the way home because I wasn't paying attention.

'Hey, Kitty Kat!' Dad shouts at me as soon as I arrive home. 'Where you been? Whatcha been up to?'

'Exciting news, Papa! There's a French exchange trip NEXT MONTH!'

'Oh right, who's going on that, then?' he asks, distracted by the vegetables he's chopping.

'Well, everyone in our French class, I'm guessing. Millie, Sam, definitely me, that's for sure,' I say

'Oh,' he says and stops chopping. 'Right, well, let's talk to your mum when she gets in.'

He grabs his phone and starts texting, trying not to look too suspicious. He's telling her about it now so that she's prepared when she comes home. He's unaware how unbelievably unsubtle he's being with it too, because he's old and doesn't realise that young people do this with their phones all the time, in fact, we INVENTED it, Dad. But we have the courtesy to do it under the table.

'OK, cool, well, I'm gonna head upstairs. Revision to do!' I say breezily. Maybe if I act like it's not a big deal, it'll rub off on them and they'll just say yes? I mean, they have to say yes, don't they? The whole class are going. Oh my god, if they don't let me go it will be the END OF THE WORLD. They CANNOT ruin this for me. I will DIVORCE THEM, or phone the NSPCC, or both.

6 p.m.
My bedroom

I have done no revision. It seems to be a theme. The revision timetable I made myself is just hanging uselessly over my desk. I've failed to make any of the goals set out on there so far this week.

Instead I am sitting on my bed lightly internet stalking Sébastien. He hasn't posted anything new so I scroll way back to older pictures on his profile and show Bea the picture of his dog, Claude.

'Fancy a French boyfriend?' I ask her. She turns her head away. I guess since we had her done she's got a little less interested in the boy dogs, but she seems particularly unimpressed with poor Claude.

Sébastien really is so dreamy, though. Imagine if I actually *did* walk into Trudy's party with him. She'd be SICK with jealousy. (Not very feminist of me, I know, but it's hard being a good feminist ALL the time.)

I need to practise my alluring-ness so that as soon as Sébastien sees me, he remembers how sexy I am and how much he fancies me, NOT how I ran away at the first sign of penis.

I am going to France to see him and I am FINALLY going to enter the adult world.

I click on to the photo of him topless on his skateboard again.

Oh god, I AM an Insta lurker.

I need to follow him and stop being a creep.

I hit the follow button and shut my eyes. I've got a strong urge to launch my phone across the room, but I don't think it's reasonable to break your phone just because you've done something embarrassing. If I did that every time I was embarrassed I'd be on my tenth phone this year.

6.03 p.m.

Sébastien has still not followed me back.

It's been ages.

8 p.m.
The kitchen

'Kat? Can we talk to you?' Dad says.

I've unwittingly walked in on what looks like a parental conference in the kitchen. All I wanted was some chocolate to help while I'm watching my phone waiting for Sébastien to follow back. Not that that's what I was doing. I was obviously actually using it to look at important feminist campaigns for next Monday's meeting.

'Sure.' I sit down, already wishing I hadn't come in here.

'We've been talking about the trip to France and we're just

not sure it's the best idea at the moment,' Dad says.

What? I feel like I'm having an out-of-body experience. Is this really happening? They can't do this. I'm staring at them, saying nothing, and my head's playing some kind of montage with pictures of Sébastien and images of me and the girls hanging out in Paris slipping through my virgin-ous fingers.

'It's just, it's not been that long since you were really poorly, and we know that you're doing better now, but we're just worried that it's too soon,' Mum says.

'What? But . . . I HAVE to go!' I feel like my mouth's moving quite apart from me. I can't believe that they're doing this. Maybe this is one of Dad's bad jokes, but he doesn't look like he's joking.

'We understand,' says Dad, 'but it's quite a big deal going on a school trip to another country and we just worry that it might be too much for you right now. What happens if you have a panic attack while you're away?' I can tell Dad's trying to use his kindest most rational voice so that I soften but I can't stop the rage and feeling of injustice from boiling.

'And with the exams coming up so soon—'

'BUT THIS WOULD HELP WITH THE EXAMS!' I shout over Mum, louder than I mean to.

I know it's not mature, but I don't know how else to deal with this. I need them to change their minds and they're not listening to me. This is why I still feel like a child – because they still *treat* me like one.

'Please don't get angry, love,' says Dad. 'We're doing this because we've got your best interests at heart.' The more

Dad uses his calm and reasonable voice, the more I want to scream.

'YOU SAID THAT YOU DIDN'T WANT ME TO MISS STUFF BECAUSE OF MY DIAGNOSIS!' I know I look like a toddler having a tantrum, but how can they not let me go? Don't they understand what it means? How important it is to me?

'I'm sorry, Kat, we've made our decision,' says Mum.

'We just don't think it's a good idea right now, and when you get a chance to really consider it properly, I'm sure you'll agree with us,' Dad says.

There's no chance of THAT happening, I think. I open my mouth to tell them but I realise that I'm way too angry to make any sense right now and just bolt from the room instead.

I race up the stairs and head straight for my bed.

8.15 p.m.
My room

I pick up my phone to text the girls and tell them but there are already messages there.

Clitoris Liberation Crew
Sam, Millie, Me

Millie: Paris here we come! FEMINISTS ON TOUR! XXX

Sam: YASSSSS! I'm so excited!!!!!
I'm already planning *Emily in Paris* inspired outfits!

Sam: Oh my god. I told Dave about the trip and he's literally SICK that he chose to do Spanish instead of French. Hahaha xxx

Sam: Although actually I am sad he's not coming xxx

Millie: Naaahh! It'll be like old times, just the three of us, having the best time, and helping Kat get into Sexy Sébastien's knickers again. Xx

Sam: A little more delicately this time perhaps, Kat? Xxxx

Millie: I think we need a more French name for this group you know . . .

Sam: Agreed!

Message: WhatsApp Group name changed by Millie:
Bonjour le France!

I feel sick. I can't believe it. We were going to have the best time and now I can't go and they'll still have the best time, but without me, because I can't go, because *I'm not allowed to go*, like a child.

I need to tell them, but first I think I need to have a monumental cry.

Buried in a stack of snotty tissues

> **Bonjour le France!**
> Sam, Millie, Me

Me: Guys, I've got some bad news.
My parents aren't going to let me go.
They don't think I'm well enough.
I'm sorry. I've ruined Feminists on Tour xxx

Millie: NOOOOO! Kat! What?! Xxxx

Sam: How can they think you're not well enough?
Surely after everything you should be allowed a
nice trip away with your friends! Xxx

Millie: We won't go without you Kat! Let's all stay home. X

Sam: Agreed! Xxx

Me: No! Don't do that. The two of you'll have an
amazing time and you should go. Just maybe
FaceTime me from the Eiffel Tower yeah? Xxxx

Sam: Kat!!! We can't go without you! Xxx

Me: Please? It would upset me more if the
two of you didn't go because of me. Xxx

Millie: I can't believe this xxx

Sam: I'm sorry dude.
This is absolute fucking bullshit xxxx

Yes. Sam, that's correct, it really is.

Message: WhatsApp Group name changed by Millie:
Je Déteste Mes Parents

10.00 p.m.
My bedroom

Dad's just knocked on my door for a chat for the third time tonight and for the third time I told him to go away. They'll be lucky if I talk to them this side of Easter. They've ruined everything: the French trip, feminists on tour, and most importantly my chance at exchange romance with Sébastien. I'll never forgive them, ever.

11 p.m.

Dad really needs to give up and move from outside my bedroom door. I bury my head into my pillow and carry on crying.

Not for the first time, I feel like a complete weirdo. I bet I'll be the only one in the French class who's not allowed to go on the trip because they had a breakdown anyway. I need to get better faster, so that my head stops holding me back.

I need to sort out my anxiety, my constant fear that people

hate me, my compulsion to touch the light switch . . . I mean, what would I do about the light switch in France? What if Sam and Millie saw me? How would I explain it? Or would I just have to try and not do it? But I don't think I could? I can't even do sleepovers at home without touching it, let alone somewhere I've never been before.

Maybe my parents are right and I just don't want to admit it?

11.30 p.m.

My phone beeps in the darkness and I reach out to see what it is.

> You have 1 new follower.

Sébastien has followed me back.

Bit late for that now, Sébastien!

3 Positive Things:
*There were loads of positive things, but then my parents
RUINED THEM ALL.*

Thursday 9th January

7 a.m.

Dad's just left a cup of tea by my bed and I didn't even roll over to say thanks or anything. I'm not drinking it.

He can shove his peace offering up his bum.

8.30 a.m.
On the way to school

'There must be something we can do!' Millie's saying again.

'It's just really unfair, you HAVE to come,' Sam's saying.

'I know, but they seem pretty certain about it. The deposit's due tomorrow, and I can't see them changing their minds before then,' I say sadly. '*Au revoir*, French trip, *au revoir* Sébastien.'

'I'm sorry, babe,' Sam says. 'I still think we shouldn't go without you.'

'No! You have to go!' I say. 'Someone still has to have fun! You'll just have to 'gram the whole thing, so I don't miss anything.'

'AND FaceTime you constantly! It'll be like you're there,' Millie says.

'We'll talk about you non-stop to Sébastien. Maybe we can even bring him home for you!' Sam says. 'Especially now he follows you back on the 'gram! A holiday gift!'

I appreciate what they're trying to do, but I feel gutted.

8.35 a.m.

We're about two metres from school when I feel a shove on my shoulder and Sienna swoops past.

'It's "excuse me!"' I shout after her as Sienna raises her middle finger without even looking back.

'Attitude much?' Millie asks.

'Wow, she's just a *peach*, isn't she?' Sam says.

'Trudy mark two,' says Millie.

What is her problem?

6.30 p.m.
The kitchen

I was really upset this morning about France but the more I've thought about it today, the more I'm convinced that I've got way too much to do here anyway, especially if I'm going to make the Feminist Society a real success. I can't go galivanting around the world chasing after BOYS. Even one as sexy as Sexbastien. I've got a mission, a purpose. I am a feminist! FORGET FRANCE!

I came home after school and put some final design touches to the Feminist Friday blog, and then I put together the agenda for Monday's Feminist Society meeting. I may not be going to France, but I am going to make a CHANGE, a feminist change.

'Hey,' I say to Dad as I walk into the kitchen. He spins round.

'Hey, love!' God, he's so eager for reconciliation. Like a needy puppy.

'Hey,' Mum says more casually. 'How was your day?'

'Yeah, it was OK. Um, I just . . . wanted to clear the air,' I say to them not sure if I should sit or stand but feeling very awkward. 'I realise that I was a bit OTT about things last night and I understand why you made the decision you made.' (I don't really, but I've moved on, like a mature adult.) 'And I'm not going to be cross about it any more.' (I am furious and you are idiots, but look how mature I am! I am not even lying on the floor screaming about it!)

'Oh right, OK,' Mum says.

'So, are you proposing a truce?' says Dad hopefully.

'Correct,' I say sitting down opposite Mum. 'And I'm sorry for being a bit of a brat yesterday.' (I wasn't a brat and I'm not sorry.)

'Apology accepted,' Mum says smugly (I am livid).

'YAY!' says Dad. 'Good to have you back, kiddo.' (Not a kiddo, a sixteen-year-old woman actually.)

'Good,' I say and then sit at the table and sigh. I must admit, I am slightly disappointed that my very grown-up behaviour didn't immediately prompt the response, 'This is so mature of you, you MUST go to France and live your dreams. You are a wonderful daughter.'

I guess it was a long shot. And ANYWAY, like I said, I have more important things to think about.

10 p.m.
Bed

I've read over the Feminist Friday blog post for tomorrow and my agenda for Monday and have now got a little buzz of excitement about it. I can't wait to see what response it gets.

I turn off the light and touch the switch three times, hoping for more luck for tomorrow.

3 Positive Things:
1. At least I won't have to worry about what I'll do about the light switch in France because I'm not going to France.
2. I am going to throw myself into feminism and the Feminist Society and do GOOD THINGS.
3. At least I won't have a chance to embarrass myself in front of Sébastien's penis again. Although maybe I'll never have a chance to embarrass myself in front of any penis again. NO! I must NOT get distracted by this! I am about the Feminist Society and Feminism!

friday 10th January

8.30 a.m.

Seeing the blog published and being viewed by people has made me a bit giddy with excitement. The Feminist Society is going to be huge. I just know it. I'm literally DRAGGING the girls to school while barely taking my eyes off my phone, watching to see if anyone likes it and constantly refreshing.

8.35 a.m.

SOMEONE HAS LIKED IT!

8.40 a.m.

TEN PEOPLE HAVE LIKED IT AND THREE HAVE SAID THEY'RE COMING TO THE MEETING ON MONDAY!

We've paused our walk to school to huddle around my phone and watch the likes shoot up and I am just starting to wonder if success will go to my head when I hear Sienna's voice behind us.

'Cool blog . . .' Sienna says sarcastically rolling her eyes at me as she walks past.

The three of us look at each other, and I just shrug.

No one can bring me down today. Especially someone who's barely been here a week.

'Must be hard hating on everyone so much all the time,' Millie reasons.

'Well, she seems to have caught someone's attention,' Sam says, pointing over to where Trudy's watching Sienna with her beady eyes.

'They're like clones of each other,' I say as all three of us shudder at the thought of them joining forces.

'At least we know for sure after that comment that she's DEFINITELY a twat,' Sam says.

10.30 a.m.
The playground

'I think I'm a feminist,' one of the boys in Freddie's year shouts

72

over at me as Sam, Millie and I wait for Matt and Nick to join us. 'I LOVE THE FANNY!'

FFS.

All three of us raise our middle fingers in a shitty salute at them.

12.30 p.m.
The cafeteria

'I can't believe the blog's got EIGHTY-FIVE likes already!' I say, staring at my phone.

'AND twenty-seven comments!' Millie adds.

'How many people do you think will actually come, though?' I ask.

'Definitely more than last time,' Sam says, scrolling through.

'I'm so excited I almost wish the weekend was over so it could be Monday already and time for the Feminist Society to reign supreme,' I say.

'OMG, LOSER!' Sam says as Millie chucks a chip at me.

'Fair point.' I giggle 'What you up to this weekend, by the way?'

'Don't know,' Millie says. 'I really need to try and get my coursework done for maths. Apparently Mum's heading to yours tomorrow night.'

'Oh. NO,' I say, feeling extreme dread. This can only mean that there's a mums' wine night planned. And now I really am wishing the weekend away.

'Yeah, my mum too,' Sam says, laughing at my horrified

face. 'Jas and I are using the opportunity to go out together before she goes back to uni.'

'PLEEEEASSSE join me while I hide in my room away from them, Millie?' I beg. 'I can't handle them on my own. I'll see if Matt's about too.'

'Sounds good,' says Millie. 'Issy'll probably be there with Freddie. Does anyone else worry that those two are going to get married before us?'

'Every day. And I'm only sixteen,' I say, stabbing harder at my jacket potato than is strictly necessary. They'll never know how much of my mind precisely is taken up with anger that my brother's love life is more fruitful than mine.

3.45 p.m.
Walking to therapy

When Sarah said we were having a break over Christmas, I fully FREAKED OUT. But it's actually been OK. At the time it felt like I was being abandoned down a well or something, but I survived, and I didn't even have to gnaw off my own arm for sustenance or anything.

4 p.m.
Therapy

I forgot how nice this room smells and how calm and comforting it is. If they made the exam hall smell like this for my GCSEs, I'd be much less scared.

'So, it's been a while! How have things been?' Sarah asks, settling into the comfortable-looking pink velvet chair opposite and crossing her legs with her hands clasped on her knee.

I realise that I've suddenly got all these things that I need to talk about, and they're all fighting in my brain to be the first out. It feels like I'm about to do the mental equivalent of handing a fitting room assistant a hundred items of clothing off their hangers.

'Well . . .' God, where do I start? 'There's a lot . . .'

'Hit me with the headlines and we'll delve in deeper,' she says.

'Well . . . they announced a French exchange next month that Mum and Dad said I'm not well enough to go on, the Feminist Society is a disaster, my GCSE revision is going TERRIBLY and I'm still worried that I'm going to fail everything and ruin my entire life, and Trudy's having a party that's going to be like prom where people need dates and obviously I'd never have one of those even though I was fantasising about bringing this French guy whose penis I accidentally patted. And I also have kind of started to think that maybe Mum and Dad are right, and maybe I'm really *not* well enough to go to France, like they said.'

Can't believe I included the bit about Sébastien's penis, but Sarah's face hasn't moved from its usual unfazed expression.

'So, let's start with the French trip. That's a shame. How do you feel about that? And why do you think you're not well enough?'

'At first I was annoyed. I feel like all we talk about is how I shouldn't let my mental health conditions hold me back, and then when it comes down to it, Mum and Dad use it as an excuse to stop me going to France.'

'Mmmmhmmm.' Sarah nods. I can't tell if she's on my side about this or if she's on their side, but I also think maybe she's not supposed to be on anyone's side? I definitely want her to be on mine, though.

'And then I realised that, actually, if I was going to go then what do I do about the fact that I can't sleep without touching a light switch three times? How do I share a room with friends without them finding out? How am I supposed to be a grown-up person travelling the world, having fun with her friends and then not be able to go to bed at night without touching a light switch? And what if I did it and someone saw and then they worked out my secret and then the whole school ends up thinking I'm a complete weirdo?'

'Well, do you think the light switch is something that you might be ready to address? There are things that we can try to help you work through that.'

I look at Sarah. The thought of not having the light switch hanging over me sounds really freeing – like, frolicking in fields of daisies with newborn lambs-style freeing – but it's also weird. It's been my secret for so long, a bit like a selfish, energy-draining, imaginary friend. The thought of saying goodbye to it makes me feel a little sad. This is probably even more reason to work on getting over the compulsion.

'I would like that, yes, please!' I say, feeling bold and brave.

'Great, so why don't we try something? We'll call it the ten-minute challenge, or light-switch challenge at first. I want you to try to go a few nights this week where you don't touch the light switch immediately after you've turned it off. The aim is to get to ten minutes without touching it. But maybe this week we just see how long you manage? How does that sound?'

Like hell.

'Yeah, that sounds good,' I say.

I used to be so scared of this little room but I seem to be getting braver every time I step in here.

5.15 p.m.
Walking home

I feel so much better now. I hadn't realised how much I'd missed our sessions over Christmas. But now I feel so much lighter and definitely ready to try and give the light switch thing a go.

9.30 p.m.
In bed, ready to start the light-switch challenge

I decided to come to bed early rather than sit on the sofa worrying about it. Best thing to do when you're worried about something is to just crack on with it.

I get in, pull the covers over me, wait for Bea to get comfy and turn the light off.

I really have to pull my hand back to stop it from instantly touching the switch. I guess it's just something that I do automatically.

But somehow, pulling my hand away without touching it makes me feel incomplete. I swear my fingers even twitched a little bit.

I put my hands on top of the covers and then feel too agitated to keep them there. I need a barrier between them and the light switch or it's too easy for me to touch it. I put them under the covers again and Bea huffs at me for disturbing the peace.

There. That must have taken up at least a few minutes, right?

I look over at the clock by my bed. Not even a whole minute has passed since I switched the light off.

I try rolling away from the clock in an effort not to stare at it, willing the numbers to go around, but I feel so uncomfortable whichever way I lie that I have to sit up again.

What if Sarah's got it wrong? What if the light switch DOES matter for me? Like, I'm sure she's right and it's just all in the mind for a lot of people, but what if I'm the exception to that rule? And by doing this I'm then responsible for someone else, someone I love, coming to harm?

I start feeling extremely hot and dizzy and turn around to look at the clock. It's saying that a minute has passed. And do you know what? That is quite enough for me tonight.

I turn the light back on, check my phone to make sure I

haven't caused any colossal world dramas and then switch the light off again, touching it three times.

3 Positive Things:

1. I did a whole minute without touching the light switch. (Shame about the other nine minutes, but I guess you have to start somewhere.)

2. I am going to crack this. I am, I am, I am.

3. The Feminist Friday blog got over ONE HUNDRED likes by the end of today. I AM SO EXCITED! I also feel slightly famous. Not Love Island *level famous but maybe* Tipping Point *level famous?*

Saturday 11ᵗʰ January

#Blessed! MY PERIOD HAS COME!

I have awoken in a crimson tide. The biggest lie is that periods work to a schedule. They don't. They just merrily bloody show up whenever they bloody like, and now my bloody period is all over my bloody bed.

FFS.

I'm frantically pulling the sheets off my bed and trying to remember where I put my menstrual cup or the period pants that Mum got me for Christmas. I've been really excited about trying those SEXY panties, where are they? To be honest, ANYTHING will do right now. They say it's never more than four tablespoons, but if that's true, why does it always look like a scene from *CSI*?

8.30 a.m.

SUCCESS! I'd put my menstrual cup in my jewellery box . . . of course, because it is precious. What kind of person wouldn't consider a cup to collect their period blood as the season's HOTTEST accessory?

8.35 a.m.
The bathroom

The good news is that I've got *much* better at putting this bad boy in, and after *much* investigation and concern, I have learned that my vagina is actually COMPLETELY NORMAL, thank you *very much*. Still not sure how I feel about anyone EVER seeing it, but I am now confident with everything inside my pants. It's just the pants themselves that may still be an issue for the fashion police.

9.00 a.m.
The kitchen

These cramps are the absolute worst. I know that they say you should be active on your period, but sod that. If I tried to run right now, I'd get two steps before collapsing in the road in the foetal position. They'd have to spend the day directing traffic around me. Exercise is not for me, not at a time like this. Not when there's hot chocolate and Ferrero Rocher in the house.

I carry my balled-up sheets to the laundry room, trying not to let anyone see. I'll text Dad about it later. It's not the first time, and he's actually very good at getting the stains out. (Should I be worried that my dad's good at getting blood out of things?) He understands the unpredictable nature of a uterus. If only my womb lining would sync with my Google Cal, rather than the moon or whatever it fancied, things would be so much simpler.

'Eww, Kat, why you changing your sheets? Did you wet the bed?' Freddie shouts from the kitchen table.

Why is it he can be so mature with Issy and then a COMPLETE JERK to me?

'Freddie, don't harass your sister,' Dad says. He's probably guessed why I'd be changing my sheets. At least I have ONE sensitive male in the family.

12 p.m.
The sofa

Finally found my period pants and they are now in situ! They're big and black and made of soft cotton. They feel sturdy, but sleek, like I'm wearing normal pants, but they seem to be doing the job. I think they are the sexiest thing that I have ever worn.

Imagine being able to just wear a pair of pants and not worry any more! I'll see how the day goes before I get too excited, though.

In other news: Freddie came in here and tried to play PlayStation, so I hissed at him and arched my back like an angry cat until he left.

7.30 p.m.
My room, hiding from wine mums

'If we stay up here then they can't reach us,' Matt says, like a fool.

Matt, Si, Millie and I have been hiding up here now for half an hour, but the sounds of pissed laughter are getting louder, and so is the sense of danger.

'They will eventually get to a level of drunk where they drag us down there,' I say, trying to keep the fear from my voice. 'You know that as well as I do. They'll want to know all the gossip, tell us things we don't want to hear from when they were young and generally cause us mental scarring that no amount of therapy can heal, and I should know.' It's nice that I'm at the stage where I can joke about therapy now. I think it's important to try and maintain a sense of humour about the whole thing.

'God, I know you're right, but I want you not to be,' Millie says, painting Matt's toenails with my black varnish.

My door flies open, scaring the bejesus out of the three of us, and Freddie and Issy burst in.

'They tried to drag us into the kitchen with them,' he says, a kind of wild fear in his eyes as Issy rushes over to us for safety.

'Ahh, come and join us in the safe room,' Matt says. 'You didn't make eye contact, did you?'

And here we all are, hiding safely upstairs away from the torment.

Three Queens
Sam, Millie, Me

Sam: I megeaaa love uuuuuu GuyyzzzzZ xx

Sam: Am at pub with Jas x

Me: Uh oh! At least your mum will be as drunk as you tonight xx

Sam: Jas is teaching me how to sexy text.

Millie: Lols, Sam. You're going to be wrecked in the morning, babe xx

Sam: I want your hand in my bra xx

Sam: Wrong chat sorry xx

Millie: OMG SAM! LOL. Don't send that to Dave xx

Sam: Too late. Oopsies.

'I do NOT want to see that other chat,' I say to Millie as we show Matt the texts stealthily, without Issy and Freddie seeing.

'Oh, I WANT to see that other chat!' Matt says laughing.

'Me too!' says Si. 'Sounds sexy.'

'EWW! You two are gross,' Millie says, throwing a cushion at them.

It feels nice to all be together like this and having fun, even if the air in here is starting to get a little hot and thick. Might crack a window. I know what Freddie's farts are like when he thinks he's doing them silently, and Issy's still too polite to let him know that he's gassed her.

I bet Sébastien doesn't even fart. If he does it probably smells of fresh baguettes. I'll never know now, though.

le sigh

9 p.m.

The stairway

We're starving *and* thirsty so Millie, Matt and I have sacrificed ourselves to go and get snacks. We've got a strategy and, if we're smart, we can get in and out super quick. All we have to do is wait until they move into the living room. Please god let that happen soon. We're poised on the stairs right now, peering round the corner waiting to make our move, and my legs are already aching from this squatting position.

'IS THAT YOUR NEW NEIGHBOUR?' Sam's mum shouts, seeing the man from number five out the window in his garden.

'Urgh, Mum's talked of nothing else lately.' Matt sighs.

He is fit, to be fair, and keeps mowing the lawn with his top off. But that's a bit attention-seeking and showy if you ask me.

'What's his name again?' Mum asks Sandra.

'Derek,' Sandra says.

'Not a sexy name,' Millie's mum says and Millie makes a face at the very notion her mum would utter the word 'sexy'.

'No, but a very sexy man nonetheless. What do you think he does?' Sandra asks.

'Stripper.' Mum cackles and I groan waiting for certain death from the embarrassment.

'GIGOLO!' Sandra shouts and then they all duck down below the window laughing, in case he's heard her.

They're worse than children.

'You should go and talk to him, Sandra,' Sam's mum suggests. 'Introduce yourself in a neighbourly way.'

'Maybe he's thirsty and would like some wine?' Millie's mum waggles an almost empty bottle.

'Oh Christ,' Matt whispers under his breath.

'Fuck it. I'm going in,' Sandra says, hoicking up her bra and downing her wine. I can feel Matt's face burn as she heads out the door and stalks across the grass, the other mums watching her at the window, mine topping up the glasses.

'Solid approach,' Sam's mum says.

'Ten out of ten for the strut,' Millie's mum says.

'Oooh! He looks pleased to see her!' Mum squeals.

'Wait, where's she going?' Millie's mum asks.

'INSIDE. They're going INSIDE THE HOUSE!' Mum puts down her glass.

If we weren't so distracted and Matt wasn't so mortified, I'd say now was a good time to get snacks without them noticing us, but sadly Matt has his head between his legs and is deep breathing.

'Oh god, am I going to have to call him Daddy?' he mutters.

'What if he's a serial killer?' Mum asks. I can't think where I got my dramatic streak from.

'Oh shit. Good point!' Sam's mum gasps.

The wine has clearly made them hysterical.

'JOHN! JOHN! WE NEED YOU!' Mum starts shrieking for Dad.

9.15 p.m.

Sandra has now been in the house of a possible serial killer for fifteen minutes and so they've elected to send Dad in to check she's not about to be buried under the floorboards.

'What am I doing? What's my motivation? My reason for going in there?' Dad asks.

'You're borrowing a cup of flour,' Mum says.

'Right. What are we baking?' Dad says.

'Cupcakes.'

'Flavour?' Mum gives him a look. 'I need to have my back story straight!' Dad says, raising his arms.

'Just go, John,' she says, as the mums all usher him out the door, towards the house of a possible serial killer.

'I can't watch any more.' Matt looks honestly slightly pale with the embarrassment as he stands up. 'I'm sorry, ladies. I have to abandon the snacks mission. I have faith that the two of you can do it, though.'

9.30 p.m.

My legs are completely dead from this crouched position and Sandra is back in the house, having secured herself a date with Dishy Derek as they're now all calling him. Weirdly *Dad* never came back from Derek's but no one seems that bothered.

Millie and I are starting to accept that we may have to simply face the lion's den.

'How are things with you and Adrian, Luisa?' Sandra asks Millie's mum.

There's a long pause and I look at Millie, wondering if we should leave, but she's staring straight ahead, ignoring me.

'Not great,' her mum finally says, and I feel like Millie might have stopped breathing. 'We tried therapy after Mum died but, if anything, it just made us realise that the only thing keeping us together now is the girls. And that's not healthy, is it? Not really? Especially when we do things like fight all Christmas.'

I didn't realise things were so bad? Aside from her putting his phone up a turkey's butt, that is. We really should go but Millie's perched, biting a fingernail and looking like she's deep in concentration. I know that I wouldn't want to move right now.

'Oh, Luisa, what are you going to do?' I hear my mum ask.

Millie's face has gone pale and I feel the true meaning of the phrase 'frozen with horror'. I don't know what to do. I feel like we shouldn't be hearing this, though.

'I don't know yet. We need to be able to have a civilised discussion about it, but every time we try, things get in the way.'

'Let us know if there's anything we can do, won't you?' Mum says.

'Same here,' Sam's mum chimes in.

'Me too,' Sandra adds. 'I'm sorry, divorces are shitty.'

Millie stands up slowly and quietly at the word 'divorce', and creeps lightly back up the stairs, with me following behind, her shoulders shaking with sobs. We cross the hallway and quietly slink into the bathroom.

'Issy can't know about this,' Millie says once we're locked inside.

'That's OK, she doesn't need to,' I say, perching on the side of the bath. 'We can just stay in here. I'm so sorry, Millie.'

I watch sadly as Millie grabs fistfuls of toilet roll to try and stem the tears that have started rolling down her face.

9.15 p.m.
In the bathtub

Millie and I have taken up residence in the bathtub. There's obviously no water in here, but we've got quite comfortable sitting either end, just waiting until Millie is sure that she's stopped crying before we head back to my room.

Matt: Where are you? Have you been taken by the winos of Eastwick? Did my mother ever return?

Me: In the bathroom. Join us but come alone.

Matt: Cryptic. On my way, MI5.

There's a light tap at the door and I scrabble out of the bath to let Matt in.

'What are we doing in here? Hanging in the bath like some kind of dry pool party?' He notices that Millie's crying. 'Oh no! What happened, Millie?' he asks as we both climb into the bath.

'We overheard something,' I say gently.

'Mum was talking about Dad,' Millie starts but can't finish because she's crying too much.

'She said they were only staying together for Millie and Issy,' I finish for her, rubbing her back.

'Oof,' Matt says. 'I'm sorry, Mills, that's rough.'

The three of us sit in silence for a bit until Matt's phone beeps.

'Hang on, is it OK if Si joins?' Matt says, turning his phone screen to me so that I can read the message.

Si: Where the fuck have you gone? I'm in proper gooseberry land. They're practically dry humping.

Urgh NOOOOOOO!

'Sure,' says Millie, blowing her nose.

There's another knock at the door and Matt kicks a foot out of the bath to flick the lock open and let Si in.

'Nuns in a jacuzzi?' Si asks as he comes in and locks the door behind him.

'Close. Virgins in a bathtub,' Matt says.

'We all know you're not a virgin, babe,' Si says.

'The rest of us are, though,' Millie says, and I'm suddenly very comforted by the fact that her and Nick haven't done it yet. I was worried they had and she hadn't told me, but of course she would. Anyway, now is completely NOT the time to be thinking about that.

'Millie overheard her mum talking about her dad and it didn't sound so great. We're trying to make sure Issy doesn't see her upset,' Matt says.

'Oh shit. Well, make way!' Si says, launching himself into the bathtub as well.

'What am I going to do?' Millie asks, putting her wet face in her hands as we all shuffle closer to comfort her.

9.30 p.m.
The bathtub, with no feeling in either arse cheek

'We should get back,' Millie says at last. 'Issy'll be wondering where we are.'

She's stopped crying now. When Matt and Si did their impression of Kim and Kourtney Kardashian fighting, it was a real turning point for her.

'I think they're probably a bit distracted,' Si says.

'They better not be being distracted in my room,' I say, panicking.

'How does my face look?' Millie dabs at the corners of her eyes.

'Stunning!' Matt says.

'Probably better than Issy's looks after all the snogging they're doing in Kat's room right now,' Si says, smirking at me.

'RIGHT! THAT'S IT!' I say, attempting to leap out of the bath and rescue my room but falling back in again due to the whole of my lower body being numb.

I accidentally land with my hand on Si's pant area.

'HEY! Hands off the merch!' Si says, laughing as I slide back down into the bath to die.

OH GOD! THE SHAME.

11 p.m.
In bed

Three Queens 👑👑👑
Sam, Millie, Me

Sam: Heyyy! Did you guys survive the wine night?

Millie: Yes, apart from overhearing my mum say her and Dad might split.

Sam: WHAT?! How? Did you have any idea? Are you ok? xx

Millie: It's pretty shitty. I just didn't think it was that bad? It was just a couple of fights? xxx

Me: I'm sorry, Millie. We love you xxx

Sam: Agreed. We're here for whatever you need xxx

Millie: 🤍 xxx

Sam: 🤍 xxx

Me: 🤍 xxx

Sam: See you tomorrow handsome xx

Sam: Wrong chat again sorry xxx

Me: SAM!!!

Millie: EWWWWW!

FFS

IS *SAM* HAVING SEX?

3 Positive Things:

1. Matt's got a new DADDY.

2. Period pants are comfy and great.

3. Tomorrow it'll be just ONE day until the Feminist Society meeting! I can't believe I am actually wishing the weekend away.

Sunday 12th January

9.30 a.m.

Three Queens
Sam, Millie, Me

Sam: OMG I cannot BELIEVE I texted you both that last night, I'm so sorry.

Me: HAHAHAHAHAHAH did Dave enjoy it at least?

Sam: He hasn't replied. 😔 So I'm doubly embarrassed.

Me: That's weird. Don't be embarrassed! Maybe he's asleep?

Sam: Maybe. How are you doing this morning, Millie? Xxx

Millie: Not so great. I forgot what happened last night for a sec when I woke up and then I remembered again. Now I feel rubbish x

Me: I'm sorry, Mills. What can we do to help? X

Millie: Make my parents go back to normal? xx

Sam: 💜 you, Millie xxxx

Monday 13th January

8.00 a.m.
Feminist Society attempt number two day!

This time I KNOW that people are coming, because they said they were on Friday, AND I'm properly prepared!

I got up extra early this morning to put the finishing touches to my agenda and print out fifty copies. I might have gone overboard, but then if all of the people that said they were coming last week do come AND bring friends, it still won't be enough. I guess people can share, it's better for the environment anyway.

I put them into a big A4 cardboard envelope and slide the envelope into my schoolbag, excited for when I get to pull it out again later.

9.30 a.m.
The toilets – pit stop on the way to class

Millie started crying right at the end of form room and so we've snuck off to the toilet. We also texted Nick with an SOS and he says he's on his way. He's a good boyfriend.

'I'm sorry, it was just Miss Mills talking about choosing our A level subjects. I tried to speak to Mum and Dad about them this weekend but getting them both in the same room is impossible.'

'If it helps, I haven't done mine either,' Sam says. 'I spent most of yesterday staring at my phone like an idiot waiting to see if Dave would text back.'

'Still nothing?' I ask, shocked.

'Not a peep,' Sam says. 'I feel so stupid.'

I stay quiet about the A level form, because I did mine as soon as we got it. I've known what I wanted to do for ages, and I was so excited about it. They don't need to hear that from me, though.

'I've just started noticing things, like how they barely talk if they're not fighting and that they're never ever together. I can't believe I didn't realise how serious it was,' says Millie through her sobs.

'It can't stay like this for ever, though,' Sam says, sensible as ever. 'They know that. There'll be some kind of solution, and things will get better.'

'Exactly. It's horrible right now, but it's not for ever,' I say.

'But what if the solution is them breaking up?' says Millie, looking up at us with red eyes.

The door to the toilet creaks open and Nick appears in a pair of sunglasses and a hat, looking like some kind of celebrity burglar. Matt is behind him, a scarf covering most of his face.

'We didn't want anyone to see us coming in here,' Matt says pulling the scarf down from his nose.

'So Matt dressed us up like Kim Kardashian sneaking into Primark,' Nick says heading straight over to Millie to enfold her in a big hug.

At least the stealth outfits have made her laugh.

11 a.m.
History

Just an hour and a half to go until the Feminist Society REALLY kicks off. I cannot wait. The agendas are burning a hole in my schoolbag.

11.30 a.m.
One hour to go!

You know, history lessons wouldn't be so boring if they included some FEMINIST history in them. Like, not just the Suffragettes. That's not the ONLY thing feminists did, you know? Maybe this can be one of the things that we talk about in the Feminist Society.

12 p.m.
Half an hour to go!

I've got butterflies.

12.29 p.m.
ONE MINUTE TO GO!

My legs are dancing around under the desk now and I can barely keep still. I want to be ready to run out of here as quickly as possible as soon as the bell goes. As the society leader, I need to be the first one there.

And . . . *RIIINNNNGGGG!*

I scramble up and out the door faster than I've ever moved before.

12.31 p.m.

Room 404

The second meeting of the Feminist Society

No one is here yet, but that's OK. I did run here pretty fast. It'll take people a minute to get here from their classes.

12.33 p.m.

Jane's here with two friends, but no one else yet. So far that means there are fewer people here than last week. I want to hand out the agenda but now I'm nervous about what Jane's going to think of it. I'll just wait until a few more people are here. More people are definitely coming.

12.35 p.m.

Another friend of Jane's just turned up so there are now four people, not including me, Millie and Sam.

I can't believe it. What happened to all the people who said they were going to come?

I feel stupid getting the massive wodge of agendas out of my bag now. Not only have I failed at feminism again, but I've needlessly wasted a tree's worth of paper in the process.

12.40 p.m.

I'm just about to hand the agendas out when Trudy comes flying through the door.

'We've got this room now,' she shouts.

'What?' I'm staring at her so intensely that it feels like my eyeballs might crack.

'Mr Clarke said we could have this room to plan my party?' she says to me slowly, like I'm stupid. 'Everyone who helps gets a VIP ticket and a free drink.'

'But he gave us this room for the Feminist Society?' I say.

'Well, he must have forgotten. And anyway, there are more of us than there are of you so can't you just go and have your little meeting somewhere else?' she says faux innocently. 'Like the toilet?'

I look past her down the corridor and see that it's not just The Bitches she has in tow, but a whole load of others as well. Half of them are the ones who said they'd come to the Feminist Society meeting. My blood boils as I slowly realise – she's done this on purpose.

I'm about to say something when Sam and Millie come and stand behind me, and I feel a steadying hand on my back.

'Fine,' I say through gritted teeth, and Trudy shrugs and shoves her way past me. She puts her stuff down on the desk I was sitting at just a moment ago and starts taking off her coat as all her minions file in to take over the space.

'Well. We should probably go anyway,' Jane says giving me side-eye while her and her friends collect their stuff and go.

I can't believe this. We're supposed to be feminists. We're supposed to be tough and strong and support each other and lift each other up, not fight each other.

I stand in the doorway, feeling like if I leave I've just rolled over, but I'm unable to think of anything I can do to turn this around.

'Let's go, she's not worth it,' Millie whispers in my ear, and I know she's right.

This morning I thought I had the whole school behind me. As I walk down the corridor, tears prick my eyes and I realise, apart from Millie and Sam, I'm on my own.

4 p.m.
Walking home

I'm pretty crushed about the Feminist Society meeting earlier, and even more disappointed that Mr Clarke thought the society was so unimportant that the room should go to Trudy's party planning, rather than something that benefits everyone at school. I guess I shouldn't be surprised, though, this is very on-brand for him. It's just not how I thought it was going to be. I thought it would be this great big huge group of activists who got shit done. By the end of last term, we'd achieved so much, and it felt really powerful.

Maybe I'm remembering it wrong, though. What if we were actually just three lunatics throwing tampons at people during the school play?

9 p.m.
In bed

I've taken my pity party to bed. I'm so disappointed in myself that I really can't be around others right now. I'm of no use to anyone.

3 Positive Things:
1. *Fuck*
2. *Right*
3. *Off*

Tuesday 14th January

7 a.m.

I woke up and instantly remembered yesterday's failure. There must be SOMETHING I can do to fix the situation, to get people to come to the Feminist Society meetings and realise that it's more important than a stupid party, but I can't think of anything right now.

9 a.m.

All three of us were pretty glum on the way to school this morning. I feel bad, like we should be trying to cheer up Millie because she's going through so much with her parents, but none of us seem to have anything much to say right now.

5 p.m.
My bedroom

I can't stop thinking about how badly I've failed the Feminist Society. Maybe if I can write another really powerful Feminist Friday blog I can win people back over again? Make them realise that the Feminist Society's more important than popularity and Trudy's stupid party.

I need some inspiration, or at least some kind of SOMETHING to do that, though. Instead, I'm just sitting here replaying in my head how easily I rolled over and let Trudy win yesterday and as a result let the Feminist Society DIE.

I'm scrolling through Instagram reading inspirational quotes and trying to find things on the Women in History account when a new picture from SEXBASTIEN pops up on my feed. He's cuddling a small kitten, and it makes my ovaries swoon.

I KNOW I'm supposed to be focusing on Feminist Friday but really today has been so miserable, I think I should be allowed at least a small minute or two to just take in this beautiful picture and fantasise about the great French romance that never was. *sniff*

5.30 p.m.
My boudoir

I've been lying here for half an hour imagining different scenarios. In this new one, Sébastien and I are having a picnic. He is feeding me brie (French AND sexy cheese) and nibbling my neck.

5.45 p.m.

My fantasy made me really fancy some brie so I headed down to the fridge in search. Unfortunately ended up having to compromise and eating a chunk of mild, plastic cheddar (must tell Mum and Dad to buy more sophisticated cheese) to try and recreate the moment, but it was a bit hard and old, and now I worry it's probably going to give me diarrhoea which is making me feel entirely un-sexy and has slightly killed the fantasy.

6 p.m.
Back in bed

I'm back in my room scrolling through pictures of Sexbastien on Instagram.

Oh god, I AM totally giving off creepy Insta lurker vibes again.

Maybe I should just message him. I could say something like:

'Hey, remember me? I slapped your crotch? Wanna have long-distance phone sex?'

I don't even know what you DO in phone sex, though, so it's probably a bad idea. I imagine I'd just end up sneezing or burping down the phone or something.

Maybe I could just send something normal and casual?

Before I know what my fingers are doing, they've typed out 'Hi' and pressed send.

HOLY FUCKING HARRY STYLES. WHAT DID I DO THAT FOR?

Three Queens
Sam, Millie, Me

Me: Guys, I've done a bad.

> **Millie:** Uh oh?

> **Sam:** Whatcha do?

> **Me:** Messaged Sébastien.

> **Millie:** Saying what?

> **Me:** Hi

> **Sam:** And?

> **Me:** Just hi.

> **Millie:** I thought you wanted to be a writer?!
> And that's all you could come up with?

I am deeply, deeply ashamed.

I am immediately going to recommence thinking about the Feminist Society and more serious matters and STOP thinking about Sexbastien and his brie.

11 p.m.

Maybe I should pretend the 'Hi' was an accident? I could just say, 'Whoops sorry wrong chat!'

Except it WAS for him.

Oh dear vaginal god, what have I done?

Maybe I just need to stop touching my phone for a bit.

I put it on the side out of reach.

I'll sit over here and the phone will sit over there.

And never the two shall meet.

Yep, no touching.

Not even looking.

I wonder if he's replied?

Can't hurt if I just touch the phone to see?

No reply.

Cool, cool.

Probably sleeping.

Right.

Like I should be.

I turn the light off, touch the switch three times, and roll over so I'm facing away from my arch nemesis, my phone. There's no way I'm trying a light-switch challenge tonight, not after what I've done.

I roll back over and grab my phone quickly again, just to check one more time before I go to sleep.

No messages.

I put the phone down again and roll back over.

11.30pm

Still no message.

Definitely going to sleep now.

3 Positive Things:

1. At least I am not going to France therefore will never have

to be face to face with Sexbastien and be embarrassed about the message.

2. I know he likes kittens, though, and kittens are good and that means that he is good and that is nice . . . STOP IT, KAT!

3. Maybe I will be a better feminist and sex-kitten tomorrow.

Wednesday 15th January

7 a.m.
Waking up not at all refreshed or rested

I roll over and check my phone for messages. Nothing. Not a single thing.

OH god, I am FREAKING out. I woke up every hour in the night worrying about the things that might happen, like:

1. He might never reply. He might read the message, and I'll see that he's read the message, and then never reply.
2. He might not see the message, and then see it when everyone is over there and ask who this weird Kat girl is that's messaged him because he can't remember the sexiest moment of my life.
3. He might see it and respond with, 'Sorry, who is this?'
4. He might see it and decide I am a stalker and report me and then I will be on a Most Wanted list of Instagram stalkers and penis slappers.
5. I will then never be able to enter France, even when I am thirty and have touched (hopefully) many other penises.

I shuffle off towards the bathroom to deal with the massacre of my period and try not to dwell too much on the idea that Interpol were probably alerted to my Instagram shenanigans.

But, what if he saw it and deleted it straight away? Rolling his eyes as he hit the big red delete tab. I really need to forget this whole thing. I doubt he's even registered it.

OR maybe I'm being too negative? Sarah would tell me to turn this around, reframe my thoughts. Maybe he doesn't look at Instagram all the time like I do? Maybe he's more aloof and actually does things rather than 'gramming about them twenty-four-seven? God, that makes him even sexier.

There's a knock at the door and Freddie starts shouting at me while I'm mid INCREDIBLY IMPORTANT thought process.

'What are you doing in there? I NEED TO SHOWER.'

'MENSTRUATING,' I shout back.

'Urgh, fuck's sake,' I hear him mumble and walk away.

I wonder how much longer that's going to scare him away for.

1.45 p.m.

On a trampoline
PE – as if things couldn't get any worse, now we have to bounce about, defying gravity and common sense.

No one's allowed to do trampolining at our school until Year Eleven. The rumour is that it's because a girl once ripped her belly button piercing out, so now you have to be old enough to watch gory horror movies to do it.

For Millie, today will be the first time she's returned to a trampoline since we were five and a TERRIBLE ACCIDENT occurred.

'How are you feeling, Mills?' Sam asks, rubbing her back.

'Yeah, I'm OK. It was ten years ago now, and lightning can't strike twice, right?' She stares at us, her wide eyes begging for reassurance.

'Absolutely,' I say. I've actually read a story about someone getting struck by lightning twice, but now's probably not the time for it.

It's hard to think about what happened that day. We were all bouncing on the trampoline in Millie's garden, having the most fun we've ever had, when little four-year-old Issy and her little four-year-old friends joined us. Unfortunately, the weight of the extra people (even though they were little) bounced Millie off to the side at a funny angle, where sadly she landed very painfully, straddling . . . actually it just doesn't bear thinking about.

We look over as she pulls two large padded sanitary towels out of her bag.

'Just popping to the toilet,' she says, waving the pads as we stare at her amazed. 'What? You didn't think I was going to go on there without full vaginal protection, did you?'

'Think you mean vulvic protection, babe,' I say, being anatomically correct.

'I need more than mineral water right now, babe,' she shoots back at me.

I think I'll leave her to it, rather than explain that she's using the wrong words. Maybe I should have padded up too, judging by the way Terrible Trudy's sizing me up from across the room. Perhaps I should put some around my head, fashion a kind of helmet? She's got a dangerous look in her eye.

2 p.m.

We're standing around the trampoline acting as buffers in case the person on the trampoline strays. Trudy and Amelie are standing opposite me and I'm one hundred per cent sure that if I bounced their way they'd rather push me off than buffer me on.

Worse luck, Sienna's also in our group, looking bored and disengaged. I doubt she'd even notice anyone bouncing off.

All we have to do is get up and bounce three times on the spot without moving from the X, arms moving in wide circles. That is all.

First up is Millie. I fear she may vomit on us when Ms Sykes shouts at her to get on the trampoline. She takes a big gulp and hoists herself up.

Standing in the middle, she does three perfect jumps. The only slight issue is when her T-shirt rides up exposing her very chunky pant area. Fortunately, no one else seems to notice.

Millie gets down from the trampoline beaming from ear to ear as Sam and I pat her on the back.

Next up: Trudy, who of course does three perfect jumps, then steps down again smugly, without even ruffling a hair.

Unfortunately, now it's my go, and Trudy's smirking at me. I try and maintain full eye contact with her while I get on the trampoline. Staring the enemy in the eye shows them you have no fear.

But I do have much fear.

I struggle to get up there, half pushing up, half falling down, the end effect being like a seal on its side, one flipper flapping desperately.

Finally, I'm up after what feels like ten thousand years. Ms Sykes is staring at me like I'm a marvel of modern science because I'm just that uncoordinated.

Why is it so high up here? I don't remember trampolines ever being so far off the ground. Is this what vertigo feels like? I am completely dependent on my peers – three of whom are actually my sworn enemies – to save me from certain death.

I hear Trudy and Amelie sniggering, but I won't let it put me off.

'For god's sake, Evans, JUMP!' Ms Sykes shouts, startling me and making me almost fall over. It's like trying to balance on a waterbed.

I take a first small jump, and it goes OK, though I swear to god if she shouts at me to jump higher or something, I will LOSE MY SHIT. Just two more to go. Second one, up and down. Done. Just one more to go.

I try to jump a little higher this time and as I feel myself going up, I look down. I'm on my way back down and just about to land, when Sienna kicks the bottom of the trampoline, causing it to ripple. I'm so freaked, I lose my concentration and my balance, I can already tell I'm not going to land on my feet and I desperately just want this to be over. I really wish I wasn't flailing my arms quite so much right now as well, but I don't seem to be able to stop myself from doing that either. It's like some kind of law of physics/chronic cringe has kicked in.

And then it's over. I land hard on my side, face smushed into the disgusting trampoline, that has had literally every single gross foot in our year on it. I'm probably going to wake up tomorrow with some kind of fungal situation: athlete's face.

I try to pick myself up as quickly as possible, but the trampoline just keeps moving and that's when I see that Sienna's still kicking the underside and making it jiggle about.

'Whoops, sorry, I get these spasms,' she says, smiling meanly at me as I manage to gather myself off the side and down to Millie and Sam and safety.

'What the . . .' says Millie. 'Did she just . . .?'

'Leave it,' I say, as I finally manage to get myself off the trampoline.

I take up position opposite Trudy again, and notice she's no longer staring at me. Instead, she's staring intently at Sienna. And smiling.

2.20 p.m.

It was bad enough when I just had Trudy to worry about. Now there's two separate forces for evil at work in this school. At least, they're separate for now. The way Trudy was watching Sienna makes me worried that soon they'll be working together – PURE EVIL DOUBLED.

2.30 p.m.

The changing room

Hiding to avoid my next turn on the trampoline

I told Ms Sykes that I needed to go to the toilet about two people before me hoping that I can miss my go and don't have to go through that hell again.

I hear a sniffing sound and realise there's someone else in here with me. I creep around the corner to where the lockers are and see Sienna sitting on a bench on her phone, and then slink back behind the lockers. I hadn't noticed her leaving. Is she crying? I didn't realise she knew how.

'I know, Mum,' I hear her say. 'It's OK, honestly. I'm fine.'

What does she have to cry about? I'm the one that she just tried to topple off the trampoline!

Despite everything, though, I feel a pang of sympathy for Sienna and wonder if we've got her wrong. But then I remember all her snarky remarks and the fact that my face has foot fungus on it now and decide just to get out of here before she sees me.

5 p.m.

My room

I can still feel the impression of the trampoline on my cheek even though I have washed my face five times.

5.10 p.m.

I'm trying to revise but I keep having flashbacks of my fall and I can't seem to shake the smell of the trampoline, which is basically the smell of feet and some kind of plasticky rubbery aroma mixed together. It isn't really something I want to be smelling for the rest of my life.

Why do people find rubber and PVC sexy anyway?

Is it the smell or the texture or what?

Or is it just that it's wipe-clean?

Do people get that turned on by something you can glide an anti-bac wipe across?

5.20 p.m.

> Google: Why do people find rubber sex— 🔍

Wait, googling that is a TERRIBLE idea, isn't it? Also, I am supposed to be revising! WHAT AM I DOING?!

6 p.m.

I've re-read the same passage of a book about twenty times and I've no idea what it says. Revision = HELL.

8 p.m.
The sofa

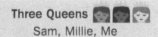

Three Queens
Sam, Millie, Me

Sam: Dave's got a football match on Saturday, does anyone want to come with me?

Sam: I still feel really awkward about Saturday. Even though we've spoken since then, he just completely ignored the sexy texts. I'm so embarrassed. Please come, so I'm not a loner as well as a sex-pest?

Millie: Ummmm, have you seen the weather on Saturday?? Will they even still play in that? Xxx

Sam: They play in any and every weather. PLEASSSSEEEE? I'll buy you hot chocolate after? xxx

Millie: OK fine. I'd rather be out of the house at the moment anyway. Nick says he'll come with so he can make sure I don't lose a tit to the cold. Xxx

Me: EW! Is he literally planning on holding your tits for ninety minutes? In public?

Millie: Don't be such a prude, Kat! Maybe you'll find a footballer that takes your fancy? Xxx

Sam: Oooh yeah! Then we can be WAGS together.

Me: I'm a feminist. I'm not a WAG xxx

Sam: Massively unfeminist to say that WAGS aren't feminists.

Me: They're literally defined by their partners.

Sam: By the media, and we know that the media is not a friend of women. You only have to look at the way they describe women for just existing . . .

Millie: Woman wears a skirt = A LEGGY DISPLAY

Millie: Woman wears a T-shirt = FLAUNTING HER CURVES

Me: Ah shit you're right. Have I also been brainwashed by the media? How did I let this happen? I'm so ashamed! As penance for my unfeminist ways, I will come and join you on Saturday. Even though there'll be no one there to keep my tits warm xxx

Sam: Speaking of someone to keep you warm . . . did you ever hear back from Sébastien? xxx

Me: Nothing from Sexbastien.

Me: Oh god SÉBastien.

Millie: LOL

Sam: LOLLLLLL

Sam: Why don't you invite Matt and Si? They can take a tit each xxx

I don't need a man to keep my boobs warm. I'm a strong, independent woman with a very padded bra, thank you very much.

8.10 p.m.

Me: Would you and Si like to come and watch Dave play football on Saturday with me, Sam, Millie and Nick? Xxx

Me: Please come. I need you

Matt: Sounds good, we're there xxx

I am still a strong independent woman, though.

11 p.m.
In bed

I don't know if I can be bothered to even think about writing this week's Feminist Friday. I mean, what's the point if no one's going to come to the meetings anyway?

I still haven't had the guts to re-open Instagram either.

Everything in my brain just feels like a big scramble. I don't like feeling this way again.

I think I'll have another go at the light-switch challenge even though things are rubbish. Maybe I can salvage something good from this mess inside my brain?

11.02 p.m.

I turn the light off and try not to stare at the clock as I force myself not to touch the switch.

The twitchy, agitated feeling in my fingers starts to build again, like last time, and bad thoughts begin to swirl in my head. Today's already been a bad day, what if I'm just making it worse?

But then again, I feel like maybe when I've got so many bad thoughts in my head anyway and it feels like things can't get much worse it's probably a good time to try this? At least that way I've got less to lose.

11.03 p.m.

Though things could just get EVEN WORSE.

Last time I did this, I thought it was all fine afterwards but, actually, the NEXT DAY we found out Millie's mum and dad are thinking about separating. And I know I'm supposed to think that isn't connected but, oh my god, what if it is?

I sit up abruptly and turn the light back on. Amazingly, I've lasted three minutes, which is an improvement on last time, but I really don't know if I should be doing it any more.

3 Positive Things:
1. My face has never been so clean after the post-trampoline faceplant scrubbing session.
2. I lasted three minutes in the light-switch challenge which is two more than before and felt IMPOSSIBLE last week.
HURRAH.
3. If I can do that, then maybe I can do the other things that feel impossible, like revision and finding a way to salvage the Feminist Society.

Thursday 16th January

Urgh. I can't believe the girls are here already. I slept so badly and just feel crappy. I have nothing to write for Feminist Friday tomorrow, no France to look forward to, no Sébastien. GCSEs are coming up and I have so much revision and my brain's just a big mushy scramble.

I do feel good about managing to go so long without touching the light switch last night, but I'm also worrying it might make things get worse. Everything's already messed up enough as it is. Right now, I just want to crawl back into bed and stay there until it's all over, especially the exams.

I sit in front of the mirror to put make-up on but as soon as I see myself, I start crying. I just feel knackered, my brain's all in a fog, and I don't feel like I can do even *one* of the things I need to do, let alone *all* of them.

'Ready?' Sam pops her head round my door and sees my crying face.

'Oh no! Kat! What's up?' Millie says coming over and giving me a hug. I feel bad about her having to comfort me when she's dealing with so much.

'I just feel so useless,' I say, throwing down my concealer stick. 'I'm not doing anything good any more. I'm going to fail my exams because I can't focus on anything. The Feminist

Society's rubbish, and I don't know what to write for this week's Feminist Friday blog, because I'm not a proper feminist. I'm just an idiot. I don't know why I thought I could do it when I spend all my time worrying about a stupid boy not messaging back anyway. Everything I do I screw up.' I'm properly crying now.

'Oh, Kat. Screw Sébastien,' says Sam coming to sit next to me. 'He's not worth it, and as for everything else, it's OK. You don't have to do it all alone. We can help you with Feminist Friday.'

'We'll think of something together!' Millie says.

'You've got this,' Sam says.

'Thanks, guys,' I say, sniffing into my jumper. 'I'm sorry. You've got enough going on at the moment without me crying on you, Millie.'

'Nahhh, nice to have someone else crying for a change, I feel like I've being hogging the tears lately,' Millie says, grabbing my concealer stick to start work on my face.

8.30 a.m.
The playground

By the time we get to school, I'm feeling much better. There's an odd atmosphere in the playground, though. Everyone seems to be staring at their phones and there's a weird buzz in the air. I'm hearing snippets of excited and appalled chatter, but I can't work out what's happened.

I see Matt racing towards us, phone in hand.

'Have you seen it?' He's all flustered.

122

'Seen what?' I ask.

'There's an Instagram account. It's called **@FittyorPity**. It looks like it's been going for a while as a private account, but someone made it public this morning.'

Sam pulls her phone out and I feel like I already know I'm going to hate whatever it is. The name **@FittyorPity** was enough for me.

'Oh my god,' Sam says.

'What is it?' I ask, Millie and I crowding around her phone.

I can't believe what I'm seeing. There must be pictures of every girl from Year Nine to Year Thirteen here, taken in really unflattering and candid ways from across the playground, and definitely without consent.

Under every picture, there's a list with a score next to it that reads:

But even worse is what they've written for one of the Year Nine pupils, Aimee Jones. Aimee's never come out as non-binary or anything, but their friends refer to them by gender-neutral pronouns. Now over their picture is just written: 'Not even a girl – zero points'. They've not only publicly outed them, they've humiliated them too. I can't even begin to imagine how Aimee feels right now.

'Are you fucking kidding me?' Sam manages to rage, while the rest of us stare at it speechless.

'Has anyone seen Aimee today?' I ask, scanning the playground.

'No. Their friends are trying to get in touch with them,' Matt says sombrely.

'God, this is just heinous,' Millie says. 'What kind of garbage person does that? Or any of this?'

'I'm NOT going to look at my score,' I say firmly.

What I don't say is that I really want to look. But I won't.

'Me neither,' says Millie.

'Me neither,' agrees Sam. 'We can't give in to this toxic masculinity bullshit.'

'This is just designed to make everyone feel crap about themselves,' Millie says.

'And none of us should,' I add.

'Who do you think did it?' Millie asks.

'I have an idea,' I say, seeing the same group of Year Ten boys sitting in the same place they always sit. laughing and joking around, as if nothing's happened.

The girls follow my gaze and we all stand with narrowed eyes, staring at them.

'It HAS to be them,' Millie says.

'But how do we prove it?' I ask.

'Can we see who's following?' Sam asks. 'Then we can pin

down their names.'

'There were about a hundred followers this morning, but it's dropped down to ten really quickly. They all just disappeared, I guess none of them wanted to get caught. Now it's just a load of bots and . . . Trudy. Surprise, surprise,' Matt says, motioning in her direction. She's striding around the playground enjoying every second of the upset and confusion happening around her.

'Look at her,' Matt says. 'If it wasn't for the fact that she got a six for her legs, I'd think she was responsible.'

I want to ask him what her other scores were, but I also don't. I don't want to be any part of it.

'She got tens for the rest,' he says, as if reading my mind.

Of course, that's why she's loving this so much. I can see her coming towards me and I'm so NOT in the mood.

'Sorry you got a two for your tits, Kat. I guess there are barely two of them anyway,' she shouts to me across the playground.

Oh great. Thanks for the spoiler, Trudy.

'Well, I guess technically it's just one each,' I hear from behind me and turn around to see Sienna leaning against the art block like some kind of cartoon villain.

A weird noise comes from Trudy that I realise is her laughing, I've just never heard it before. The Bitches all look as taken aback as I am.

'New girl! Come hang with us?' Trudy asks Sienna.

Tiffany and Amelie stand with their mouths hanging open in shock as Sienna grabs her bag and coolly struts over to Trudy. Has she just been invited to join The Bitches? In eleven years, no one new has been allowed in. And yet Sienna seems to fit in perfectly as they all stride off together to find more victims to destroy.

'*What* just happened?' Millie says, turning around.

'I think we've just witnessed the joining of two very dark forces,' Sam says as we watch them walking away.

'I'd give your tits at least an eight, by the way,' Matt says. 'At least they won't sag.'

'Thanks, Matt. That means a lot. Love you,' I say, giving him a hug.

The bell rings and as we all start to move inside, I comfort myself with the thought that at least I know exactly what I'll be writing this week's Feminist Friday blog about.

9.00 a.m.
Form room

Sienna swans into form late and sits behind us, already smelling of Trudy's signature scent, or as we like to call it, Eau de Piss.

I hate that she sits behind us and I can't see what she's up to.

'Is it wrong that I really want to look at my scores?' Millie asks.

'Yes!' Sam and I say.

I have to admit, I also really want to look at mine. BUT THAT'S WHAT THE PATRIARCHY WANTS ME TO DO!

I turn slightly to see Sienna behind us smirking. Just because she's too new to be on the list, doesn't mean she should be enjoying every other girl at the school being shamed. She really is perfect for The Bitches.

Sam follows my eyes to behind us and realises what I'm staring at.

'Eugh, what's up with her?' she says.

And I can't help wondering the same thing. What kind of person starts a new school and is immediately drawn to the most toxic group around?

10.00 a.m.
Biology

I couldn't resist. I know it's self-destructive behaviour, but I looked at my scores.

The picture is a creepy stalkerish shot taken from across the playground – gross and intrusive.

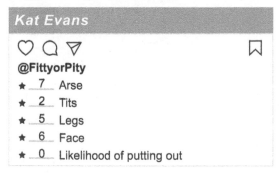

Great, I've got the highest score for the thing that's constantly behind me. Although, it's right about one thing, I'm VERY unlikely to 'put out' with whoever made this list.

Patriarchy 1 – Kat 0

Me: I couldn't help it, I looked at my scores. I'm sorry x

Millie: Me too.

Sam: Me too. I guess it's just natural to be curious about this stuff xx

Millie: It didn't make me feel good x

Me: Me either x

Sam: Me either x

12.30 p.m.
The cafeteria

'This whole thing is nuts,' Sam says as we watch two Year Ten girls have a shouting match – one accusing the other that she has got a real ego since getting a ten for her legs.

'Oh god, I think she's about to throw spaghetti at her!' Millie says.

The whole cafeteria is watching and it's clear that every girl in this school has been affected by the account in some way, whether they got good scores, bad scores, or no score at all. It's

128

the younger ones I feel sorry for. Imagine feeling like the only thing you have to look forward to when you grow up is being judged for your physical attributes and competing with your friends over how someone else views you.

'Fuck this, I'm going in,' I say, unable to sit and watch any more.

I stride over to the fighting girls, my blood boiling.

'Hey!' I shout. 'You're just giving the monsters that did this exactly what they want! We need to stick together – don't let them tear us apart!'

They both stare blankly at me. One of them is still holding her plate of spaghetti so I'm very much in the danger zone here, but I'm going to keep trying.

'They want to turn us all against each other so that we can't be strong. So that we're distracted by all this bullshit. You're playing directly into their hands. What do those scores even matter anyway? Who devised them? Someone who has absolutely no experience with women probably.'

'What scores did you get?' one of them asks, eyeing me suspiciously. She's clearly NOT been listening to what I said.

'I didn't look,' I lie.

'She got a two for her boobs,' the one with the bowl of spaghetti says to the other. I don't even know her, and this is the main thing she knows about me.

Everyone in the cafeteria laughs. I push down my humiliation and press on. 'What scores we got is *not* the point!'

'Yeah, totally,' says the other one. 'Since she got a ten for her legs, she's behaving like she's some kind of model.'

'Oh, screw you, can't you be happy for me?' And before I can stop her, she launches herself at her 'friend', spaghetti bowl in hand.

I don't know why, but for some stupid reason I jump between them. And then I feel it hit my face and shoulders. Spaghetti is dribbling down my back. It's up my nose and all I can smell is tomato. I think I might have inhaled some. What if I have tomatoes in my lungs now? All because I was trying to be a good feminist.

Both girls stare at me. Frozen.

I wipe spaghetti from my eyes and realise that now, with everyone staring at me, is the perfect moment. I climb up on to the nearest chair, nervous about slipping with all this sauce over me.

'DON'T LET TOXIC MASCULINITY WIN! COME TO THE FEMINIST SOCIETY! MONDAY 12.30, ROOM 404!'

'Join the Feminist Society and beat @**FittyorPity**!' Millie joins in also standing on a chair, while Sam climbs up next to her.

'You are more than just a score!' shouts Sam. 'Read the Feminist Friday blog tomorrow for more information!'

I look around. Everyone's staring at us blankly.

In a film people would be cheering right now. But this isn't a film. It's me standing in front of the whole school, with spaghetti in my bra.

Of all the things I wish would slide into my bra, cafeteria spaghetti is not one of them. But as Sam, Millie and I stand on our chairs, I can't help but feel slightly triumphant.

4.30 p.m.
In my room, after a shower

Oh good.
    I'm a GIF.

4.35 p.m.

Honestly, no sooner had I washed the spaghetti off my person than some dickhead made me into a GIF ensuring I can never wash it off my SOUL.

4.40 p.m.

I'm going to be Spaghetti Girl for ever now, aren't I?
    So far this term I've:
- Been floored by Chanel
- Walked around with 'Is this my clitoris?' on my arse
- Become SPAGHETTI GIRL – the worst superhero on the internet

It's only January and I've already been a gif, a meme and a mess.

6 p.m.
My room

I've been writing for over an hour now, my anger fuelling my fingers.

I write about how the Instagram account is designed to tear people down, to objectify them and reduce their value to how sexually attractive they are.

I write that we have to find out who did this and make sure it never happens again. Whoever made this cannot be allowed to feel that it's acceptable or that they've got away with it.

I add a clear call to action for people to join the meeting on Monday, so that we can discuss next steps and how we think we should respond.

I ended with 'All welcome' – because that's what feminism's really about. Equality.

Is it terrible that an upside of this whole scoring malarkey is that I feel useful again? I feel like I have a job to do. I also feel shitty because someone has scored me as not a very attractive person but the fire it has ignited in me seems to overshadow that.

I've finished. Ready to post tomorrow morning.

I feel like I've gained some of my credibility back.

But inside, very, very deep down, I know I deserve a higher score.

6.05 p.m.

Someone's done a video of the moment I got spaghetti-slapped with 'That's Amore' playing over the top.

That's *not* amore.

No (a)more, PLEASE.

6.30 p.m.

It's spaghetti for dinner.
　　Dad's trolling me.

11 p.m.
Bed

I've been lying here thinking about what we can do and how we can prove whether it's definitely those guys from Freddie's year that made the account. What if it's more widespread than just one group, though? What if there are people in other years too?
　　The whole thing just feels so seedy and creepy.
　　We can't stand by and just let this happen.

3 Positive Things:
1. My tits may be small, but they're actually perfectly formed, thank you very much.
2. You can take your 2 and shove it up your arse.
3. @FittyorPity has given me a RAGE that I shall use for feminist good.

friday 17th January

7 a.m.

I woke up to Bea licking my face and at first thought it was part of a dream I was having where Sexbastien was kissing me and telling me what a great feminist I am.

8 a.m.

In my room.

Ready to go into full hibernation mode if this all goes wrong

'KAT! KAAT!' I can hear Sam and Millie running up the stairs calling for me.

'Oh my god, KAT!' shouts Millie, bursting through my door. 'Your post!'

I posted about ten minutes ago, then shoved my phone in a drawer and jumped in the shower to stop myself thinking about it.

My heart is RACING now as I see the excitement on their faces.

'IT'S GOT TWO HUNDRED LIKES!' says Sam thrusting her phone at me.

'AND THE COMMENTS!' Millie's gushing.

I race over to the drawer and take out my phone. I can't believe it. They're right – there are two hundred and twenty likes now. And climbing. And the comments are amazing. People agreeing with me, people outraged and upset, people embarrassed about spending a whole day disappointed that they got a three for their legs rather than raging against it as they should have been. And almost all of them saying they're coming to the meeting on Monday.

OK, one person has commented to ask if I was the girl who flung a menstrual cup at a boy's feet. And there are comments from anonymous users on there too, not nice ones. One person calls me 'a bitter ugly troll-whore'. Probably Trudy TBH.

But the good more than outweigh the bad.

I look up from my phone and see the girls' grinning faces. They pounce on me and we all fall back on my bed laughing. Bea, sensing excitement, jumps up to join the celebration too.

9 a.m.
Form room

Still, though . . .

Troll-whore.

Troll. Whore?

How can I be a troll-whore when my likelihood of putting out was 0 on that stupid account?

Arghhhh! Why am I even thinking about this one comment when all the other ones were so good?

The hallway

People have been walking up to me all day saying that they're going to come to the meeting, asking for more information, telling me how great the post was and how pleased they are that someone's spoken out about it. I feel like I'm gliding through the halls, on a high.

'Oh, here she is, queen activist, spaghetti-head,' Trudy shouts at me as I'm walking down the corridor to meet the girls. 'Ruining everyone's fun just because she got shit scores.'

Even Trudy can't bring me down today, though. I turn around, which to be fair was probably my mistake.

She's standing with all The Bitches behind her and Sienna next to her, making me wonder if Sienna's been promoted straight to some kind of Second-Bitch-in-Command position. Tiffany and Amelie do look a little put out.

'What do you want, Trudy?' I sigh.

'Just to remind you what a loser you are.'

'Boring,' I say and turn back around and keep walking.

I can hear her and Sienna laughing behind me and I'm trying my best to remember what my mum's always said about Trudy – that her behaviour must come from a place of deep unhappiness.

Maybe Sienna's does too?

Or maybe they're both just from places of pure evil.

136

4 p.m.
Therapy

As the bell for end of school goes, I'm excited to remember that I've got therapy this afternoon. I can't wait to tell Sarah about everything that's happened this week. I know that she's going to ask me how I did on the light-switch challenge too, and I'm pleased that I can tell her I managed a whole three minutes, even if I did worry that the world was going to end afterwards.

I feel like I can really tackle this compulsion now. I can and *am* smashing the patriarchy and if I can achieve that in our messed-up school, then I can achieve ANYTHING.

Shame about being a troll-whore, though.

5.10 p.m.
Walking home

I felt so high from the reaction to my blog that even talking about my freakout after doing the light-switch challenge this week couldn't bring me down. Sarah asked lots of questions about when I first started touching it, and why, questions that I would normally get annoyed by and would find intrusive and shy away from. But I feel bold today. I feel like I can overcome anything, even my biggest secret.

It's really hard to talk about something that's been a secret for so long, but today, when I'm feeling strong, was exactly the right day to do it.

This week the plan is that I need to try and not touch it for the full ten minutes after I turn it off, at least once. Sarah said I need to sit with the uncomfortable feelings that it gives me, knowing that there'll be a resolution. It's called exposure therapy apparently.

Tonight, is the night – I'm going to make it to ten minutes.

It's time to start facing this head on.

I want to be free.

8 p.m.
The sofa

Everyone's busy tonight, Mum's with the mums, Freddie's with Issy, even Dad's got his new BFF Derek from number five round to play computer games. I'm the only friendless loser in this house.

Oh, wait! What's this . . . I've got a message on Instagram! There it is – the little red dot of joy in the corner of the screen. It MUST be from Sébastien. FINALLY. Today really has been AN EXCELLENT DAY.

I should wait and savour the moment, open it in a controlled manner . . . fuck it, I'm GOING IN.

Oh. It's not from him.

It's from Aimee in Year Nine.

'I saw your blog, is it OK if I come to the meeting on Monday?'

My heart lurches and I respond immediately.

'Hi Aimee, OF COURSE it is. I'm so glad you want to come!'
I watch and wait as the three dots appear.

'Cool, thanks. I just didn't know if it was only for cis women or if non-binary people would be welcome too.'

'Of course non-binary people are welcome. Feminism is for everyone – for anyone who wants equality . . .'

I want to say more and try to remember the definition of intersectional feminism – how people experience different levels of discrimination depending on their race, class, religion, sexuality, gender identity. I guess this is really true for Aimee.

'Equality should be for everyone,' I go on. 'Not just whoever society decides is worthy of it. I'm so sorry about those idiots . . . we'll prove who it was and make them pay!'

I really hope I helped and said the right thing. I want Aimee to feel supported and included.

'Thanks, Kat! 😊 See you on Monday!'

Phew.

Oddly I don't feel disappointed that it wasn't Sébastien now. I guess deep down I know that talking to Aimee was more important.

10 p.m.
In bed

Spurred on by everything that's happened today, I'm ready to go to bed and try another light-switch challenge.

10.01 p.m.

I steel myself and turn the light off.

Actually, this isn't so bad. I had to stop myself from touching it automatically. But now I've done that, I'm just lying in the dark, hands clasped under the duvet, waiting for the timer to go down.

I'm trying not to think about all the bad things that might happen and instead I try to remember all the good things that *have* happened today.

10.06 p.m.

This is the slowest ten minutes ever. It felt easy at first, but it's getting harder with every second.

I hate feeling like this, like I'm going to pop, like I can't breathe properly until I touch it. There's no way I can sleep until I do it, that's for sure. I keep running over the events of today to try to keep my momentum and positivity up, even if my palms are sweaty and my head's spinning.

How is Bea so calm? She's just lying there sleeping next to me when I'm so anxious.

At least I think she's asleep.

What if something bad HAS happened and she's stopped breathing?

The room starts to go a bit fuzzy and everything feels a bit further away than it was before. I think I can hear my heartbeat in my head. It's echoing.

10.08 p.m.

I lurch up in bed and turn the light on, unable to take any more.

Bea groans as my sudden movement disturbs her. I guess she is very much still alive and now just a bit annoyed that I woke her up.

I give her a big hug to say sorry.

She groans again. It's possible she's annoyed at me for being so dramatic.

I'M annoyed at me for being so dramatic.

Still, eight minutes is a really long time, and maybe, like Sarah suggested, I should be kind to myself and maybe even proud each time I manage a bit longer than before.

10.10 p.m.

It does feel odd afterwards, though. I want to text the girls and ask if they're OK. I want to check on Mum and Dad and Freddie too, but they'd all think I was weird.

I look out the window and see Matt, Si and Sandra next door in the conservatory. So at least I know they're OK.

10.35 p.m.

I can hear Mum getting home downstairs and Freddie's in his room, so I think they're OK. Dad's still playing with Derek in the study.

I feel exhausted but take deep breaths remembering that today was a good day. I did good things, and no one can take that away from me.

Now I've just got Monday to prepare for. THE BIGGEST, MOST IMPORTANT FEMINIST SOCIETY MEETING EVER.

I turn the light off and touch the switch three times.

3 Positive Things:
1. I have done good things today.
2. I am using feminism to smash the patriarchy and fight for equality for EVERYONE.
3. I am NOT a troll-whore (must repeat this to myself hourly).

Saturday 18th January

8.45 a.m.

I am looking super sexy right now in ten thousand layers of clothing INCLUDING a thermal vest. IS there anything sexier than the words 'thermal' and 'vest' together? I think not.

I have really gone for the layering style today. I'm also dressed to protect myself from the stupid football, should it ever veer my way. I have to be careful. I'm already Spaghetti Girl and Troll-Whore. I don't want to add Ball Bitch to the list.

I keep telling myself that we're doing this to support Sam. I know that Sam is really worried about Dave's behaviour lately. So who cares if we'll be standing in the cold, perilously close to a flying football? We're FRIENDS. This is what friends do. Even on Saturday mornings in January.

I feel like the marshmallow from *Ghostbusters*, except less evil. I start walking downstairs but actually have to swing my legs slightly out to the sides to try and move. I just don't know why the chic Parisian boy has not made immediate contact with me and my sexy thermal wear. He really is missing out.

10 a.m.
The sidelines of sporting greatness

'You're twice your actual size!' Sam laughs at me.

'Are you wearing everything you own?' Millie asks.

'Everything except for her sexy clothes.' Matt chuckles.

'Don't listen to them, Kat, they're just jealous because they didn't think to wrap up as well,' Si says.

'Thank you, Si, at least one of you is sensible,' I say, catching him smirk slightly, the little shit.

Nick appears behind Millie.

'Morning, everyone. Kat, you look . . . wow.'

FFS.

10.20 a.m.

Kick-off

Hypothermia has set in despite everything

Kick-off has only just happened. I repeat, it has ONLY JUST happened. We have been standing here for twenty minutes. We have NINETY minutes more, not including half time which apparently they insist on taking because they get tired. I've not seen enough movement to warrant tiredness yet. I've moved more through shivering than some of these 'players'.

'Dave's quite good, isn't he?' Nick says encouragingly.

'I've just never found footballers that sexy,' Si says, apropos of NOTHING. 'It's all a bit dirty for me. I like a boy who keeps his knees clean.' They're chuckling to themselves. Must be an in-joke.

Oh.

I think they're making a reference to blow jobs.

God, I am SUCH a virgin.

'Huh?' Millie says, pointing down the field. 'What are THEY doing here?'

We follow her gaze to where Trudy and Sienna are walking towards the pitch, in matching faux-fur jackets, with those woolly headband things round their heads, and the rest of The Bitches trailing behind them. I've never understood those bands, what are they warming?

'Seriously, though, why are they here?' Sam asks.

'They're dressed like the cast of *Made in Chelsea* on a ski trip,' Matt comments.

They're all making quite a lot of noise about arriving. I guess Trudy wouldn't want to be upstaged by an actual entire football game.

'I find it so weird that new girl has opted to be friends with Trudy,' Matt says.

'And that she's somehow now Trudy's BFF,' says Millie. 'I've never seen someone burst through the ranks of The Bitches with such ease, without even so much as a bitchy initiation.'

'Très peculiar,' Sam admits.

'Does anyone know anything about her yet?' Si asks.

'Just that she was expelled from some posh girls' school and her parents begged for her to be able to come to our school to sit her GCSEs,' Sam says.

'The latest rumour I heard was that she set something on fire. Like, deliberately,' Millie says.

'Woah. That's pretty big,' Si says.

'Yeah, that's, like, arson. Wouldn't she be in prison?' Sam says.

'I mean, the first person she made friends with was Trudy. That says a lot about a person,' I say.

'If she DID do that, should she be at ANY school now?' Matt asks.

'Regardless of what she did, though,' I say trying to steer things back to the point, 'HOW has she got up the rankings to vice principal bitch so fast when she doesn't even know anyone here? And why haven't the others kicked off about it after years of loyal service to the dark lord?'

'Well, she seems to know Dave,' Nick says as Sienna and Dave smile and wave at each other.

'Erm, what?' Sam says, staring over at them.

She looks like she's about to drag him out of the game right now and demand answers.

12 p.m.

Football is long. It has ONLY JUST FINISHED and so unfortunately has my relationship with my extremities. Goodbye, fingers, toes and tits.

We've been dutifully waiting for Dave for the past fifteen minutes. How can it take him so long to change? What's he doing?

'Oh, wait, he's over there already,' Matt says, pointing to where Dave is.

We all wince as we spot Dave in the crowd talking to Sienna.

'WHAT?' Sam says, spinning round and looking at them. She's watching them interact, completely silent. I can't even tell if she's still breathing. 'Well, that's not a big deal, is it? I'm not the kind of girlfriend who gets funny about their boyfriend talking to another girl.'

But she doesn't sound too sure about this.

And neither would I be. It's uncomfortable to watch Sienna twirling her hair around her finger and sticking her boobs out so close to his face that it's a wonder he can see past them.

But Dave's always been crazy about Sam. So surely we don't have anything to worry about. I say WE, because if you cross one of us, you cross us all.

'Right, well I think I might just go over there and politely reintroduce myself, as Dave's girlfriend,' Sam says, heading over to them.

2 p.m.
Scoops

I'm spooning cream and marshmallows off the top of my hot chocolate into my mouth and I'm incredibly relieved to be inside.

Sam managed to prize Dave away from his new BFF and we're all in Scoops warming up and talking about Trudy's party.

'Who announces a party over A MONTH in advance anyway?' Si asks innocently.

'Trudy, obviously!' Matt says. 'Keep up!'

147

'Where is the party?

'The Den.'

'Filthy. Theme?'

'Prom.'

'Tacky. We're there.'

'Absolutely.'

I love watching Si and Matt together. It's almost like they have the same brain sometimes. I often wonder if when they're alone they don't really have to talk to each other, and just communicate telepathically. I can't imagine ever having anyone like that in my life. Well, romantically, anyway, I've obviously got Sam and Millie.

'So we're going, then?' Dave asks as if that whole exchange was confusing for him.

'Of course we are,' Sam says, taking a sip of hot chocolate.

'How do you know Trudy's new BFF?' Si asks him, batting past the elephant in the room.

'Oh, Sienna? She's Luca on the team's twin sister,' he says.

'Huh, I didn't know Luca was a twin,' Sam says.

'She's been at this boarding school for years.' Dave's answering in short sentences, his eyes fixed on his hot chocolate.

'Did she really get expelled from her last school? For a FIRE?' Millie asks.

'I don't really know. She doesn't ever talk about it. I just know her because she lives with Luca now and we're round there all the time after practice,' Dave says, not noticing Sam's face change to show fear and concern.

My desk

Attempting to revise and FAILING because my phone keeps beeping

Message: WhatsApp Group name changed by Kat:
I lost my toes to hypothermia for you Sam

Sam: I don't have to worry about Dave, do I? xx

Millie: In what way? xx

Sam: You know. With Sienna.

Me: No way! He loves you. And she's just Luca's sister xx

Sam: Yeah who he seems to have been hanging out with a lot.

Me: Yeah but he's with you, he wouldn't be with you if he wanted to be with someone else. That would just be silly xxx

Sam: You're right. Why am I being so paranoid? Xxx

Millie: Because you've just found out your boyfriend's been hanging out with someone massively shady. But I'm with Kat on this one. You can trust him xxx

Message: WhatsApp Group name changed by Millie:
We 💜 SAM

8 p.m.

The sofa at my house AKA Loserville

I literally cannot believe that I am SIXTEEN now and STILL I do not have cool plans for a Saturday night. This is against everything I was led to believe by *Hollyoaks* or those American teen movies where they're always having fun and going to parties, even on school nights. (Who has parents that let them go to parties on a school night and HOW do they get away with it, please?)

8.10 p.m.

Mum's put on a film called *Hysteria*. Freddie ran out the room as soon as he realised what it was about. I want to leave too. WHY HAS SHE DONE THIS?

It's basically a film where two doctors use masturbation to cure female illnesses and eventually invent the vibrator. This is TOO MUCH.

Does she know about my inability to masturbate? This is not normal mother behaviour.

I repeat, WHY IS SHE DOING THIS?

Dad is sitting in the corner trying to distract himself. Mum keeps trying to talk to me about the film.

'See, Kat, they thought that women being horny was actually an illness. Apparently it was fine for men to rage about the place with erections like bulls in china shops, but when women felt a tiny urge or a little bit of desire they were called

150

hysterical and sent to a doctor. MEN!'

Dad tries to sneak out of the room without getting spotted.

I think her and Dad might possibly have had an argument . . .

We 💙 SAM
Sam, Millie, Me

Millie: Can you guys talk? Xxx

Me: Always xxx

Sam: Of course, what's up? Xxx

Millie: Dad's left.

Me: WHAT? XXX

Sam: I'm doing a WhatsApp call xxx

I answer as soon as the video call rings and see Millie red-faced and crying. I hate that with video calls you can't hug someone.

'Oh, Millie, what happened?' I say.

'I came back from the football with you guys and he was packing a bag. Issy came home and they told us he's going to live with Uncle Alex. A trial separation apparently.' She's crying through the end of the sentence, so I have to strain to work out what she's saying.

'Oh god, Millie! I'm so sorry,' I say.

'I'm sorry, Millie. Maybe it won't be for ever?' Sam suggests.

'Maybe, but Mum sounded pretty certain before. Nick's on his way over.' More bonus points for Nick.

'What can we do?' I ask, struck by the fact that I have no idea what she's going through. I feel utterly helpless.

'Can we hang out tomorrow? I think I need some Scoops time and some seriously trashy films,' she says, sniffing.

'We can do that,' I say.

'Just let us know when you're awake and we'll be over,' Sam says.

> **Message:** WhatsApp Group name changed by Sam:
> We 💙 MILLIE

3 Positive Things:

1. Sadly, Trudy and Sienna did not get taken out by rogue balls at the football match, but I enjoyed imagining that they might.

2. It was touch and go but I do still actually have all my fingers and toes.

3. It's hard to think positive thoughts when Millie's going through such a terrible time. Is it bad that I'm still looking forward to the Feminist Society on Monday? Is it OK to enjoy things when your friends are having a hard time?

Sunday 19th January

10 p.m.

Sam and I spent the day with Millie trying to help in whatever way we could. In the end we went for distraction – the three of us working on an agenda for tomorrow's big Feminist Society meeting and re-reading the messages of support on the Feminist Friday blog.

By the time we left Millie's place we'd roped her mum and sister into preparations as well which distracted them too. It felt like feminism was doing what we needed it to do today, giving us all strength in a difficult time. And most importantly, by the time we all hugged goodbye and squashed her, Millie seemed much better.

Tomorrow, though, FEMINISM SHALL PREVAIL. I'm too excited to sleep.

3 Positive Things
1. The Feminist Society
2. Feminism
3. PATRIARCHY SMASHING

Monday 20th January

The first REAL meeting of the Feminist Society happens TODAY!

7.45 a.m.
My room

I'm sitting yawning at my dresser after a bad night's sleep. My head was buzzing with too much excitement to rest and I kept waking up every five seconds wondering if it was time for the meeting yet. Two adorable bereted heads pop round my door just as I finish mascara-ing my tired eyes.

'Reporting for activism, miss!' Sam says, saluting.

'It felt like a beret kind of day!' Millie says, tossing one at me.

She looks exhausted and like she's doing her 'pretending to be cheerful' thing, but I'm hoping that smashing the patriarchy is at least still providing a welcome distraction.

She's right about the beret, though. If I'm to lead a feminist resistance, my beret is definitely the way forward.

'Thanks, Millie,' I say, arranging the beret so it stays on properly. 'How are you feeling?'

'I don't think I've slept properly since Saturday, but we did talk to Dad last night and he seems to be having a great time with Uncle Alex.'

'That's good?' Sam suggests.

'Yeah, it's just . . . I haven't seen him that happy with us in ages.' Millie shrugs.

'That's not to do with you, though. It's got nothing to do with how he feels about you,' I say.

'I guess,' Millie says but I don't get the sense she believes it. 'Anyway, today is FEMINIST DAY! And we've got too much to do to waste time wallowing!'

She gives me a brave smile and the three of us head out TO FEMINIST.

8.30 a.m.
The playground

Five days after the account first circulated, the playground's still abuzz with **@FittyorPity** chat, which is bad for humanity, but good for the Feminist Society, because loads of people have said that they're coming along today as a result.

'Matt's going to come along to the meeting and show his support . . .' I say to the girls as we meet up with Dave.

'Nick said he'd come too,' Millie says and the two of us look at Dave until he takes the hint.

'Oh, I'd love to come but . . . football practice . . . sorry,' he says.

Sam's glaring at him, furious. I'd hate to be him right now.

'I'm sorry,' he says again, arms raised as he leans in and kisses her forehead.

Ever since Hot/Shit Josh kissed me on the forehead, I've

found it quite a patronising gesture. Especially in this instance, when he's using it to apologise for not coming to the meeting, to effectively silence her when she's upset about something.

'Ah well. Sounds like there'll be plenty of other people there anyway,' says Sam, her eyebrows knitted together in a hard, angry stare at Dave.

12.30 p.m.
Room 404

FINALLY the Feminist Society meeting is here, after the longest Monday morning ever. I think time actually stopped during History.

As we head excitedly up the corridor, I briefly allow myself a moment of doubt and wonder if it's just going to be another disappointment. What if Trudy's there again, commandeering the room? Or Jane has to take over because of my ineptitude?

But as we swing through the double doors at the top of the corridor leading to Room 404 we all gasp. There are people spilling all the way down the corridor, lining up outside the room, all of them waving and saying hi as we walk past.

I keep heading for the room, wondering if this may actually be some kind of joke arranged by Trudy, but when we get through the door the room's full and Trudy's nowhere to be seen.

It's not just girls here either, there are boys too, ready to fight the patriarchy alongside us. I'm so pleased to see Aimee sitting with their friends, laughing and joking. I look around and feel my breath catching in my throat, and briefly feel like I might cry. As the three of us stand at the entrance to the room and the great crowd, we look at each other with big beaming smiles on our faces, eyes sparkling. And then we dive in.

Nick and Matt have fought their way to the front with a group of girls from the Sixth Form and they wave at us excitedly as we come in.

At first when I try to get attention there are too many people and it's too loud, so Matt stands up, giving me his seat, and motions for me to stand on it. I'm nervous about talking to this many people but I know that we're all here for the same reason and I have faith in what we're doing.

The usual cold, stale feeling in this room has been replaced by something warmer and energetic and as I climb up on to the chair, I can look around properly and register just how many people are here, their eyes all turned towards me hopefully.

Now I just have to not be weird.

'Hey, so, welcome!' I shout, feeling like an absolute dweeb.

What are my hands doing?

It's like a mixture of jazz hands and the dinosaur from *Toy Story*. Jesus, put them away, Kat. Matt's smiling and nodding at me encouragingly, but I know that he's going to make fun of my dinosaur jazz hands later.

'So I guess, umm, we're all here for the same thing, because we saw *that* Instagram account, and now we're angry, right?'

I'm hoping if I ask questions it will make it less about me talking.

'RIGHT!' a few people say and nod along, while others are just staring at me. God, there are so many people looking at me right now I feel like I might fall over. Aimee catches my eye, smiling, at the front, and I take a deep breath. I can do this.

'We have to act!' I shout. 'We need to find out who's responsible. We need to make sure that the school take this seriously. We need to make sure it never happens again!'

'Mr Clarke didn't even talk about it this morning in assembly, though,' says Jane, 'and I overheard him telling Miss Mills that he felt like it was an "outside-school issue" and not one that they should be concerning themselves with. He also said, "Boys will be boys, Miss Mills," Jane mimics his voice and gets a little chuckle from the room.

'Right, well, that answers the first question about whether we can go to Mr Clarke about this,' I say and Jane nods at me while I feel the hope in the room sag. It's shitty to realise someone responsible for your care won't support or protect you, but we can't let this deter us. We've got to forge ahead.

'I think this is part of a bigger culture at our school, though,' says one of the girls next to Jane. 'I've seen boys taking pictures up girls' skirts on the stairwell, I've seen girls who have fun with guys being called sluts while guys that do the same thing are patted on the back and called heroes. There's so much toxic masculinity here, I don't know how we'd tackle it all.'

There's a small rumble of agreement in the room.

'Well, thankfully, upskirting's illegal now so we can speak

up about that knowing that the law's on our side. And no one should be slut-shamed, that's completely unacceptable,' I say frowning. 'Has anyone had any experiences of this sort of stuff first-hand? Only if you're OK sharing it. Don't feel you have to.'

One girl stands up. 'Hi, I'm Denise, and I'm absolutely sick of boys always talking about my boobs,' she says. 'They're always shouting things at me, calling me names. They know I can hear. They just want a reaction or to make me feel ashamed and I won't.'

YES, DENISE! I note that she does have absolutely MASSIVE knockers, and it's probably not OK that I am noticing that and now staring at them and I need to stop.

Oh my god, I'm just staring at her boobs and saying nothing.

I look like a pervert.

Stop looking at her boobs, Kat.

Why are you STILL looking at her boobs, Kat?

I blink and hope that no one noticed that I've just been staring at Denise's chest for at least the last ten hours.

'Oh my god, me too!' Another girl stands up and now I appear to be staring at hers also. At this rate I've just invited a bunch of women into a room to stare at their boobs and that is NOT FEMINISM.

'I get called names because I *don't* have any boobs,' another girl shouts out from the back. She looks very young, probably only in Year Seven, so of *course* she doesn't have boobs. She's probably not even started puberty yet, FFS!

'Me too!' says another voice from inside the crowd.

'The boys in my year keep calling me a slut because I got fingered at a party last term and the guy told everyone,' I hear from the back, and recognise a girl from our year called Susannah.

Susannah looks like she might cry. I want to hug her, but she doesn't really know me, and people have probably already found me creepy enough during this meeting. Thankfully the girl next to her puts an arm around her.

One girl stands up in the middle of the room and says, 'The boys in my year keep trying to look up my skirt and take pictures whenever I walk up the stairs.'

Every time someone sits down, another person stands up.

'I got off with one of the lads in the football team and wouldn't let him go any further than kissing so he told all his friends we'd slept together and now they all send me pictures of their dicks and call me a slag.'

'A guy I was dating in the year above said if I didn't send him a picture of myself he'd break up with me. When I did he broke up with me anyway and showed all his friends.'

The more people that stand up and speak, the more come forward. The room seems to gain strength and momentum from itself. The stories make me angry, and some make me feel like I might cry. There are people hugging each other and raging together and in between all of that are people, sitting, listening, feeling shocked, upset, embarrassed at other people's bad behaviour. But the thing that we all have in common is that we believe each other. We believe each other and we want to make sure a change happens.

Room 404 isn't cold any more – it's filled with warmth and energy and compassion, though alongside that sits the awareness that what brings us together are experiences that none of us should have had to go through in the first place.

I look at Sam and Millie. I'm suddenly nervous that when I'm writing the blog later and I'm trying to convey what's happening here and work out how to address it, I'll lose this feeling, this energy, and that I'll forget these stories that need to be honoured or won't do these people and their experiences justice. And then I have an idea.

'What if we get everyone a piece of paper, and you all write down something that you've experienced at school that's made you feel uncomfortable or upset?' I say. 'And then on Friday I'll publish them all – anonymously – in the Feminist Friday blog. Let's get the attention of parents and teachers and make sure we've got as many people on our side as possible. Then we can start trying to change the rules.'

'Good idea,' says Jane, as she, Sam and Millie start tearing up small scraps of paper and pass them around. 'We should fight for a zero-tolerance policy, especially when groping and upskirting are actually illegal.'

Some of the boys in the room stand up and help pass the paper around, and I see some of them writing down things. I guess it's not just girls having a hard time.

There's an air in this room that feels slightly magical, but it's a sad kind of magic that should never have had to exist in the first place.

1.15 p.m.
Heading to my locker

'That meeting was pretty tough, huh?' Matt says as we head to my locker with all the bits of paper.

'Yeah, really tough,' I say. 'I had no idea half that stuff was going on, you know?'

'Well, now we have our eyes wide open,' Sam says. 'And you've just given all those people a safe space where they can talk and feel supported. Well done, Kat.'

'You were AMAZING, Kat,' says Millie, giving me a big hug. 'We're so proud of you.'

'And we're gonna fix this!' says Sam.

'Thanks, guys,' I say, feeling a lump in my throat. 'I'll write the blog and publish all these stories on Friday, and then we need to talk to Mr Clarke. See if he still thinks it's just "boys being boys" after that.'

'Good plan,' Sam says.

'Let us know if there's anything else we can do to help, though, yeah?' Nick says.

I look at his kind, sweet, helpful face and I'm so pleased that one of us has someone like him. It reminds me that it's not the majority but the minority doing this stuff. Most people are good.

'Yeah, what he said,' Matt says, making a move to leave.

'Oh, and byeeeee, Kat!'

Matt replicates my dinosaur-jazz-hands wave from the start of the meeting with a flourish as he walks away from me backwards, grinning.

Dammit. I knew I wouldn't get away with that.

4.10 p.m.
My bedroom

I settle myself down with Bea on the rug next to my bed and empty the envelope full of toxic masculinity. Sixty odd bits of paper come fluttering out, and I watch the patriarchy falling to the floor. I take a deep breath and prepare to dive in.

I'm worried that I'm not good enough to do this. That I'll let everyone down and won't write something representative enough of everyone's feelings and experiences. I know that I'm not individually responsible for instigating change, it's a group effort, but I'm scared that if my piece doesn't do the situation justice, and I don't express the severity of these experiences and the way they've made people feel, we'll fall at the first hurdle.

I turn over all the bits of paper until they're all face up. They're just paper, they can be torn and screwed up, but each one demonstrates the strength of the person writing it. As I read them I hear each person's story and the bravery it's taken to come forward.

Just like in the meeting, each story seems worse than the last. And with each story my sense of rage and dread increases.

'Someone on the rugby team keeps pinching my arse in the hallway. He leaves bruises and red marks on it and it makes me feel embarrassed and ashamed.'

'There's a group of boys in our year who wait until we're heading up stairs and then stare up our skirts yelling out about who needs a bikini wax. They take pictures too.'

'A boy in the year above I've been dating secretly keeps asking me to send him pictures. At first we were having fun but now he says that I'm tight and frigid because I won't do it. I'm scared of him losing interest but I don't feel comfortable doing it. He says he can't tell his friends about me until he knows I'm serious because he's worried I'll mug him off and embarrass him, and if I send him pictures, he'll know I wouldn't do that.'

'A tampon fell out of my bag last year. It was one of the super ones. Now the boys tease me, saying I've got a wide vagina. They call me Big Vagina Emily.'

'My ex-boyfriend asked for pictures of me all the time, he said that it was just for us and that he loved me so I sent one. We were getting on really well and I believed him when he said the picture was just for him. Then we had sex and he dumped me. Now he's sent the picture to all his friends. They've all seen me naked and I feel so violated.'

There's so much in here: upskirting, harassment, period-shaming, slut-shaming, revenge porn. And that's before we even get on to @**FittyorPity**. A lot of this stuff's illegal. Surely Mr Clarke has to sit up and listen to the evidence here.

I'm no longer tired or anxious – I'm furious. This can't carry on. We thought Shit Josh was the worst, but it turns out he was just the tip of the iceberg.

Why do they think they can behave like this? What have they learned that teaches them that this is OK? And how can we break that down and let them know that it's not?

6 p.m.
My desk
Typing away, my trusty feminist dog by my side

I've been writing almost non-stop for hours now, mostly fuelled by anger.

'Kat! Dinner!' Dad shouts up the stairs.

It's probably for the best that I take a break and come back to this anyway. I think it's done, but I might need to check for excessive use of swear words.

6.05 p.m.
The dinner table

'So, how was the Feminist Society meeting today, Kat?' Mum asks.

'It was good, thanks,' I say, not sure how much I want to mention after clitoris-gate the other week. The last thing I want is to set that kind of chat off again.

'I'm so proud of you for all the work you're doing. Starting a society like that takes guts,' Mum continues. 'It might take a while, but you'll see, there'll be loads of you soon, making the world a better place.'

I don't have the energy to explain to her exactly how bad things are at school, especially not when she looks so proud of me. I don't want her to know that, actually, I've been completely unaware of so many awful things happening.

We're all silent for approximately five seconds before I hear Mum gasp so loudly that I nearly drop my fork. She rushes over to Freddie.

'Oh my GOD, FREDDIE!' she says, launching herself towards his neck. 'Is that a LOVE BITE? A HICKEY?'

Dad gets up and comes round the table.

'Let me take a look at that, son!' he says as Freddie shrugs away from Mum's grip and buries his head in his hands on the table.

'Oh my god, go away, go away, GO AWAY!' he says, muffled into the tablecloth.

'Awww, c'mon Freddie, show us the hickey!' Mum says. 'Did you try and cover this with make-up?'

'Might have.' He shrugs as my ears prick up.

'Whose makeup did you use, Freddie?' I ask, sitting up like a meerkat.

'Eerrrrrr . . .'

'FREDDIE!' I shout at him, giving him a two-second warning with my eyes before he knows I'm going to pounce. He maintains eye contact, then I fling myself at him and he launches himself off his chair and out of the door. I'm chasing behind him, coming fast up the rear as we head for the stairs. He'll never out-run me, although I can't think of anything to do when I catch up with him apart from give him one HELL of a wedgie.

'Kat! Freddie! CALM DOWN!' Dad is shouting at us, but it's too late now. I thought I'd expressed QUITE clearly that he was NEVER to get his grubby fingers in my make-up bag.

6.10 p.m.

We've been separated. I've got a tuft of hair sticking up where he got me in a headlock and he's still trying to recover his underwear from his butt crack where I hope I've lodged it so far up that he never gets it back.

We're now eating our dinner on opposite ends of the table with Mum and Dad between us at the sides, but we're maintaining eye contact.

It's really quite hard to eat peas when you're maintaining eye contact.

The floor is a sea of pea.

There is even a pea on Bea.

11 p.m.
Bed

I feel exhausted and anxious. I know that in the meeting I was confident that speaking up would help solve the problem, but what if it doesn't? What if simply calling guys out doesn't solve it? What if we're all sharing our painful experiences for nothing?

I guess we'll have to see what Friday brings.

I need to try doing another light-switch challenge tonight, but I don't know if I have the energy to manage it.

11.05 p.m.
Halfway through ten minutes of stress

This is horrible. I know the theory behind this is that I'm supposed to sit with the anxiety, with the uncomfortable feelings and the fear, but I don't want to.

I feel annoyed about how weird this makes me feel. I feel like I do when I'm forced to run too far and too fast in cross country, except I'm lying completely still.

11.07 p.m.

God, why am I doing this to myself? I'm not even going to France now.

But then, this is part of why I'm not going. If I can crack this, I can start to get better. I need to keep going.

If I could JUST bring myself to get into wanking then at least I'd have something to take my mind off it now. But honestly, whenever I think about it, my vagina feels like a foreign country. Like the rest of me is England and my vulva's Australia.

My clitoris is probably Mars.

11.08 p.m.

That would give me a very long vagina.

At least thinking about *not* wanking is helping to distract me.

11.09 p.m.

I wonder when wanking was first discovered? Like who was the first person to wank? And how did they know that they were the first? Because no one ever really talked about it back when it was first invented, did they? Unless back then they were way more open than we give them credit for. Maybe actually they were super open and it was like, 'Just having a self-care night tonight, washing my hair and fiddling with my fanny.'

I wonder if Sébastien wanks?

Or if he hasn't been able to touch his penis since I SLAPPED it last year.

Oh god.

I wonder if you can break a person's penis?

11.10 p.m.

I did it! The light switch, not the other thing. Still not a wanker.
I can hear my vagina sighing with disappointment.

I can't believe I DID IT!

However, I also need to google now to check whether you
can actually break a person's penis. I'm worried I've been
laughing about this, but maybe I did some serious damage to
Sébastien? Is this why he never replied to me?

I know I'm going to get some dodgy results, but I have to set
my mind at ease.

> Google: Can you break someone's penis?   Q

11.12 p.m.

Oh god, you can. And that was more detail than I wanted.

It turns out penises must, from now on, be treated like
precious china.

11.50 p.m.

This is such a double-edged sword. I'm really proud of myself for
making it through the full ten minutes, but I'm also really
nervous now that I have broken a man's penis. Jesus. The
anxiety giveth and then taketh away.

It's a weird thing to be proud of yourself for something that other people don't even have to try to do. Like, I am really proud of myself and what an achievement, but I'd rather that my achievements were more along the Pulitzer Prize lines, rather than being things I can never tell anyone about.

11.55 p.m.

All I can seem to think about now is the health of Sébastien's penis.

What if I broke it and it's going to come after me on its own to seek revenge? Like one of those terrible eighties horror movies. It'll be holding a little axe in its penis-y grip, running at me.

Now I can't stop picturing being killed by a small, angry, axe-wielding penis.

Should I tell Sarah about this? Perhaps I am sicker than we all thought?

Sod it. I'm just going to ask Matt.

> **Me:** Matt, you don't think I broke the French penis when I patted it, do you?

Matt: Well good evening to you too. Nah, there would have been loads of blood if you'd done that.

Matt: You are quite a funny little onion xx

Not a penis slayer after all.

Quite relieved.

3 Positive Things:

*1. We are starting a movement and making a change at
school – I am an excellent feminist!*

*2. I don't think anyone noticed me staring at Denise's boobs
for ages.*

*3. I beat the ten-minute challenge at last and have also
definitely not broken a penis (we think), and I have only spent
forty per cent of my most feminist day thinking about penises
(actually maybe fifty, or sixty . . . seventy-five . . . that's my
final offer)*

Wednesday 22nd January

12.30 p.m.
The cafeteria

'They've taken it down, look, it's completely disappeared!' Jane appears breathlessly in front of us.

She thrusts her phone screen in our faces, jabbing at the lack of results for **@FittyorPity** and we all stare at it.

I had half a fork of baked beans headed for my mouth when she appeared waving her arms around in celebration, and it's still there, suspended in mid-air, yet to reach its destiny (my mouth).

'We've done it?' I ask, blinking at it.

'Well, we've got rid of the **@FittyorPity** Instagram account anyway, but if Monday's meeting's anything to go by there's still a long way to go. They've run away scared, here, though,' Jane says looking proud.

'With this and your blog on Friday, Kat, by next week we might have freed the school from all the toxic masculinity,' Sam says as I finally put my fork down so I'm not just wafting beans at everyone.

'Well . . .' I start, just staring ahead.

I don't want to jinx it, but I feel extremely positive right now.

10 p.m.
In bed

It's two days until the Feminist Friday blog publishes and I keep reading it over and over again. Tweaking it and making sure it's perfect. I feel like I'm trusted to do such an important job and I want to do it well. Every time someone in school comes up to me and says how great the meeting was on Monday or how much they appreciated last Friday's blog I feel more spurred on, knowing that we're helping people feel less alone.

I feel excited that something I'm doing has such an impact and will help people, but I also feel a bit sick that these things are happening in the first place.

3 Positive Things:

1. I am another day closer to making a change.

2. There's no way Mr Clarke can read this blog and not want to fix things.

3. At the start of the term I thought France and having a date to Trudy's party really mattered. Now I know that what matters is what I'm doing right now.

Friday 24th January

Toxic Masculinity at Our School: Keeping Score

It's been nearly a week since the school was rocked by the unveiling of the @FittyorPity Instagram account and with it the aggressive rating of girls from Years Nine to Thirteen.

To rate a person based on their physical appearance and likelihood of engaging in sexual encounters reduces their value to nothing more than the judgement of men. This way of thinking has exposed a lack of respect and a culture of toxic masculinity bubbling under the surface of our school.

On Monday, the Feminist Society took charge of the situation, holding a special meeting to discuss our plans to find out who was responsible for the offending Instagram account and how best to address the concerns it raised.

Unfortunately, what the Feminist Society uncovered is a far more shocking and painful story than any of us were aware of. Stories of upskirting on the stairs, sexual harassment, groping, period-shaming, revenge porn and slut-shaming appear to be rife. Today, Feminist Friday would like to give a voice to those that have suffered as a result of this.

We need to work together, collectively, to defeat this culture of toxic masculinity in our school. We invite everyone to attend the next Feminist Society meeting where we plan to lay out a new agenda for our school, a list of rules. We'd like to call it the Feminist Manifesto, banning toxic masculinity from our school and making these acts of aggression and oppression punishable.

We commend the bravery of those who shared their stories with us on Monday. Below we publish these stories anonymously.

8 a.m.
My bedroom or, as I now like to call it – Feminist HQ

'Have you seen all the likes and comments, Kat?' Sam says, bursting into my room.

To be honest I've been trying not to look at the post again, I'm too afraid that I'm going to have done it wrong, disappointed people or let them down. The fear's like last week times one million. So, every time my fingers reach out for my phone I've shakily drawn them away again. Just in case what I see on there makes me feel awful.

'There's already a hundred likes and loads of comments!' Millie hands me her phone as I stand open-mouthed.

The girls both crowd around me on my bed and we scroll

through. The excitement hits me and I finally feel like I have proof that I've done something good.

The comments are mostly supportive, people saying how great they think the blog is and how well it conveys what's going on. Then there are people who are shocked that these things are happening because, like me, they hadn't realised that they were going on either.

I feel so good about the blog and the response it's had that it doesn't even bother me when I see a comment from @KatsFishyVagina.

Grow up, losers.

8.30 a.m.
Walking to school

We're still scrolling through the comments while we're walking to school. More and more are being added and the likes just keep going up.

'I can't believe someone's written #notallmen and something about boys needing more protection from false allegations,' I say, rolling my eyes.

'Um, 'scuse moi?' Millie asks. 'BOYS need more protection from FALSE allegations?'

'None of them were false!' I rage.

'They've made themselves look like idiots, though, because your article proves that it's happening and it's happening a lot.' Millie says.

'You've smashed it!' Sam says. 'And we're so proud!'

I'm beaming, and by the time we arrive at school I feel like I'm gliding through the gates and across the playground, head held high, having the best morning of my lif—

'KATERINA EVANS!' Mr Clarke is standing by the entrance to the school. He looks like he's been waiting for me. 'MY OFFICE. NOW.'

8.35 a.m.

The beigest office there has ever been
Complete with beige crusty seats and a filthy beige carpet to go with Mr Clarke's beige outfit

Miss Mills is already waiting in the office when I get there and she looks furious.

'Sit down, please, Kat,' Mr Clarke says as I take a seat next to Miss Mills. I feel like we're both on the side of the desk that's about to be made to feel really small.

'Kat, when I agreed to your Feminist Friday blog and your Feminist Society meetings, it was to give you the opportunity to educate your classmates. It was NOT to create fear and scaremongering and write elaborate stories about things that simply AREN'T HAPPENING.'

I start to protest and tell him that they ARE happening, but he raises his hand to silence me and carries on talking.

'This morning I've had phone calls from concerned parents who I am now personally having to reassure that we do not have a culture of toxic masculinity in this school and that these are the words of an overdramatic wannabe journalist, searching for a "scoop" where there is none.' He looks down at me like I'm a toddler he's telling off, his fingers still in bunny-ear quote position. 'I've also had a call from the school board who I have thankfully also been able to reassure that this is just a girl with an overactive imagination. And they've agreed to take it no further.'

Overactive imagination? There's definitely someone in this room with an overactive imagination but I'd say it's more likely to be the man telling me that nothing's wrong and everything in the school's fine.

I look at him sitting behind his desk, fingers steepled under his chin, in some kind of power pose. A pose to tell me that he's in charge and I am a silly little girl causing drama and extra paperwork for him. A silly little girl who no one will believe.

'But I think from Kat's blog we can clearly see that there is.' Thank god for Miss Mills. 'Why can't we believe girls when they make these allegations? And support them? If we're not believing them now, at school, how are they going to go out into the world and feel able to speak up? Just because it's not convenient for you to deal with it doesn't mean there isn't a real problem in this school. We have a duty to safeguard these kids! I mean, come on!'

'Miss Mills, I think I've always been very supportive of girls at this school and in particular of Kat's "Feminist agenda".' His bunny ear-ed quote marks are starting to really get on my tits now. 'But this is taking things too far. Why is this the first time I've heard of any of these things happening? It seems to me that she's creating a frenzy out of a small group of boys doing a silly Instagram account. It's no more than that, and these fantastical stories and elaborations are too much. And, I suggest you adjust your tone and remember who you're speaking to.'

What is he saying? Why isn't he getting this? I feel my rage hit boiling point and I become dizzy with it.

'But you clearly haven't been supportive, though!' I protest, watching his face get redder and redder. 'All these pupils have had these things happen in YOUR SCHOOL!'

'According to *you*, Katerina. I've not heard this from anyone else, and I suggest you lower your voice,' Mr Clarke says in a dangerously patronising tone. 'There was no need to whip up hysteria around the school and as a result I feel justified in letting you both know that you're treading a VERY fine line.'

Hysteria? Is it hysterical to want to be safe?

'What's more, I have re-evaluated the Feminist Society and Feminist Friday blog. I don't think that at this stage they are an asset to the school. And so, I'm shutting them down, effective immediately. I've already removed the blog to contain the spread of misinformation and prevent more parents becoming concerned about something that simply isn't an issue. This isn't a game, Katerina. You cannot create drama in this school simply to further your journalistic endeavours.'

'MISINFORMATION?' I shout, exploding out of my chair, not sure where to even begin.

'You can't just pretend a problem doesn't exist because you can't see it, sitting at the top of the food chain, enjoying your male privilege!' Miss Mills has it spot on and Mr Clarke looks furious.

'I won't tell you again, Miss Mills. Please respect my decision. Any further trouble on this matter would result in me considering both of your positions at this school.'

I can't believe what he's saying. I can't believe this is happening. Just when you think that the world's changing and people are getting a fairer shot at equality, you're reminded that there's always someone in a position of power ready to silence you and block your way.

Miss Mills looks like she might cry. I feel like I might too.

I've let everyone down.

8.55 a.m.
Walking to form room

'I'm sorry, Kat.' Miss Mills looks slightly glassy eyed. 'I'm so angry, for you and for all the others at this school who've experienced this stuff.'

I don't feel like I can speak because if I do, I'll cry. My head's spinning and I don't understand how I could have gone so quickly from the proudest I've ever been of something, to having it completely taken away. I feel impotent. I can't change his mind and I can't help anyone. Rather than helping people, my blog's just made the situation even worse. Now there's no safe space and no one's allowed to speak up.

Form room

'What happened?' Sam whispers hurriedly as I sit down and Miss Mills goes to the front of the class, still looking flustered.

'He's taken the blog down and shut down Feminist Friday and the Feminist Society. He said we were just creating hysteria in the school,' I say, my voice catching slightly.

'WHAT? So he's just going to deny any of this happened? Pretend nothing's going on in the school? Just leave everyone who's had these experiences to basically rot?' Sam says.

'Yeah, it seems like it. He doesn't believe any of them ever happened in the first place.'

We hear a snort of laughter behind us and even before I've turned around, I know it's Sienna.

'Chill out, Germaine Greer,' she says without taking her eyes off her phone, sniggering.

Urgh.

5.10 p.m.

Walking home after therapy

It's always SO cold when I finish therapy. I wonder if all my worries and stresses are somehow keeping me warm, and then I give them to Sarah, and I'm lighter, but I haven't got my big jacket of stress shrouding me?

I told Sarah everything about the Feminist Friday blog, and

the Feminist Society meeting, and how I worry that I've ruined everything. That me trying to help has done the opposite and meant that rather than amplifying oppressed voices, I've directly contributed to them being silenced.

I told her how angry I am. All the hard work, all the bravery people showed sharing their stories, and all the time spent telling people that their experiences mattered and were valid, was for nothing. Just as we're about to make real change, it's all been taken away from us. And I feel completely gagged. When Mr Clarke announces the cancellation of the Feminist Society next week everyone at that meeting will know I've let them down.

Sarah says it's not me that's let them down it's Mr Clarke and I wish I could believe that but earlier I remembered that I did the light-switch challenge on Monday and now I can't shake the feeling that what happened with Mr Clarke today happened because of that. Because I hadn't touched the light switch.

Sarah pointed out that bad things have happened with Mr Clarke previously when I *was* touching it. Which is a good point, well made. But I guess I'm still having trouble believing it. She wants me to try and do some more this week and she was trying to get me to see it as a positive, saying that I should be proud of myself for achieving it. And for everything I achieved with the Feminist Society, even if it was shut down.

I want to see these positives but it's so hard. Especially when deep down I feel like I've failed.

What I don't tell Sarah is that I've started to question whether Mr Clarke might in some small way be right. I keep running over his words in my head and wondering if it's my fault. If maybe I went too far? Or maybe I imagined it was all that bad and it's really just silly boys that we're making too big a deal out of? After all, he's the adult, he's supposed to be wise and in charge.

But I was THERE in the meeting. I heard all those people talk. I read the things they wrote down. I'm so confused and I'm questioning myself so much now that I'm starting to wonder if I can trust my brain at all.

6.30 p.m.
The dinner table

It's just me, Mum and Dad tonight because Freddie's at Issy's which means all the attention's on me and, because I don't feel much like talking, that's making it even worse.

'I tried to read your blog after work but couldn't find it, will you send me a link?' Mum asks, not realising how much of a loaded question that is.

I squirm awkwardly in my seat, wishing I could ignore the question and just make it go away. I'm so tired and confused about the whole thing. I feel silly when I remember the things that Mr Clarke said to me today.

'Mr Clarke's cancelled the Feminist Society,' I say in a small voice.

'What do you mean?' Mum says as her and Dad both put down their forks.

'Something about us disrupting the school,' I say, trying to keep it simple.

'Well, you can't have a bit of activism without disruption,' Dad says jovially.

'Exactly and he's always been a bit funny about it, hasn't he?' Mum asks cheerfully. 'You'll win him round again, don't worry, love.'

If only they knew how badly I screwed up this time.

7.30 p.m.
The sofa in Lonersville

Why am I ALWAYS in alone on Friday and Saturday nights? WHAT IS THAT?

Matt and Si have gone to the cinema. Millie's at Nick's, and Sam's doing some art coursework.

I, however, am sitting on my sofa, with only my parents and the choice of *EastEnders* or *Corrie*. FML.

8 p.m.

I just can't believe that's that. The Feminist Society's over, and it's probably all my fault. Either way I have to accept it or face getting expelled right before my GCSEs. Not only that, but Miss Mills could lose her job. What a shitty day.

8.10 p.m.

I'm just wondering if I can take another minute of this lameness, when my phone lights up.

I feel like I've not spoken to anyone who isn't my parents for ten thousand years. I don't know who I am any more. Am I a teenage girl or have I now leaped straight to OAP?

I'm stretching out the fun of receiving a notification because it's the ONLY INTERESTING THING THAT'S HAPPENED ALL NIGHT.

Right, well, best see who it was.

Oh my god. What?

Am I hallucinating? Have I wanted something to happen so much that I'm now imagining that it has?

Sébastien HAS MESSAGED ME BACK.

He's said . . .

Hi.

> **We 💜 Kat – Feminist Society FOR EVER**
> Sam, Millie, Me

Me: Umm, HE'S MESSAGED ME BACK! XX

Sam: Who??

Me: Sébastien!

Sam: FINALLY!

186

Millie: JESUS, HOW LONG DID THAT TAKE?

Me: 10,000 years. I am a very old woman now, like the old lady at the end of *Titanic*.

Millie: WHAT DID HE SAY?!

Me: Hi

Sam: Imaginative.

Millie: What did you say to him again?

Me: Hi

Sam: Christ, it's steamier than Fifty Shades in your DMs.

Millie: 🙄

Me: SHUT UP.

Millie: Sorry Kat, what are you going to message back?

Me: How are you?

Sam: Too formal.

Millie: Agreed. Send him a peach emoji. 🙄

Me: OMG you two are no use. Whatsoever.

Sam: Sorry, Kat.

Millie: Sorry.

Me: I'm changing the subject to stop me from feeling like a TOTAL LOSER.

Me: What time are you meeting your dad tomorrow, Millie?

Millie: He wants to take us for breakfast at 9AM!! It's inhumane!

Sam: EWWW!!! So early!!!

Me: Gross.

Millie: I know, things have been more chilled at home and they both seem happier, though. Maybe now they've had a little break they'll get on better and we can all go back to normal?!

I want to be encouraging about this, but I'm worried that's not how it's going to work.

8.30 p.m.
Still on the sofa

Still no idea what I should say back to Sébastien.

'How's your penis?'

I think not.

Maybe it's best if I just leave it. I mean, it's not like I'm ever going to see him again. I side-eye Mum and Dad, remembering how they've RUINED my life.

I can't believe that now not only do I not have any chance at a reconciliation with Sébastien, I don't have the Feminist Society either. I've got nothing.

Being sixteen was not supposed to be this shit.

8.50 p.m.

I will never lose my virginity and am destined to spend all my Friday nights alone. My vagina will end up as a house for bats and I will be known locally as The Batcave.

3 Positive Things:
1. My vagina is to become a bat sanctuary and I will probably get an OBE for services to nature.
2. Sébastien messaged me back.
3. But . . . because of me there is now NO CHANCE of us battling the culture of toxic masculinity at our school and I am struggling to feel positive about that.

Saturday 25th January

7 a.m.
Dreams just like real life

I had a dream where I was sinking slowly down a big well and screaming for help but the only person who could hear me was Mr Clarke and he just kept walking past as I sank lower and lower. Just as I was about to be completely submerged in water, I woke up gasping for air with a pressure headache.

10 a.m.
My bed

What's the point in getting up when I don't have the Feminist Society, Feminist Friday OR any French coq to look forward to? What is the bloody point?

WE ❤ KAT – FEMINIST SOCIETY FOR EVER
Sam, Millie, Me

Sam: Guys, I think I might be doing something weird.

Me: Unlikely, compared to the things I've done lately, but what?

Sam: I'm watching the football game from behind a parked car, I'm kind of stealth hiding so that Dave doesn't see me.

Millie: Why don't you want him to see you??

Sam: Because he's with Sienna. I came to surprise him, but he's here and Sienna's here with Trudy, and Dave and Sienna keep chatting to each other and flirting. Then I got really upset and started crying and now I feel like I don't know what to do so I'm just stranded behind this car. I hope no one comes to move it.

Me: Oh, Sam. We're coming xxx

Millie: Just at brunch with Dad, will finish up and head right over. Feminist rescue mission on its way! xxx

Me: Love you, Sam xxx

10:30 a.m.

Behind a parked car by the football field

When we found Sam, she was crouched behind a Prius in the mud, crying. She said she'd been there for so long she no longer had feeling in her thighs.

I'm hoping we're far enough away that no one can see our three sets of eyes peeping over the bonnet of this car but I'd say that Dave definitely hasn't clocked us because he's just gone over to Sienna, mid game, and started doing keepy-uppies with the ball, while she giggles at him. There's a whole pitch of footballers behind him waiting for the ball to go back into play while he shifts it from knee to knee in front of her, flirting with his big muddy ball.

I can't believe what I'm seeing. It's disgusting.

We need to find a way to remove Sam before anything else happens, and without anyone seeing. I pop my head up. Trudy and Sienna are still wrapped up in Dave's peacocking. They're dressed in Made in Chelsea ski-trip chic again, boots, big puffer jackets with fur collars, and fluffy mittens. The rest of The Bitches are nowhere to be seen, which is interesting. I guess Sienna really is Second in Command now?

'Right, we just have to wait until the ball goes up the other end of the field, and then we can make a run for it,' I whisper. 'If only our team weren't so shit and could actually get the ball up the other end. Or just anywhere within twelve feet of our goal.'

'Don't let Dave hear you say that. He thinks he's the next Messi,' Sam says.

'He's not,' I say bluntly. 'Nick was just being kind the other day.'

'Jesus, my legs hurt already, how strong are your glutes that you haven't fallen face first in that mud?' Millie asks, leaning on poor Sam while I peer over the car.

'We could be here a while,' I say. 'They really are quite shit.'

'Crap, I'm sorry, guys,' Sam says, putting her head in her hands.

10.35 a.m.
Still behind the car

'Why didn't you tell us you were still worrying about Dave after

192

last week?' Millie asks, trying to stretch out her legs from a crouching position without her arse hitting the ground.

'I just felt silly and embarrassed. I never thought I was the type to be insecure before, but he's barely been about these last couple of weeks and I just kept feeling worse and worse. I know he's at Luca's house a lot, and I started to get paranoid and doing things like looking through Sienna's Instagram. He's liked ALL of her pictures,' she says.

Warning signals are going off in my head like mad right now. I can't believe Dave's being such a shit.

'Maybe he was just being kind because she's his friend's sister?' Millie suggests. 'I sometimes like Freddie's Instagram posts.'

'I've noticed,' I say raising an eyebrow at her. I saw her like the one where he caught me with moustache bleach on my face.

'But all of them?' Sam says, looking at us pleadingly while giving in and settling on the ground on her knees. 'And on one of them he'd used the angel emoji.' I see a tear roll down her cheek, and join her in the mud. Some things are more important than getting a muddy bum, and if one of us is going to get one, we all are.

'Well, that's pretty weird. Maybe his thumb slipped? Remember when I accidentally thumb-slipped and put a wink on BTS's picture?' I suggest, but the evidence is stacking up.

'Kat, you did that on purpose. You even said 'gotta be in it to win it' at the time,' Sam says.

Livid that she's remembered the BTS incident in such detail.

I was high on strawberry laces. No one should be held accountable for the things they do on strawberry laces.

'Maybe it's because I've been so busy and caught up in exams and stuff? I thought if I showed up and surprised him, he'd be pleased, and we could hang out after the match, just the two of us. But then when I got here, he had his hand on her arm.' I've never seen Sam like this before, and I'm furious with Dave but also at myself for not noticing sooner. I can't believe he's behaving like this.

'What am I going to do?' Sam asks.

'Why don't you message him?' I ask. 'Normally if someone's doing something shitty, you call them out. You should call him out too.'

'Maybe,' Sam says which makes me worry even more. She'd normally just confront someone who upset her.

'I think first we need to get out of this mud,' Millie suggests, 'and down to Scoops for some serious hot chocolate.'

10.45 a.m.
Escaping from our muddy prison

'Right . . . NOW! GO, GO, GO!' Millie whispers, once she sees the coast is clear.

We all try to clamber up as quickly as possible but my legs are completely dead so I nearly fall flat on my face. We all end up doing a kind of squatted run from behind the car. I'm not sure my knees straighten out any more.

I'm sure the three of us squat-running out of the car park would have been a funny sight, but fortunately no one saw us.

I hope.

11 a.m.

Scoops with massive hot chocolates

'Why don't we hang out today? All day? Put revision on hold,' Millie suggests. 'Nick's just texted saying he's on his way with Matt. They've got some kind of surprise for us.'

'AND I saw on Insta that Polly Perkins is having a party tonight,' I say.

'What if Dave's there?' Sam asks.

'Why don't you text him and try and talk to him beforehand? Maybe there's some explanation?' Millie says.

But I'm not so sure. I'm starting to think Dave might be a massively shady twat.

'And maybe you going out and having fun will make him realise what he's been missing out on by not hanging out with you, and he'll start being normal Dave again?' Millie suggests.

'Good plan,' I say. 'We go, we make sure you look fabulous – which you always do – and we'll have a massively fun time in the process.'

'I thought you were against making yourself look hot for a man?' Sam asks, half laughing.

'You're not doing it for him, babe, you're doing it for YOU. And either way, it's all part of having fun with your girls!' I say as

Millie and I frame our faces. 'That's us, by the way.'

11.20 a.m.

'I wonder what Nick's surprise is?' Sam asks.

'God knows. I'm a little scared, to be honest. He's been spending a lot of time lately looking at pictures of footballers from the seventies with mullets and saying how cool they are,' Millie says.

'Oh god, no. If he's done that, we'll hold him down and you just shave his head,' I suggest.

'Plan! Thank you,' Millie says just as we spot Nick coming in, with a healthy and normal head of hair, accompanied by Matt and Si.

'Here they are! No mullet! Thank god!' I think the mullet was a very real concern for a minute there.

'Guess how we got here!' Matt asks with way too much enthusiasm, considering it was probably the bus.

'The 38?' I suggest, making a face at him.

'NOPE! OUR BUS DAYS ARE OVER!' We're all staring blankly at him until I see that Nick's twiddling something in his hand.

He holds up a car key with a huge grin on his face.

'I PASSED MY TEST!' he says.

'WHAAT! OH MY GOD! Congratulations!' Millie says, running over and MOUNTING him, much to the dismay of the other, much older, people in this cafe. She needs to calm down, there's already some very iffy blood pressure in here.

11.45 a.m.
Still in Scoops

I was worried that a second hot chocolate to celebrate Nick's news would make me feel a bit sick, but actually I'm OK. I guess it's about building your tolerance, and I've worked hard for this glory.

'So he was with Sienna in what way?' Si asks Sam.

'Like this . . .' Sam turns to me, clearly pretending I'm Dave, or Sienna, I'm not sure which way round we are, but she stares deeply into my eyes and laughs, then puts her hand on my arm.

'Oh, and the Instagram thing Kat mentioned earlier?' Nick asks as he and Si exchange a look.

Sam passes her phone over to Si and Matt.

'Oh,' Si says sadly.

'We said she should message him and just ask him what's going on,' I say.

'I think that's right,' Matt says.

'Do it,' Si agrees. 'Maybe it'll clear things up, and if not, he's a knob and we'll help you forget about him and have a great day.'

We try not to stare at Sam while she's texting him, resulting in us all staring at the ceiling. I've never noticed before, but the Scoops ceiling could use a lick of paint.

11.50 a.m.

'OK, how's this?' Sam asks, holding her phone out to us.

'Hey, I think we need to talk. You're being off with me and I don't know why.'

'Fierce, to the point,' Matt says.

'YAS, QUEEN!' Si says.

'Do it!' I agree. It's direct and to the point and very Sam.

'Perfect!' Millie says and Nick nods in agreement.

'Right then . . .' Sam says, pressing send.

11.51 *a.m.*

The six of us have since proceeded to stare at Sam's phone in silence.

'We should probably talk about something else,' Sam says. 'Before I start crying again?'

'Right, yes, of course,' Matt says as all of us shuffle uncomfortably in our seats.

Suddenly there's a text tone noise and we all stop.

'Ah,' Nick says sheepishly. 'That's me, sorry, guys . . .'

He hangs his head and puts his phone on silent.

12.30 *p.m.*
The Sainsbury's car park where we will have to live now

We get bored of waiting for Dave to text back, and all agree it will happen quicker if we stop staring at Sam's phone, so decide to take Nick's driving licence for a spin and feel the grown-up freedom of the open road.

It turns out that you don't have to be the best driver to pass your test. Nick has been trying to get out of this parking space now for at least fifteen minutes. So much for having the freedom of the open road.

'Why don't I get out and direct you?' Matt suggests for the fifteenth time.

'Fine.' Nick sighs. 'I'm sure the other cars weren't this close when I pulled in. THAT guy –' he points to the car on his right – 'IS OVER THE LINE!'

We all nod in agreement, heads tilted to the side, a look of sympathy on our faces as Millie pats him on the arm.

'Has anyone got anything that I can use as paddles? Like they do with aeroplanes? Just so we can make sure you can see me!' Matt declares.

'I don't think—' Nick starts saying, but Matt interrupts him.

'If I'm going to do a job, Nicholas, I'm going to do it PROPERLY,' Matt says as Nick rests his forehead on the steering wheel.

We all start rummaging in our handbags.

'I have a copy of *The Feminine Mystique*?' I suggest.

'I have a tampon?' Sam says.

'I have my housekeys and a lipstick?' Millie offers.

'Christ, has anyone ever told you three how on-brand you are?'

'The tampon's a super plus, he'll definitely be able to see it,' Sam reasons.

'Right. Give me the book and the tampon. I'm going to get

us out of here!' Matt says, triumphantly holding the tampon aloft like a trophy.

He gets into position, keeping the tampon up in the air and starts kind of wafting the book towards him.

'I think that means come back in a straight line,' Si deciphers.

We crawl backwards *very slowly* until suddenly Matt thrusts the book and the tampon urgently into a cross shape. Nick hits the brakes so hard that all of us jolt forward, seatbelts now cutting into us.

'I think I was just nearly garrotted,' Sam says.

'My left tit is deceased,' I announce.

'Sorry, guys.' Nick seems embarrassed so we all try to be a bit more supportive.

'You got this, Nick,' I say, rubbing my boob (not in a sexy way, more in a CPR way).

Matt is now waving the tampon to his right energetically. Two old ladies have stopped with their little shopping trolleys and are pointing at him. They're squinting at what's in his hand.

Matt starts waving the book and Nick swings the steering wheel to the right. We've made significant progress and I think we may soon be free.

Si opens the window.

'You're doing great, babe!' he says.

'You're doing great too, babe!' Millie says stroking Nick's arm.

God, you'd think someone was giving birth in here the way people are carrying on. We're squeezing out of a parking space, not a birth canal.

We're free, though! We're finally FREE! We're all celebrating when I see the two old women approach Matt – handbags aloft – and start battering him with them. He's running back to the safety of the car but I hear them shouting, 'DIRTY BASTARD!' at him and, 'THOSE ARE WOMEN'S THINGS! PERVERT.'

'Oops, I think they might be talking about the tampon,' I say.

'Different generation.' Sam shrugs.

'Guess they didn't get the memo about us all being open about our periods now,' Millie says, as poor Matt takes a whack to the back of the legs.

At last he gets away from them and makes it back to the safety of the car.

'FYI, IT'S NOT JUST CIS WOMEN THAT MENSTRUATE, YOU KNOW!' he calls out.

I think that revelation along with the sighting of a tampon out in the wild may have blown their minds.

'Honestly, women!' he declares, squishing himself back into the car, still clutching his tampon. 'I can't believe I've just been period-shamed!'

'Um, can I have my tampon back, please?' Sam mutters.

3 p.m.
Sam's closet

We've been having a super nice time, just the three of us, and now we're sitting amongst the clothes in Sam's tiny walk-in closet. It feels like it used to before boyfriends and spending all our time either constantly revising for or worrying about our exams. On the outside, everything is a mess – Millie's parents, Sam's relationship, the Feminist Society – but at least we have each other.

'Have you heard from him yet?' Millie asks.

'Nope, still nothing,' Sam says.

We've managed to distract her quite well, but now she seems to be staring at her phone constantly. I don't blame her. It's bullshit that he hasn't replied. Imagine getting that message from your girlfriend and not immediately thinking you'd been a massive shit. Or at least thinking it warranted a reply.

'Well, maybe he just hasn't looked at his phone?' Millie says.

'Yeah, maybe,' says Sam.

'Hey! Have you heard from SEXBASTIEN at all since the hi, hi incident?' Millie says, trying to distract Sam.

'No, and I think it's for the best that I leave it at that. After all, I'm not even going to France, am I?' I say.

'Oh, but wouldn't it be fun to have a little flirt?' Millie says. 'I reckon it would certainly cheer Sam up!'

'Oh, it WOULD!' Sam says, finally putting her phone to one side. 'Message him!'

'NO!' I put my phone in my pocket.

'YES!' Millie shouts, trying to wrestle the phone out of my pocket.

3.10 p.m.

They won, and we've been composing a message to him for the last few minutes.

It turns out it's actually very complex to send a sexy message. We've finally settled on:

'How's it going?'

And frankly I'm not sure what grounds either of *them* have for teasing *me* about my original 'hi' message.

3.15 p.m.

'WHERE DID THESE BABIES COME FROM?' I ask, waggling the THIGH-HIGH boots I have just found in the back of Sam's closet.

'Oh, they're Jas's,' says Sam. 'Mum never let her out of the house in them, though.'

'I can't think why!' I say, looking at the SEXIEST footwear I have ever touched. 'I'm going in. I HAVE to try them on.'

3.20 p.m.

Turns out that if you're five foot one, thigh-high boots are NOT thigh high. Thigh high boots are actually fanny-high boots.

And just like that, I have invented a new fashion.

Fanny-high boots.

Come AT me, designer labels, I've got you a money-maker.

I get up and try to walk in them but I guess you can only walk like a robot in fanny-high boots. Sam and Millie are laughing at me and videoing me roaming about like a chic robot.

I eventually fall over into a pile of clothes and I'll admit they may not be QUITE what the fashion industry is waiting for. There's also something very odd about tucking your knickers into your boots.

Also, I can confirm, there is chafing.

3.30 p.m.

Caught one of my many stray pubic hairs in the boot zip. Let's just say I have glimpsed the world of bikini waxes and I don't need to see any more than that.

I am having a lie down in the clothes while the girls fan my crotch area to calm the redness.

7 p.m.

In The Shaggatron —

AKA our name for Nick's car. It's actually a very old Nissan Micra, and the LEAST sexy thing I've ever seen. So SHAGGATRON seems about right.

'Maybe they won't even be there?' Sam says hopefully. 'But then, if neither of them is there, do I just assume that they're together? That would be awful!'

Mille and I are trying to comfort her, but Nick petrifyingly told us just as we got in the car that this is the first time he has

EVER driven in the dark, so we're also a bit distracted by extreme fear. Our fears also weren't helped by him not knowing how to turn his headlights on. He's got them on now but they seem to have got stuck on FULL BEAM mode, so we have been blinding any cars we come across.

Matt and Si are supportively holding hands and praying to the great god RuPaul to save them.

'Whatever happens, babe,' I say, 'you know that WE'RE here. And we're way more fun and important than him.'

I've never seen Sam like this before, she looks so lost and confused and I'm SO angry.

'Exactly,' Millie says. 'And if you want to go home at any point, we can go home. We only stay as long as you want.'

'Matt's been dying to get out of this party anyway,' says Si. 'He thinks Polly's house is tacky.'

'The carpets give me static shock,' Matt says, rubbing Sam's arm. 'This is the last time this evening I'll be able to touch you without giving you an electric shock, my little poppet.'

7.10 p.m.

The full beam is actually quite useful on the country lanes where Polly lives because there aren't any streetlights or houses. We'd definitely die without it. Also, it means we can actually see the entrance to her ridiculous driveway.

As we pull in, we see two figures in the dark, kissing.

At first we're too far away to be able to see who they are.

But as the full beam of the headlights lands on them, we all gasp.

It's Dave and Sienna, caught like rabbits in the headlights.

7.12 p.m.
In the back of the car

Sam's mouth has been open for two minutes. Sienna and Dave are frozen ahead of us. Nick has been trying to turn off the headlights this whole time. He's just hitting things trying to make them stop now. Windscreen wipers are swishing, emergency lights are flickering and he's just sprayed Sienna and Dave with the screen washer jet thingies which is the only bit any of us enjoyed. No one knows what to do but everyone wants this to end.

'Right,' Sam says from her seat in the middle as she unbuckles and starts clambering out over Matt and Si to get to the door. 'Excuse me, I need to break up with the shithead in the headlights.'

Matt and Si bump her over their laps and out of the door. Millie and I follow – for support obviously, but also because we're not entirely sure Sam isn't about to commit murder.

'Sam . . .' Dave says, jumping away from Sienna who actually still has her arms around his shoulders with absolutely no shame. 'It's not what it loo—'

'It is,' says Sam, cutting in. 'And you two are welcome to each other. We're done. You are released from your duties. I can do better than a massive wanker.' She turns on her heel and heads back over to us.

Sienna's smirking, confirming my opinion that she's a spiteful prick. At least they're as awful as each other. Sam really does deserve so much better.

'What do you want to do?' I ask as Sam rejoins us, looking fierce.

'I don't know,' Sam says, deadpan. She seems strangely together, all things considered. I'm wondering if she might be in shock or something.

'We can go home if you want?' I suggest.

'Yeah, then none of us have to get potentially lethal static shock as well?' Matt offers hopefully.

'No way,' says Sam. 'I'm not going to hide away just because of them. Fuck it.' She stares at me and Millie with the same fury and determination on her face as when Krish's friend Tom pushed her over in the playground age five. 'We're going to that party, and I'm going to show him exactly how little he matters to me.'

All of us stare at Sam in awe.

'Right then! You heard the woman!' Matt says, putting an arm around her. 'We stick together! And there's an extra ten bonus points if anyone can push Dave over, preferably on to something painful.'

7.20 p.m.
The driveway

Nick's finally managed to turn the headlights off and the car only rolled back a tiny bit before he realised that in all the faff he'd forgotten to put the handbrake on. (Honestly, he's a completely safe driver . . .) Now we're all standing on the driveway, staring at the party like it's our nemesis.

'Right,' Sam says, taking a deep breath.

'Ready?' I ask with my arm around her shoulders.

'Ready!' she says.

And so, the lot of us walk towards the door, Millie and I with our arms linked in Sam's and the boys behind us.

'Christ, we look epic,' whispers Si, so as not to ruin our fierce silence.

'*Nobody* puts Sam in the corner,' Matt whispers back.

Walking into the party is a bit like walking into a disaster zone. There are people skateboarding down the stairs and the noise of things breaking around the house.

'Kitchen?' Si suggests, and we all nod as we make our way through the house, trying to keep our fierce line going even while we dodge flying objects and mess.

7.45 p.m.
One very sticky, very gross party kitchen

'This party is super lame,' says Si, resting his head in his hands on the kitchen counter. 'There's no FUN, just mess.'

'Agreed,' says Matt.

We've been sitting watching people tamper with the punchbowl which, along with alcohol, also now contains soil

208

from a house plant, tea leaves, chilli powder and some grass from the garden, added by a girl wearing a crown made of half dead, mouldy leaves.

'Maybe we should go?' I suggest to Sam but she's not paying attention.

Millie and I follow her gaze and realise what she's silently staring at. Dave and Sienna are on a bench outside, kissing. They're not even sitting on the bench, they're lying on it. They might as well be shagging in front of her.

'OH, FUCK THAT!' Millie shouts, full of rage.

She grabs the punchbowl and marches with it out of the back door, then pours THE ENTIRE BOWL over them. They screech like a pair of horny street cats and we all fall about laughing.

'You looked like you needed cooling down,' Millie says before striding back through the door.

She stomps over to us, plonks the bowl back on the side and grabs Sam's hand.

'Come on guys, we're leaving.'

And with that, we leave, as fierce as we came in.

8.15 p.m.
Pulling up outside Matt's house

Sam started crying as soon as we got into the car.

She maintained a steely look in her eye the whole way out of the house. Then I guess the first wave of grief hit her and that's when the tears came.

We weren't quite sure where to go, so Matt suggested we bring her to Sandra. She knows a thing or two about cheating men. (Matt's words.)

'Are you sure she's in?' I ask as we get out of the car and see that the house looks pretty dark.

'She said she was having a night in watching *Sex and the City* reruns,' Matt says, looking suspicious. 'Maybe she's watching it in the dark, to give herself a cinema experience?' He puts his key in the lock and we all pile into the porch.

'Mum!' he shouts as we spill into the hallway, turning on the lights.

The living room's pretty dark and it's hard to make much out at first but then to my horror I realise what we're seeing – it's Sandra and she's not on her own, nor is she in a very conventional position. I hear a crash and swearing as I see two figures, lit by one single candle, scrambling up from a pose that even a top yogi would struggle to recreate, across the coffee table.

'MUM!' Matt shouts, clearly horrified. 'OH MY GOD!'

All of us have frozen in the hallway. I'm really not sure what the protocol is here. What do we do? How do we make it go away?

'Reverse!' I shout. 'REVERSE! BACK OUT! ABORT!'

I'm covering my eyes and urgently shuffling backwards in a fit of pure panic. Poor Sam's already been through enough this evening. She'll be even more traumatised now.

It's only when I'm back outside that I realise who her coffee table companion was.

Derek (DEFINITELY NOT a serial killer) from number five.

9.15 p.m.
Matt's kitchen

As we tried to work out if we should abandon Sandra's ship because she already had too many people aboard, she came out, wearing more clothes than before (although the outfit she was wearing seemed very durable, and probably also wipe clean), and now we're all sitting in their kitchen watching as she makes hot chocolate. Derek from number five has disappeared, but his naked image lives on in my mind.

'I'm sorry about that, kids. Matt didn't tell me you were coming,' Sandra says breezily with only a hint of embarrassment. Good for her, though. I mean, it's tricky seeing your friend's mum shagging over the coffee table, but I'm pleased she's met someone, and so local too. Very convenient.

'You didn't tell me you had company tonight,' Matt says as if he's about to launch an inquisition.

'I didn't know I was going to. He just popped round to borrow some milk.'

'Your milk brings all the boys to the yard,' Si mutters raising an eyebrow, making Sandra giggle even though Matt's still glaring at her.

'Will he be borrowing milk regularly? Or is he just going to run off into the night with the milk, never to return?' Matt sounds like an overprotective father rather than her son at this point, but I guess he's had to deal with the aftermath of a lot of men running off with her milk.

'We've made plans for in the week.'

'Interesting.' Matt seems to have relaxed slightly at this.

'Anyway, this is about Sam now, Matt!' Sandra says, enveloping Sam in a hug. 'Come here, pet. What happened?'

9.30 p.m.
Many tissues later

'No, you mustn't think that you've done ANYTHING wrong here,' says Sandra. 'This has nothing to do with you. He's an idiot and you can do better than someone who's head got turned by the first person who came along.'

Sam's finished telling Sandra everything. Including some stuff I didn't know, like that she was planning on having sex with him to stop him dumping her. I'm really pleased that she didn't. I just wish she'd told us she was feeling like this sooner.

'I know it hurts now, but cry all you need to, get it out. Soon you'll wonder what you were ever bothered about. He'll be a distant memory and you'll be better off,' Sandra says, signalling to Matt to get another box of tissues as poor Sam has already cried her way through that one.

'Thanks, Sandra,' she says, sniffing through the tears.

'And we're going to Paris next week!' Millie pipes up.

212

I try not to show how much this upsets me. I wish I could go even more now. I feel like the three of us need each other more than ever at the moment.

'Well, there's no greater place to recover from a broken heart than Paris!' says Sandra. 'Just take some time for you, reconnect with yourself. You're going to be absolutely fine.'

Sam looks like she might actually stop crying as Sandra heads round to the stove to pour out some hot chocolate and marshmallows for us all.

'ARGHHHHH!' We all turn abruptly at the sound of Matt screaming from the hallway and running back into the room. 'MOTHER! Next time you hide a man in the cupboard please remember he's there before sending your son in there to get something for you.'

Derek from number five comes in, still naked but for a pair of white socks pulled up high (not high enough to hide anything, though) and his hands cupping his bits. Sam, Millie and I put our hands over our eyes while Si tries to sneak a glance. Perv.

'I . . . couldn't find my clothes . . .' he flusters while Sam, Millie and I peek slightly through our fingers.

'Oh god, sorry,' Sandra saying, frantically trying to throw tea towels over his modesty.

Si's now doing the international sign language for MASSIVE PENIS over Sandra's head.

We shall now for ever call him Big Dick Derek while being mentally scarred.

12 a.m.

In bed

I can't get over how much of a dickhead Dave is. I always thought he was so great and that they were solid. Sam's going to be fine, though. Millie and I are going to make sure of it.

And they've got Paris of course.

I'm just gutted that I won't be able to go with them.

3 Positive Things:

1. Sam will be better off without Dave and we will look after her, and Dave and Sienna will regret the day they messed with our friend AND be miserable for ever.

2. I will no longer feel bad thinking mean things about Sienna.

3. We know that Sandra is having a LOVELY TIME.

Sunday 26th January

8 a.m.
The kitchen

I'm still recovering from the events of the previous day, standing at the kitchen counter waiting for the kettle to boil so I can make myself a nice cup of tea, when Mum and Dad slide in either side of me, chins on their fists, mimicking my pose. Oh god. What now?

'So, hear you saw Derek last night?' Mum says.

'He texted me apologising this morning because he thought you might have seen something you shouldn't have,' Dad says.

'Very traumatised actually,' I say, hoping this will make them stop.

'What was he doing over there? What did you see?' Mum asks and I just stare more intensely at the kettle, willing it to boil.

'Are they dating?' Dad questions as I contemplate whether a lukewarm cup of tea would be THAT bad.

'Were they on a date?' Mum presses as I feel like my brain's about to explode.

'STOP IT! HAVEN'T I BEEN THROUGH ENOUGH!' I shout as the kettle finally boils and Mum and Dad look slightly taken aback until the penny finally drops.

'Oh, they weren't . . .?' Mum asks raising an eyebrow.

'They were.' I nod, stirring the milk into my tea and hoping this can be an end to it.

'I should phone her!' Mum squeals.

'I should phone him!' Dad says as the two of them hustle out excitedly to talk to their disgusting friends.

'Your sixteen-year-old, impressionable daughter's fine by the way . . . Not traumatised at all,' I whisper into the abyss.

8.10 a.m.

In my room
Hiding with my hard-earned cup of tea from my weird parents

> **Message:** WhatsApp Group name changed by Millie:
> We 🩶 Sam

Millie: How you doing, babe? xxx

Sam: I can't believe we've actually broken up. This time yesterday we were together and now we're not. How does that happen? I just didn't see it coming before. I trusted him so much Xxx

Millie: He's an arsehole, you're better off rid, I promise. What shall we do today? Shall we come over? xxx

Me: YEAH! Let's have a film marathon xx

Millie: Yeah, we can spend the day together making voodoo dolls of Dave and Sienna, watching cool films and listing the reasons why you can do MILES better xxx

Sam: Thanks, guys. I'd love that xxx

Might help me take my mind off the fact that there's no Feminist Society to look forward to tomorrow too.

10 p.m.
My bed

We have had the best day just the three of us. The girls and I talked about EVERYTHING and then we started looking at an Instagram account of Jake Gyllenhaal doing normal everyday things but looking sexy.

Jake cleaning the toilet – sexy.

Jake in the supermarket – sexy.

Jake blowing his nose – sexy.

I know I'm supposed to be doing more light-switch challenges this week, but I don't think I can. Since starting them, Feminist Friday and the Feminist Society have been cancelled, Millie's dad's moved out and now Sam and Dave have broken up.

Obviously, my rational brain knows that not touching the light switch can't be responsible for these things, and I know that Sarah said that too, but I just don't feel like I can do it. I'm so cross with myself. I don't want to be like this for ever but right now I just can't.

3 Positive Things:
1. Jake Gyllenhaal cleaning the toilet
2. Jake Gyllenhaal in the supermarket
3. Jake Gyllenhaal blowing his nose

Monday 27th January

7 a.m.
In bed

It feels like there's no point in getting up on a Monday when there's no Feminist Society. Bea's come to sit on my head as if to confirm this for me too.

8 a.m.
Sam's room

Millie and I go to pick up Sam this morning, because today may be difficult for her. We poke our heads around her door, wearing our berets.

'Beret for you, m'lady?' I say as Millie offers her the hat.

'Ahh, thank you!' Sam says, taking it.

'You OK?' Millie asks.

'Can I skip school and the humiliation and just stay in bed instead?' Sam asks.

'You're going to be absolutely fine. We'll be with you at all times, plus . . . we're getting a lift to school!' Millie says.

'Oh, sweet!' Sam says.

'As long as Nick can get out of the parking spot without tampon assistance this time,' I say.

Millie giggles, then makes a stern face. 'Never say that in front of him.'

Sam grabs her beret and affixes it to her head. 'Right then,' she says. 'Better get it over with.'

'If you need cheering up at any point please remember I can always flash my vulva at you?' I say without a hint of joke in my voice.

'I mean this in the nicest possible way. Nothing is so bad that you need to show me your vulva. Ever.'

So ungrateful. (But thank god.)

9 a.m.
Assembly

Driving past everyone else walking feels SO cool, even if you're in a Nissan Micra and some people are actually walking faster than us. We also managed to avoid seeing Dave or Sienna until we walked in the hall. They're obviously sitting together but he now has to sit with Trudy and her friends so HAHA the joke's on him.

Mr Clarke, or MR COCKHEAD as I now call him, stands at the front, ready to take assembly.

'Some announcements this morning: there will be no Feminist Society meetings until further notice, effective immediately, and the toilets in Humanities are blocked, please avoid if possible.'

I can't *believe* that he's casually shoved the MURDER of the Feminist Society in with an announcement about blocked toilets.

9.05 a.m.

Now he's banging on about how people are to conduct themselves on overseas trips.

Overseas trips that I'M NOT EVEN GOING ON.

I know from the Feminist Society meeting that there are WAY more people in this room who have been upset by being cat-called, groped, and rated one to ten on their sexual availability than there are French people who've been mildly offended by a naughty student on a school trip.

Why isn't he concentrating on making sure that the boys are model citizens? Or at least decent human beings? Why can't he concentrate on making sure that they conduct themselves correctly towards the women IN THIS SCHOOL?

This whole assembly is about making sure we make HIM look good. But he's not good, he's rubbish. He's failing so many people at this school and there's nothing I can do about it.

And then I remember all the things he said on Friday and I start questioning myself again. I wish I could trust myself, be surer about everything but I know that he's in a position of responsibility and if he's saying it's not an issue he has to be right? Right?

Or is he wrong? And everything's upside down?

I just don't know what to believe any more.

12.30 p.m.

The canteen

Jane just walked past me and I swear she gave me a look that suggests that I'm responsible for all the bad things happening in the world *and* the failure of the Feminist Society.

I've let everyone down.

12.35 p.m.

Dave's sitting over on the other side of the room with The Bitches and we're trying not to look, but it's so weird that he's over there with THEM, I can't stop myself. Trudy looks especially smug today revelling in Sienna and Dave's actions and the closure of the Feminist Society. Earlier she cornered me at my locker and did a mock crying face shouting, 'Boo hoooo, did your little club get shut down?'

I tried my best to take the moral high ground and had to walk away before I kicked her in the shins.

'Last week, he was my boyfriend sitting here with us and now he's over there like an honorary member of The Bitches. Brutal,' Sam says, sadly swishing her fork around a plate of spaghetti hoops.

He doesn't even look embarrassed or glance over at us or anything.

'So weird,' Millie says, glaring at him. 'I know it's not helpful, but I googled to see if I could find anything about why she was expelled from her last school and couldn't find any results about a fire with her name.'

'Can we talk about something else? I think I need distraction again,' Sam looks down at the hoops.

'Of course,' Millie says, rubbing her arm as I get my phone out, poised to show her some more photos of Jake Gyllenhaal doing normal tasks.

This morning I noticed a new one: Jake crossing the road.

So cute.

9 p.m.
In my room reading The Handmaid's Tale

It feels appropriate.

Imagine if *The Handmaid's Tale* actually happened. I wonder if they'd get away with it or if the feminist resistance would be strong enough to take them down?

Probably not if I was in charge.

10.03 p.m.

Mr Clarke would probably like to live in Gilead.

10.05 p.m.

I wonder if he has a wife that he calls OfClarke?

Although actually it would be his first name.

His first name is Ronald. OfRonald.

Poor wife.

10.10 p.m.

Just imagined Mr Clarke having sex.

It's things like that that are probably making me incapable of masturbation.

10.15 p.m.

> Google: What do people masturbate ove—   Q

WAIT this is a bad idea.

Porn lies here.

But why aren't girls supposed to watch porn? Why is porn considered, like, a man thing? When it's just people having sex? There's porn to suit every sexual orientation. Why shouldn't women watch it? Maybe I should start watching porn immediately, as an urgent feminist issue?

Maybe it'll stop me from being wankingly challenged?

10.20 p.m.

Maybe another night.

Bit tired.

10.30 p.m.

I can't get the image of Mr Clarke having sex out of my mind.
My phone's just beeped. Please, god, be a distraction from my
perverted brain.

> **We 🩶 Sam**
> Sam, Millie, Me

Millie: Guys, are you awake? I need to talk.

Me: Always. What's up?

Sam: Of course xx

Millie: Mum and Dad came home from
dinner early to talk to us. They're splitting
up permanently. Dad's even already found
a flat, he's moving out xxx

Sam: Oh my god, Millie, I'm so sorry xxx

Me: Oh, Millie, I'm sorry Xxx

Millie: They said that they've tried to fix things
and that they wanted to hang on until after the
GCSEs but they realised that they were making
us all miserable xxx

Me: Oh god, Millie 🩶 xxx

Sam: Three-way call?

Millie: Yes, please xxx

12 p.m.
In bed

We talked for ages, until Millie started yawning. Issy and her are going to come by here first thing tomorrow and we'll all walk in together. Including my smelly little brother.

Poor Millie, poor Sam. Why are so many shitty things happening?

3 Positive Things:
1. Positivity
2. Is
3. Dead.

Tuesday 28th January

8 a.m.
My room

Issy and Freddie are downstairs and we're having a quick pre-school debrief in my room. Millie's eyes are red and I can see that she's been crying all night, even though her concealer is on point.

'I just feel so shit,' Millie says. 'I don't even want to talk about it because I'm so angry at them.'

'You don't have to talk if you don't want, we're just here,' Sam says.

'Exactly, you just let us know if there's anything we can do, and we'll do it,' I say.

But what can we do? I can't help Millie, I can't help Sam. I can't even help myself.

Why is everything going wrong? And why am I so rubbish that I can't help them the way they helped me last year?

Thursday 30ᵗʰ January

11 a.m.

Chemistry – the worst class (why do they call it the periodic table when it has nothing to do with periods?) in the worst week in school history, that I can't help but think is about to get even worse as I read the message that's just been delivered to my phone.

We 🤍 Millie
Sam, Millie, Me

Sam: Sienna and Dave had sex x

Millie: What? WHO SAYS? x

Sam: Trudy was just talking to Amelie about it right next to me in Physics, loudly so I'd hear, now she's side-eyeing me xx

Me: That's definitely not proof. She'd do that just to wind you up xxx

Millie: What Kat said, there's no way. Not this quick. Trudy just wants to upset you xxx

Sam: She's making it seem very convincing. Apparently it was in the shed where we used to hang out at the bottom of his garden xx

---

12.45 p.m.

The canteen

The three of us are sitting at our usual table but none of us are eating. It seems like wherever you turn there's someone talking about how Dave and Sienna have had sex and I for one am sick of hearing about it so I can't imagine how Sam must be feeling.

'Honestly, Sam, he's really not worth it. I promise you,' Millie says with her hand on Sam's back.

'Yeah, and who has sex in a shed in this weather anyway? It must have been freezing in there. I hope they both get piles,' I say matter-of-factly, because my nan once told me that failure to wrap up 'your nethers' properly in the cold can result in piles. I don't want to know how she found this out.

'It's just, it was our shed.' Sam stares sadly at a wilted piece of lettuce while Millie rubs her back.

'I'm sorry, Sam,' I say.

I'm so angry that Dave's made her feel this way, and that the whole school's talking about it, so she's got literally no escape. I don't know what to do to help my friend and I feel so helpless.

Surely things can't get worse than this?

'OH my GOD, so tell me EVERYTHING,' I hear Trudy say right behind me and immediately remember that where Trudy's involved things can always get worse.

I spin around and see Trudy and Sienna on the table behind us and know that they've sat there on purpose. Pure evil has no boundaries or compassion after all.

'Well,' Sienna throws us a dramatic look that makes me feel sick. 'We were in his shed . . .'

'Can we go, please?' Sam asks in a tiny voice, smaller than I've ever heard her use before.

'Of course,' Millie says as the two of us spring up and join arms with her.

The three of us walk out in a line.

Absolutely broken.

5 p.m.
Scoops

Everything's shit. I feel crap about the Feminist Society and missing the French trip when it feels like my friends need me the most. Millie obviously feels crap because of her parents, and Sam feels crap because all anyone's talked about all day is Dave and Sienna having sex in that gross little shed. I wish she could see that she's had a lucky escape.

So we've come to Scoops, putting revision, coursework and

all other life on hold (not that any of us can concentrate anyway) for some serious hot chocolate time.

'The French trip'll be rubbish without you, Kat,' Sam says.

'I'm sorry, I wish I was coming,' I say.

'The only reason I really want to go now is because at least Dave and Sienna aren't going to be there. Five blissful days without seeing either of their twatty faces.'

'It'll be nice to be in a different country from my parents,' Millie says.

'Why are grown-ups so shitty?' I say, feeling especially angry that mine aren't letting me go on the trip now.

'Agree with that,' Sam says. 'I finally told my mum about Dave last night and she said, 'Oh well, he's just your first boyfriend, best to get it out of the way and move on.' Like I can't be heartbroken about it. She just doesn't understand, at all.'

'Parents!' Millie says.

'Twat-rents more like,' I add.

'I just want to go back to feeling OK again and stop getting a sinking feeling every time I see them.' Sam looks like she might cry. 'I know she's prettier than me and there's no way I could compete with that, but I thought he loved me. I didn't realise that was all it would take to stop someone being in love with me.'

'She is so NOT prettier than you!' I say.

'AND you're wayyyy cooler than her,' Millie says.

'He's an idiot. A big fartface,' I say maturely.

'Massive fartface. Huge penis-head,' Millie confirms, making Sam giggle a little bit as she gestures a HUGE penis coming from her head.

'Have you packed yet?' I ask, subtly moving the conversation away from Dave.

'Yeah, obviously. My bag's been done since Monday,' Millie says, like I've suddenly mistaken her for someone with no organisational skills.

'Doing it tonight,' Sam says. 'I looked at the weather and it's mostly freezing.'

'Berets and jumpers?' I ask.

'I can't wear my beret without you!' Millie shrieks.

'YOU MUST!' I take both their hands in mine and stare earnestly into their eyes. 'You and the berets must be strong. You must go on without me. I believe in you.'

'OK, Princess Leia,' Sam says as we all have a small hug.

6 p.m.
Glaring at my parents across the kitchen

It just feels like all the parents are getting it wrong right now. My parents won't let me go to France, Sam's parents are belittling her heartbreak, and Millie's parents . . . well . . . they're behaving more like teenagers than we are at the moment. Honestly, it's a disgrace.

11 p.m.

Lying in bed, unable to sleep

I can't help but think that the Feminist Society would have done better with someone else running it. I thought what I was doing was a good thing, but as usual I managed to screw it up so badly that I've made things worse. People trusted me with their stories, they trusted me with their trauma and I let them down.

I know I'm lucky that I have a therapist and she says when I have these thoughts I'm supposed to acknowledge and challenge them and tell myself why they aren't true, but I can't help thinking that if they weren't true they wouldn't keep happening?

I have all this support from my friends and my family and all this help and I'm still too rubbish to get anything right, or even to properly support my friends when they're going through a hard time.

I can't help Millie and Sam like they helped me.

I don't deserve friends and maybe the truth is that I don't deserve a trip to Paris.

Friday 31st January

7 a.m.
The Bedcave
(Not to be confused with The Batcave)

Waking up on a Friday morning without the Feminist Friday blog happening feels rubbish enough, but the trip to France being tomorrow really adds another crappy layer to the crap cake.

I feel incomplete not posting my blog. Like I'm about to leave the house with no knickers on or something.

4 p.m.
Therapy

At last this week's over and I'm back in therapy again where it's safe and cosy.

'So, how's this week been?' Sarah asks, settling into her chair with, bless her, no idea of all the badness I have to tell her.

'Bad,' I say, staring at my feet, because I don't really want to talk about any of it. I just want someone else to give her the rundown and then I'll join in for the discussion after. I really don't think I've got the energy.

5.15 p.m.
Walking home

I feel exhausted. But I also feel empty.

I told Sarah everything that's been happening, that I feel like I'm letting everyone down, I'm failing all my friends and my family, and everyone from the Feminist Society.

Sarah reminded me that there wouldn't have even been a Feminist Society in the first place if it wasn't for me. No one would have had their voices heard at all. She reminded me that depression and anxiety will be fuelling my feelings of worthlessness and that they lie to me. And I can't let them win.

But even when I'm trying hard, it's difficult to see the positives right now.

5.30 p.m.
Arriving home

The girls are both under strict instructions from their parents to have early nights tonight ahead of the trip, so we're FaceTiming later and then I'm waving them off with coffee at the coach tomorrow. And then it's just me, on my own.

It's probably good to have some time alone so I can focus on my exams anyway, I need to knuckle down and work really hard, then maybe I can at least make sure I don't fuck those up the way I've fucked everything else up.

I need to snap out of this before I start spiralling again.

I open the front door and toss my keys on the side, abandoning all my stuff at the door. The house is eerily silent. Normally by this point on a Friday there's at least someone about. But I can't see or hear anyone as I head to the kitchen. I guess if I have to get used to the loneliness, why not start early?

'SURPRISE!' Mum and Dad jump out at me as soon as I shuffle into the kitchen.

They're wearing moustaches, striped tops and berets, and they're sword-fighting with baguettes. Are they taking the piss? I'm tempted to walk back out again.

I narrow my eyes at them as Bea runs towards me wearing a tiny dog beret on her head. If she had opposable thumbs, she'd have called the RSPCA by now.

'Why are you doing this?' I ask. This is insensitive even by their standards.

'Take a seat, Kitty Kat, there's something we need to talk to you about,' Dad says gesturing to the kitchen table.

'I know we said that it was too soon after everything that happened last year, and that we didn't think you should go to France . . . but we got it wrong. With everything you and your friends have been through together, you deserve this trip and I know you'll look out for each other.' Mum sits down at the kitchen table and I sit down opposite her. 'And I feel like it's important for us to own it when we get something wrong and do what we can to make it right.'

'We also don't want you to miss out because we made a bad decision. That's not fair,' Dad says looking somewhat sheepish.

I can't believe this is happening.

Are my parents 'apologising'? Admitting they got something

wrong? Is this real?

'So, we spoke to your teachers today and they can squeeze you in, and would love for you to join in *if*, that is, you want to go,' Mum says.

'We know it's short notice and we know it's a lot to take in, so take your time and don't feel pressured to go,' Dad says.

I stare straight ahead at them both, not sure what to say. This is the best news EVER, but I was NOT expecting it.

'God, just say yes you idiot,' Freddie says, sauntering into the kitchen. 'I can't wait for you to be gone for a few days.'

'OH MY GOD, I CAN'T BELIEVE IT!' I shout, ignoring Freddie. 'Of course I want to go! Thank you so much!'

Bea looks at me pleadingly as I start jumping up and down.

'Sorry, Bea,' I say, and take the beret off her. She's never been one for costumes.

'I need to tell the girls! OH MY GOD!' I say.

'You could always leave it and surprise the girls tomorrow morning?' Dad suggests.

Actually that's not a half bad idea. I'd LOVE to see their faces.

'Come on, let's pack your bag!' Mum says and we run up the stairs together excited.

6 p.m.

VERY excited packing with Mum who's throwing more pairs of knickers at me than there are days in the week, 'Just in case!'

236

In case of WHAT?

TWO MEN AND A LITTLE LADY
Matt, Si, Me

> **Me:** Oh my god, Matt! Si! I'm going to France after all!

> **Me:** Don't tell the girls, I want to surprise them tomorrow.

Matt: Whattttt?! How? Whatttt? This is amazing news. Now you can finally get that French coq!

> **Me:** It's not all about the coq, Matt.

Matt: Keep telling yourself that, babe. 👍

Si: Enjoy the coq, babe!!

Thing is, though, I've barely even thought about Sébastien this week. He hasn't replied to my message from last weekend and it's just not bothered me. This is not about him. It's about having the trip of a lifetime with my girls.

Though I may have packed my secret thong somewhere away from the hoards of massive nana knickers that Mum's put in the bag.

But that's obviously got nothing to do with it.

237

6.30 p.m.

Too excited to eat dinner/starting to get anxious because I can't seem to just ENJOY myself

Obviously, my anxious brain has now begun making lists of worries.

So far I've got:

1. What if the coach crashes and we all die?
2. What if the ferry sinks and we all get stranded out at sea?
3. And then we die? Dropping each other in the sea like Kate with Leo at the end of Titanic. THERE WAS ROOM FOR TWO ON THAT PLANK.
4. What if I get off the coach for some reason and the driver doesn't realise I'm off the coach and leaves and then runs me over and I die?
5. What if I get there but can't get to sleep without touching the light switch?
6. What if I have to touch the light switch but it's so far from my bed that people see me, and the whole year finds out that I'm a loser?
7. What if something bad happens because I can't touch the light switch?
8. What if I can't touch it all week then we die on the trip home?

And those are just starter worries. I know that my brain can create more in a flash. But I do my best to put my worries aside. Why can't I just be normal? I'm supposed to just be pure excited about this. Not worrying! I'm young! I'm going on a surprise trip TO ANOTHER COUNTRY with my besties! I canNOT let my anxious brain ruin this for me!

I need to stop worrying and remember that this time tomorrow I'm going to be with Sam and Millie, in PARIS! And that's literally THE BEST THING EVER.

8 p.m.
FaceTiming with the girls

I'm being oddly quiet because I don't trust myself not to give the game away.

'What will you do while we're gone?' Millie asks.

'Revise and probably continuously FaceTime you?' I say, trying to be vague and not look happy in any way, at ALL.

'I can't believe you're not coming,' Sam says.

Oh god, I might have to cut this call short because I can't stop myself from smiling. I'm going to give myself away.

9 p.m.
On the sofa

What if this is my last night on earth and I've spent it watching *Coronation Street* with my parents?

11 p.m.
In bed

Am now anxious that I'll forget to touch the light switch. Anxious that I'll forget to do the thing that I'm anxious about. Those are some layers of anxiety right there.

12 p.m.

Maybe I shouldn't go.

12.10 p.m.

I am not letting my brain stop me.
  I'm going.

3 Positive Things:
1. I am going to France – YAY!
2. I am going to have the best time with my two best friends.
*3. I am definitely not worrying about dying on the French trip and the Feminist Legacy that I would leave behind me if I do which would stand at a long list of failures and the permanent spray painting of #Tim on the playground. Oh well, never mind. **I'M GOING TO FRANCE!***

Saturday 1st February

7 a.m.

My bedroom

I AM GOING TO FRANCE TODAY WITH MY TWO BEST FRIENDS!

In France I will be brave and bold and have the best time. I will say yes to everything! Or 'oui!', as they say in France (oui oui . . . wee wee . . . *snigger*. Oh god, maybe I'm not mature enough to be going after all) and I will make the most of the whole experience!

I managed to stay up most of the night worrying about things that could happen and eventually at about 6 a.m. I managed to convince myself that I need to stop worrying about what *might* happen and instead focus on having a good time.

I AM GOING TO FRANCE!

I am knackered.

9 a.m.

The school playground

I'm standing with Millie and Sam looking really sad while my co-conspirators (Mum and Dad) hide around the corner with my bags.

'I'm going to miss you, Kat,' Sam says while Millie snogs Nick's face off like he's oxygen. 'I think they've actually got suctioned together and instead of going to Paris we're going to have to go to hospital to get them surgically removed from each other.'

'One of them has to come up for air soon, surely . . .' I say, waiting for Millie to come over before I go in for my big reveal . . .

'Heard your parents won't let you come on the French trip, loser!' Trudy shouts on her way past me with ten thousand items of matching luggage.

A slow smile begins to spread across my face. Even Trudy can't ruin this for me.

Millie's walking over now too, although still clutching Nick's hand tightly.

It's time.

'Well, actually . . .' I say, 'I AM coming!'

'WHAT?' Sam says, turning to me.

'HUH?' Millie says.

'Yep! I'm coming! Mum and Dad changed their minds.'

'OH MY GOD!' We all jump up and down squealing for a full minute, until I feel dizzy, as Trudy huffs off with Amelie towards the coach.

9.10 a.m.

'RIGHT!' Madame Rauche shouts to get everyone's attention as the three of us control our excited noises. 'We're all here. So get yourselves on the coach. Please let me know if you suffer from travel sickness or have any other medical condition I need to know about.'

#Tim rushes over to her straight away and I don't want to

know what he's confessing to.

Miss Mills and Mr Hope are coming on the trip too which is nice, although Miss Mills already looks like Mr Hope's annoying her. Poor Miss Mills.

Trudy and Amelie head for the back seat and I wonder if Amelie will use this week to try and get her second-in-command title back? Or maybe she's still Second in Command but she just serves two head bitches now?

'STOP SNOGGING, MILLIE, YOU FILTHY WENCH! IT'S TIME TO GO!' Sam shouts at Millie, who gives us the finger from her position, reattached to Nick's face.

'Aww, sweet! Kat, you're coming!' Krish says, walking past and high-fiving me.

'I AM!' I beam back at him.

Finally, Millie and Nick separate. We're going for five days not five months!

'I'll text you all the time,' Millie says, clinging to his hands as she slowly walks away, glassy eyed. Ever the drama queen.

'Oh dear,' I say rolling my eyes.

'Did you bring tissues?' Sam says.

'Crap, no.'

9.15 a.m.
On the coach

The three of us have had to spread across two aisles but that's OK because it means I get two whole seats to myself. I've already swung my legs round to make myself a kind of bed. Millie's started gently weeping like a character in a film while she waves out the window mournfully at Nick.

'You OK, babe?' Sam asks.

'Yeah,' she says, sniffing bravely.

She'll get over it.

Oh no, no, no, #Tim's started wandering up and down the bus looking for a seat.

There's plenty of space next to Trudy and Amelie at the back, so *why* is he approaching MY seat? Keep walking, pal. KEEP WALKING. Why has he stopped? Stop stopping! KEEP WALKING.

'Hey, ladieeess, this seat taken?' he creeps, pointing to the seat next to me.

'Yes,' I say, spreading my legs out even further to make a point. I will WOMANSPREAD my way through this.

'Unfortunately, I can't sit at the back as it's bad for my travel sickness,' Tim says with a sly grin, 'so this is really the only place I can sit.'

He starts pushing past me, saying, 'I have to sit by the window too,' as the girls watch open-mouthed. I don't believe a word of it but accept that I'll have to move pretty quickly or risk him touching me.

URGH. I do not want to spend Paris week with #Tim.

9.20 a.m.

'Umm, how about this?' Sam says as she holds out a sick

bag for Millie.

'Um, what?' says Millie.

'To wipe your eyes and blow your nose . . . it's just a little thicker and shinier than your usual tissue, that's all,' Sam says brightly.

Millie shrugs and takes it from her.

And that is how Millie came to dry her eyes with a vomit bag.

So far this trip has been non-stop class.

9.45 a.m.
We're on our way!

I can't believe this moment is actually here. After everything. I am on my way to Paris! I am a strong independent woman off to explore the world! I am going to be a pain au chocolat connoisseur!

I am going to be . . . I HAVE A MESSAGE FROM Sébastien!

What? I mean obviously, I'm not bothered because this trip is *not* about him.

But I need to tell the girls! I reach over the aisle with my phone.

'Guys. He's messaged me!' I say.

'Who?' Sam looks at me like I'm a lunatic as I try to scooch away from #Tim's grubby ears.

'Sébastien!' I insist as if *she's* the lunatic.

'OOOH!' Millie looks like her eyes might pop.

'What does it say?' Sam asks very reasonably.

'I don't know, I haven't opened it yet.'

'OPEN IT!' Sam practically shouts, leading a few people to turn around, but I don't care. I'm busy looking at the message.

> **Sébastien:** Hi Kat, you come to Paris this week? 👍

'He wants to know if I'm coming to Paris,' I tell the girls.

'Well, just say yes, don't be weird about it,' Sam says like she's talking to a toddler.

'Yeah, nothing weird.' Millie nods, giving me a pointed look.

Urgh, why must they know me so well? I type out various different variations of yes, rejecting 'oui!', 'Oui Oui!' and 'Indeed I shall be there!', and finally settle on: 'Yes, I am' with a thumbs up to match his.

I show the girls my thrilling message before I send it because we know I can't be trusted on my own and click send.

He replies almost immediately with another thumbs up. What's with the thumbs up? IS THE THUMBS UP IN ANY WAY SEXUAL?

Probably not. No one wants a thumb up the vagina. Do they?

God, a polite thumbs up and I read it as sexual?

I think I've caught pervert from #Tim.

10 a.m.

We've been on the road for about half an hour and I can tell you that without a doubt the cause of #Tim's travel sickness is most likely to be his own overpowering smell of Lynx.

246

10.30 a.m.

I keep having to shuffle further and further away from #Tim so that his smell doesn't make me puke. This means sliding further and further off my seat. I've got one cheek on and one cheek off right now.

11 a.m.

Half a cheek on now.

11.05 a.m.

This is very uncomfortable. But the smell just keeps wafting at me.

11.10 a.m.

Just a whisper of my thigh touching seat now and STILL I can smell it.

11.15 a.m.

This is like doing a long-term squat. I'm relying solely on my glutes to keep me up and I don't know if they'll hold out to Paris. If they do, I'll have the strongest thighs on this bus.

11.20 a.m.

I fell.

11.21 a.m.

I have the most bruised arse and pride on this bus.

Trudy and Amelie laughed so loudly that I think they broke sound barriers. #Tim offered me a hand up, WHICH I REJECTED because it's HIS FAULT.

Madame Rauche shouted at me to stop messing around. I'm not messing around I'm trying not to be gassed by the smell of eau de creep.

I slump back down on to my seat and cover my face with my jumper.

Millie and Sam are laughing and even though this is NO LAUGHING MATTER, it's good to see them both looking happy.

12.30 p.m.
On a ferry – FREEDOM from #Tim

This ferry is like a time warp. I know I wasn't alive in the nineties to know what they were like, but I'm pretty sure they were like this. Also there's a general smell of sick which is added to by the fact that it turns out quite a few people are seasick in our year.

I don't enjoy other people's pain – obviously – but I did feel smug that Trudy was being sick and I wasn't. #Tim tried to 'help' her and as a result is sitting in the corner nursing his balls, and at least we can be sure that his right hand won't be getting any vigorous action this trip now.

Really, the only good violence Trudy has ever done.

2.30 p.m.
BONJOUR, FRANCE!

We're out of the ferry and in FRANCE. For a minute we thought that #Tim had forgotten or lost his passport. We were all quite prepared and happy for him to be deported alone.

Sadly, he found it. Also sadly, we got to see inside his suitcase, filled with lube and condoms. Possibly even the same lube he tried to gift me.

We should send some kind of warning to the women of France.

3 p.m.

Everyone's laughing because Comedy Krish keeps making wank gestures at the other drivers.

'Hey, Krish! Catch!'

Tom, who's sitting next to Krish, has just thrown an unwrapped condom right in his face. I can feel the grossness from here.

3.10 p.m.

MAYHEM has ensued. There are unsheathed condoms from #Tim's stash everywhere, and the smacking sound of people flicking each other with unravelled prophylactics fills the air. I laugh as someone thwacks one in Trudy's direction only to feel one land in my hair two seconds later and stick in it.

GROOSSSSSSSSSS!

'Let me help!' #Tim dives to help me untangle the sheath from my hair and I duck out of the way.

3.20 p.m.

The bus has stopped. The driver is angry. He's shouting at us while removing a condom from his forehead, seemingly completely unaware that another floppy sheath dangles from his right shoulder. Miss Mills is trying to look cross with us, while Madame Rauche stands next to the coach driver, stony-faced.

No one knows who was responsible, but Comedy Krish has come off his seat and is curled in the foetal position in his footwell.

4 p.m.

Squatting at the side of the road – why do I always seem to be squatting? WHY?

The bus would not restart and, as a result, carrying on the

classiness of this trip, Sam, Millie and I are currently squatting in a bush – hopefully one without stinging nettles, or poison ivy – trying not to hear each other pee or get any pee on ourselves. We've got three different spots in this bush and it's just like being in our toilets at school except that nature is our toilet cubicle.

It's so cold out here that I worry my vulva will get frostbite. Also, can wee turn to ice as it's coming out of you? What if I get icicles dangling from my urethra and I have to wait until I go somewhere hot enough for them to thaw and melt?

Suddenly I feel the weirdest sensation. Like I'm still weeing but the wee is everywhere. It takes me a while to realise that it's started to rain. Honestly, weeing while it starts to rain on you is very odd.

'Finished!' Sam shouts.

'Me too!' Millie shouts from her section of the bush.

'I can't tell if I'm still weeing or if it's just the rain!' I shout back, panicked.

There's complete silence from the rest of the bush and I'm starting to worry that they've left me and I'll just be here for ever, in wee limbo. Or at least until the rain stops. I'm at nature's mercy. This is not what I meant by saying wee wee to everything.

'Guys?' I ask, starting to feel slightly frantic. 'GUYS!'

And then I hear laughing and I know they're still there, just messing with me.

'Sorry, Kat,' Sam says.

'We just didn't know what to say.' They're both still laughing – pricks.

'I think it's just the rain, Kat,' Sam says, spluttering.

Unbelievable. I'm having a urine-based crisis and they're laughing at me. Fine. I think Sam must be right. After all I can't wee for ever and I looked down and there's definitely no stream coming from down there. I pull my soggy jeans back up on to my soggy legs. If there was any stray wee, the rain's probably washed it away anyway, so I've probably got a soggy combination of wee and rain happening. I must smell delicious. Either way, it's better than #Tim's smell.

4 p.m.
Still in the layby

Glad we went for that wee when we did. Outside looks like the apocalypse, but inside this bus smells like fart and cheese.

This is not the life I deserve.

4.30 p.m.

Finally! A wonderful French man has come, shouting things, he has a can of diesel. It turns out we just ran out of fuel. What kind of coach driver doesn't keep track of the fuel?

4.45 p.m.
On the road again . . . da da da . . .

PARIEEEEEE, here we come!

4.50 p.m.

#Tim has started to creep closer again. Surely the damp rain/
wee smell on me would put him off?

5.30 p.m.
WE'RE IN PARIS

It's everything I ever imagined it would be. As we drive through
the city, I take in the glamorous, busy streets and those buildings
with the shutters. Everyone looks so sophisticated and well
dressed (and here I am in my pissy jeans).

It's so beautiful, all of it. So much nicer than London. Not
that I've been to London that often. But I once heard that a girl
in the year below spent twenty-four hours there and when she
came back her snot was black from the pollution. I bet Parisians
don't even have snot, let alone black snot.

5.32 p.m.

I've come to sit on Millie and Sam's laps so I can look out the
window and finally get away from #Tim. It's so much fun just
watching actual Paris in actual real life! Kinda weird that we
haven't stopped yet. I'm sure we will soon, though.

We're going over a bridge and it looks amazing. I'm imagining
waking up tomorrow and walking over the bridge to get coffee.

5.45 p.m.

We're still driving and Paris is starting to look a little different. If I didn't know any better, I would think that we're coming out the other side of Paris?

Maybe we'll go back in? Maybe it's one of those one-way systems like they have around the big shopping centre at home? It wouldn't make any sense because traffic is actually going the other way right now, but then neither would saying that we're going to Paris when it's not Paris?

5.50 p.m.

'Right, we're nearly at the hostel. So everyone start gathering yourselves together!' Madame Rauche shouts.

Thank god, because I was starting to wonder where on EARTH we were going. At this rate we were about to end up in Germany or Spain or something (Geography has never been my strong point). Although, this doesn't look anything like the Paris in *Emily in Paris*?

We pull up outside a bleak-looking building, paint peeling, shutters falling off. I don't know where we are, but we CANNOT still be in Paris. Maybe we're going to some other building behind this that's a bit nicer? Like sometimes when you go on holiday and you have to go on a bit of a roam to find the lovely resort behind a bit of a strange facade. I'm sure it's that. Except that we're being led through the front doors and the flashing neon sign over the door says *'auberge de jeunesse'* which even from my very limited French I know means youth hostel.

I guess we've arrived.

6.00 p.m.
Hell Hostel

Millie, Sam and I stand in front of it before we go in. There are definitely going to be bugs in there. We're looking at each other, frozen to the spot.

'Urgh, MOVE!' Trudy says, shoving us out of the way and marching through the doors to misery, Amelie following behind. Trudy looks furious. I bet she'll be on the phone to her parents immediately bemoaning the lack of five-star facilities.

We pick up our stuff and follow her into the mouth of hell.

6.01 p.m.

Inside it's actually better than I thought it would be, but mostly because it's very dark. There are only a few lights and candles. At the front is a bar where a few people are drinking and playing cards and generally making a bit of a racket. But apart from that it's quite sparse. Candles, two lamps and a smell of joss sticks. Like it's the sixties.

'OK, guys!' says Madame Rauche. 'We've got rooms on the first floor. Back in here at 7.30 for dinner. Three to a room!' She marches off ahead while the rest of us stare around blankly.

6.40 p.m.

I swear I just heard a cow moo.

This is not the city.

7 p.m.
Our room

Trudy and Amelie have got the room next to us. We didn't want the biggest room anyway, but it seemed like Trudy was willing to go to GREAT lengths to get it. Miss Mills has confessed that although we are technically in Paris, we are right on the outskirts, which is where our exchange school is. But she says that we're still going into Paris tomorrow, so all is not lost. No idea how we're getting there, though, because in the dark this very much looks like the arse end of Nowheresville.

We've picked our beds and we're just trying to work out what in the room is actually clean and touchable.

'NOOOOO!' Millie screams and leaps across the room away from a drawer she's just opened. 'WHAT IS IT?' She points a shaking finger at the drawer.

Sam and I look at each other before slowly creeping towards whatever horror has just petrified her. I've got a shoe in one hand and Sam's got a magazine. Between us we're armed and ready.

We're hovering to the side of the drawer as we make eye contact with each other, nod, and then take a small peek over, from a sensible and safe distance.

Inside is the biggest cockroach I have ever seen. I can see its EYES and it's looking at me like I'm dinner.

'ARGHHHHH!' Sam and I both scream and all three of us run out of our room and into the corridor.

'What do we do?' Millie asks.

'We get a boy or a teacher to deal with that shit!' Sam says.

'Oh no! Absolutely not!' I say. 'WE are FEMINISTS! We do NOT need other people to fight our battles for us. WE can do this. WE CAN DO THIS!' I say, thrusting my shoe higher in the air.

'Well, one for all and all for one . . . We'll be outside in safety,' Sam says as the two of them run away.

Unbelievable.

It's just a bug. Women have dealt with worse, I think to myself as I march towards the bug and imminent danger. I mean I've just sat next to #Tim for the last ten thousand hours in a confined space. I can do this.

I'm getting really quite close to the drawer now and my fight or flight instinct is screaming FLIGHT.

I'm a strong feminist, I can DO THIS . . .

I peer over the edge of the drawer, lock eyes with the monster, raise my trainer and . . .

'FETCH A BOY!' I scream as I run into the corridor, trainer still aloft.

7.10 p.m.

Scared and ashamed

People have started coming out of their rooms to see what the commotion is, including Miss Mills.

'What's happening?' she asks.

'Cockroach,' Sam says.

'This place is disgusting, I'm calling our lawyer,' Trudy says in the background.

'Show me where,' says Miss Mills as if it's nothing.

'I'll sort it for you!' Mr Hope says.

'That won't be necessary, but thanks,' she replies.

Miss Mills follows me into the room and peers into the drawer while I point to it from the other side of the room.

'SHIT, that's a bigun!' she says, before putting her hand over her mouth. 'Tell no one I swore,' she says with a wink. 'And pass me that glass and exercise book. We'll see if we can transport this big little guy out of here.'

I hand her the glass and the exercise book and I'm no longer afraid of it. If she can be so calm, I should be too. It's fine. It's just a bug. I watch as she expertly puts the glass over the cockroach, then slides the exercise book under it before carrying it to the window.

'Open the window for me, would you?' she asks, voice as steady as her hands.' Then she flings the big little cockroach out into the night.

We high-five as we head out into the corridor.

'Right, well. That's that. Who's ready for dinner?' she asks.

Miss Mills is one seriously bad-ass lady.

9 p.m.
Back in the room

Dinner was . . . interesting. I think most of us stuck to the chips on account of the fact that we actually knew the French name for them. What is the point in a French GCSE if we don't even know how to order dinner? I feel a bit disappointed in Madame Rauche at the lack of life skills she's given us actually. Or maybe I just wasn't paying attention . . . come to think of it . . .

The teachers are all still in the bar and they've sent us to bed. I know the teachers don't want us roaming about outside alone, but surely that doesn't mean we have to be in bed at nine! Although hanging out in our room, just the three of us, listening to music is pretty great.

9.30 p.m.

Sitting in bed with the covers pulled up, listening to what's happening outside.

It started with just a small patter of feet that then got bigger and now we're listening to people whispering and running between rooms in the corridor.

'Should we go and see what's happening?' Sam whispers.

'We could, or we could just hang out by ourselves and save

ourselves the disappointment?' Millie suggests. She's mostly glued to her phone texting Nick anyway. She could be anywhere right now.

'I think we should go,' I say, eager to find out what's going on.

'Me too. That's two against one. Sorry, Millie. You're out-voted. You can always stay here if you want, though?' Sam says throwing her covers off.

'Stay here? By myself? And risk being eaten by that GIGANTIC COCKROACH when it comes back inevitably seeking revenge for being turfed out of its home? No thank you!'

Millie might have a point there. I hadn't thought about the cockroach coming back. And what if it's got family?

WHAT IF IT COMES BACK WHEN WE'RE ASLEEP AND BITES OUR FACES AND THEN WE TURN INTO COCKROACH–HUMAN HYBRIDS?

Get a grip, Kat.

'Let's go!' I say, leaping out of bed in my bunny pyjamas, eager to get away from possible flesh-eating cockroaches.

'In our pyjamas?' Millie asks.

'Yeah, sod it. We'll just peek round the door, see what's going on. Then if nothing's happening, we can just go back to bed. I can't be arsed to get changed,' Sam says.

9.40 p.m.
Peering out into the corridor

None of us want to commit to joining in with something that looks lame, so all three of us have our heads popped round the door and we're just peering down the corridor, assessing the situation.

There doesn't seem to be anyone out here at the moment.

'They must be in a room,' I whisper to Millie and Sam.

'Which one, though?' Millie asks.

'Trudy's?' Sam suggests.

'We'd be able to hear them through the wall.'

I point to the wall between ours and Trudy's room. Millie creeps back into the room and tiptoes over to the wall. She stands on the bed with her ear against it.

'They're not in there,' she says after a minute, ear still against the wall.

'Maybe it's Krish's room?' I suggest.

'We might as well go and find out. What's the worst that can happen?' Sam says optimistically.

We tiptoe out into the corridor trying to work out which door it is, stealth-mode fully engaged. Just as we're being as quiet as we possibly can be, Trudy's door wrenches open and her head comes flying out.

'What are you doing?' Trudy asks as all three of us jump.

'Toilet,' I say quickly.

'Together?'

'Yes, it's scary.'

'Lesbians,' Trudy retorts.

'So what if we were lesbians? It's not an insult,' I say, rolling my eyes at her ignorance.

'Whatever.' Trudy rolls her eyes back and then shuts the door.

A second later, Comedy Krish opens his.

'PSST! QUICK!' he kind of shout-whispers at us as we run into his room. He manages to shut the door just in time before we hear Trudy's door re-open again.

Oh wow.

Comedy Krish has the entire year in here plus two French girls I've never seen before. Where did they come from?

'Welcome to Casa Krish!'

He sweeps his hand around a room full of people passing round bottles of wine that have clearly been snuck from the bar. #Tim is trying his luck with one of the French women who, petrifyingly, seems to be finding him hilarious.

'Sorry for the subterfuge. We don't want Trudy and Amelie to get wind of the party and come in and ruin the vibes,' Krish says, and I can completely understand it. 'She always makes a party about her and she's been so negative all day. I'm bored of it.'

Sometimes I feel bad when I hear things like this because I wonder if actually Trudy is just a deeply unhappy person, and as a person with mental health issues I wonder if I should be more understanding. But then when I wrote a blog about my mental health last year she called me 'a sad mental'. So probably not.

11 p.m.
Krish's party casa

This little gathering is pretty great, but I don't know how it's not been shut down yet. To be fair everyone's just chilling and having a nice time chatting to each other. It's not like it's a wild party or anything.

Weirdly both of the French girls now seem to be finding #Tim hilarious, much to Krish's dismay. Apparently, they're staying in the hostel too. Krish spotted them in the bar and invited them over but sadly they're more interested in #Tim. This might possibly be because he's lying to them. I heard him say to one of them that he has a castle in the English countryside where he is a lord. Sam spat out her drink laughing at that. They MUST know it's a lie, though. Right?

There's a tap at the door and Krish puts his finger to his lips, everyone shuts up and freezes exactly where they are. It's a bit scary actually. Like we're about to get caught by the police.

'There's definitely something happening in there, miss.' We hear Trudy through the door. 'I can hear them. He's having a party!'

'Krish?' I hear Miss Mills's voice. 'Are you OK in there?'

'Yes, miss, what's going on? Just sleeping,' he replies in a faux croaky voice.

'Can you open the door a minute?'

'Sure.'

Krish looks panicked but messes up his hair and TAKES OFF HIS TROUSERS, while all of us shuffle to the other side of the room. He opens the door a tiny crack and pops his head out, while we're all left to stare at his boxer-clad butt. Not being funny, but he's got quite a good pair of legs. Oh god, I'm

#Tim-ing over Krish. STOP IT NOW, KAT!

'Hi, miss, sorry I was asleep. Is something up?' he asks sleepily.

'Not at all,' I hear Miss Mills say, slightly slurred. I'm guessing the teachers are probably just trying to have a quiet bit of French wine themselves. 'Just Trudy imagining things. Go back to sleep. And, you too, Trudy. I'll see you both in the morning.'

'Night, miss, sleep well,' Krish says in a charming voice before shutting the door, finger to his lips and locking it behind him.

We all wait frozen to the spot.

'I know you're having a party, Krish!' Trudy shouts through the door. 'And my parents WON'T be happy if they find out this kind of thing was happening while the teachers were all pissed in the bar!' she finishes, clearly for Miss Mills's benefit.

I suspect at this point Miss Mills has had too much wine to care. 'Go to bed, Trudy,' she shouts as we hear her head back down the stairs to the bar.

We sit quietly waiting until we can be sure that the coast is clear before carrying on with the nicest and chillest night ever.

3 Positive Things:

1. *I am in France.*
2. *I have had the best night ever.*
3. *This place may be a shit hole but so far, it's quite good fun.*

Sunday 2nd February

7.30 a.m.
Our room

I open my eyes but I can't see. I'M BLIND! WHAT IS GOING ON? WHAT IS THE BANGING? WHERE AM I? I tap at my eyes, find the edges of my eye mask and peel it away. In front of me, Sam and Millie are collapsed on top of each other on Sam's bed. I think it was about 2 a.m. when we came back to bed and, while I hadn't been drinking, the two of them had been at the local wine and were a tad sloshed.

'GET UP, GIRLS! GET UP! YOU'LL MISS BREAKFAST!' Madame Rauche is shouting and banging on the door.

'Oh my god,' Sam's mumbling, putting her pillow over her head.

'Got it, miss! We'll be there in a sec!' I shout back cheerfully. Anything to make her GO AWAY.

7.35 a.m.

I lie in bed, looking around me. Something feels different, apart from just being in a different country, I mean. I can't put my finger on it.

Oh my god.

I DIDN'T TOUCH THE LIGHT SWITCH BEFORE BED!

I feel a bit hot and panicked. Is it OK?

Everything seems OK . . . it is. And I . . . did it.

I DID IT!

And I didn't even know I was doing it.

7.45 a.m.

'Well, I guess I'm going to go and find out what the hell is happening with those showers,' I say, feeling happy about the light switch and forgetting that I'm probably about to be washing in a petri dish of athlete's foot and verrucas. Or is it verrucae?

Are there any less sexy words than 'communal showers'?

8 a.m.

I actually feel surprisingly clean after that shower. I have definitely caught many verrucae, but apart from that I'm OK.

Can you ever use too much hand sanitiser on your feet?

I think I'm about to find out.

10 a.m.
The train

Confirming that ACTUALLY we're nowhere near Paris is the fact that we have been on this particular train into Paris for around half an hour now. We are not 'staying on the outskirts'.

I suspect we are staying in Switzerland.

You can tell who was in Krish's room last night because they've all got red wine lips, although I've noticed a lot of teachers are afflicted with this too. Mostly people are looking VERY quiet and sorry for themselves this morning. Except for Trudy, who still looks furious. And Krish, who really seems to be enjoying Trudy's fury.

The wind will change, and she'll get stuck like that.

10.30 a.m.
PARIS!

We've made it! And *finally* our day in Paris can commence! I'm so excited about the surprise that Millie and I have planned for Sam.

Madame Rauche has gathered us all outside the Louvre. We're crowded around her trying to pay attention but everyone's eager to get away and do their own thing.

'OK, now you're all free to do what you want for the next few hours. PLEASE meet back here at 4.30 p.m. You have our phone numbers if you need anything. No late returners. I'm here if you want to ask me any questions about things you should do, I lived here for a very long time.'

Everyone scatters immediately, and I don't think they're planning on enjoying the art and culture. Trudy has made herself a shopping map of all the boutiques she wants to go to, and Krish is already talking about 'hair of the dog'.

Madame Rauche looks disappointed that no one wants to use her expertise and ask her a question. I feel like asking one out of pity. I can see Miss Mills wants to scatter too and is itching for some alone time in Paris but is trying not to look too eager.

'Would you like to go in?' Millie asks Sam, pointing to the Louvre.

'Into the Louvre?' Sam asks

'Yeah, we're treating you,' I say as Sam's eyes light up like a five-year-old at Christmas.

'What? Wouldn't you guys find that boring?' she asks.

'Not if it makes you happy!' Millie says.

Sam looks like she might cry. I've never seen her cry as much as she has over the past week and I hate Dave SO MUCH for that, and Sienna obviously.

'Come on, you,' I say, putting an arm around Sam. 'Let's get you in to see some art!'

We go in through the pyramid. Millie and I look at Sam and I can see she looks COMPLETELY overwhelmed. It's excellent.

'I could spend all day in here. I don't know what we should do first!' she says.

'Well, we know it's a bit of a cliché, but we sneakily pre-ordered some of those skip-the-line tickets to see the *Mona Lisa*, if you'd be up for that?' I say.

'WHAT? OH MY GOD, OF COURSE I WOULD!!'

11.15 a.m.

I don't think I'd ever realised how SMALL the *Mona Lisa* is. I mean, I'm sure in real life she was normal adult-sized and all, but up close, she's tiny. Also, there are about a MILLION people here to look at this one small painting. Sam's in her element though. She's pushed right to the front and she's completely absorbed in it. I feel like we'll have to tear her away at closing time, if she doesn't get moved on first.

12 p.m.

Sitting in the middle of one of the painting rooms

I've seen a lot of boob and a LOT of bush in this room. Male painters really like a naked lady, don't they? There are far fewer painted penises on show, I've noticed. I wonder if, back in the old days when they were painting, before photos and stuff, that was their version of porn. Like if they'd have a good wank over an oil painting or something?

WHAT IS WRONG WITH ME? Literally ALWAYS thinking about sex, ALL THE TIME.

'Oh my god.' Millie nudges me and points ahead, disturbing me from my FILTHY thoughts.

#Tim is standing ahead of us as close to a picture of a naked woman as it is possible to be. Her boobs are at head height. He may as well be motorboating her.

I can't cope. Maybe my prediction wasn't far off? Maybe

#Tim was a renaissance wanker in a past life?

4 p.m.
Walking down the Seine

I can't believe I'm actually in PARIS walking down the Seine with my friends. It's SO BEAUTIFUL and this is so cool, and we've had the perfect day.

We left the Louvre shortly after #Tim noticed us and tried to get our attention. We weren't about to associate with a renaissance pervert. Sam said she'd seen everything that she had wanted to and it's such a lovely sunny day (bit nippy, but we've obviously got our berets to keep us warm) and we wanted to see as much of Paris as we possibly could.

We went to Shakespeare & Co, the amazing Parisian bookshop that's always in films and books. I don't think I'd realised how COOL it is. It's so romantic. Small and winding, with loads of little nooks. It felt magical to just be in there. I stood in front of the fiction section and just for a TINY second looked at where my book would be if I ever published one. Although if I'm to be a hard-hitting feminist writer, maybe it would be in the non-fiction section? For it to be anywhere in that shop would be completely mind-blowing, to be honest.

Now we've got crêpes from a street vendor and we're walking down the river chatting and watching people. There's so much happening and I can confirm that my suspicions were correct, French children are very well dressed and, no, this is not a sweeping generalisation. I just saw a little girl in a peacoat with a beret on and, honestly, she's my style icon now.

Paris is beautiful. I know this is supposed to be the city of love but seeing it with my two best friends seems way better than seeing it with anyone else. And maybe it's not about romantic love: maybe friendship love is even more important? They've definitely both perked up after their early morning hangovers too.

I take a deep breath and savour this moment. I've not thought about Sébastien all day and I feel like I'm miles away from any of my worries from home – GCSEs, the Feminist Society, or toxic masculinity. Is that bad? Shouldn't I always be tirelessly thinking about that and trying to find a way to fix things? But everything here just feels so magical and calm. I feel like I've got space to breathe for the first time in ages.

'It's so nice to be away from everything, isn't it?' I say.

'SO nice!' Sam says, breathing in deeply, and Millie nods.

'I've barely thought about Mum and Dad or anything,' Millie says.

'Me either. Who's Dave?' Sam says. 'Can we just stay in Paris?'

'I wish,' I say before taking the last bite of what may be the most delicious crêpe I've ever tasted – possibly the only crêpe I've ever tasted but still . . . great.

It's starting to get a bit dark and the river looks even more romantic than it did before, lights twinkling from the cafes and bars either side, the air filled with music from street performers. I never want to go home.

'I'm getting cold. You know what I think it might be time for?' Millie asks.

'HOT CHOCOLATE?' Sam asks hopefully.

'Yes!' Millie says, adjusting her beret for business.

I definitely didn't need any French coq to make this trip special. My friends have already done that for me.

9 p.m.
Bed

We've been in bed gossiping for a while. Everyone was pretty exhausted after last night and seemed to just drip off to bed after dinner. Apart from Trudy, who tried to gain revenge for last night by inviting everyone except Krish to her room. Krish didn't seem bothered, though, and I caught him rolling his eyes and the two of us ended up laughing. Somehow, I don't think I'd be welcome, but TBH by the time she'd finished laying out the RULES I doubt anyone was interested. I think she lost most people at, 'Don't touch anything, you may sit on the floor but not the beds.'

Way to be hospitable, Trudy. Can't wait for her birthday party!

I'm enjoying myself so much, I find it hard to believe that we've only been here one day and that I didn't even think I was coming until two days ago.

I know I'll have to start thinking about how I deal with the light switch soon, but I just want to enjoy this experience and not let the anxiety in yet.

'I am exhausted!' Millie yawns from her bed.

'Me too,' Sam says.

'Me three. Who knew Krish could throw such an amazing party?' I catch yawns from Sam and Millie just as Millie's phone beeps.

'What IS he on about?' Millie mutters, staring at her phone.

'What?' I ask.

'Nick's sent me some weird text banging on about Gary Lineker?' Millie says, eyebrows knotted.

'What's he said exactly?' Sam asks, sliding over to Millie's bed to take a look.

'"They lost football yesterday, Dave pulled a Gary Lineker. So embarrassing! What a douche."?' Millie reads from her phone.

'I think we might just have to ask what he means,' I say. I don't even know who Gary Lineker is.

'Good shout, I don't know why he thinks we care about Dave's footballing career either.' Millie whispers the last bit because we don't want Trudy in the next room hearing us talking about Dave.

Millie's phone beeps again and she gasps putting her hand over her face and turns it round to face us. He's sent us a video: 'Gary Lineker describes the day he shat himself while playing football'.

'OH MY GOD! He SHAT himself? Playing football?' Sam shout-whispers. 'Please tell me more! And, Kat, don't give me anything about taking the moral high ground. I DON'T WANT TO!'

'I wouldn't dream of it! I need to know exactly what happened too!' I crowd around the phone with the two of them.

'I need to know more!' Millie's whispering frantically at her phone and furiously texting Nick.

'Well, couldn't have happened to a nicer bloke.' Sam smirks.

'Oh. My. God,' Millie whispers, eyes popping out of her head as she texts. 'So Sienna was at the sidelines and just walked off, disgusted. No one knows if they're still together. Apparently, they'd been out on the Friday night and he'd eaten a bad kebab. No one's heard from him since he ran off the pitch in his brown shorts, and no one's heard from Sienna since she stormed off with Tiffany, Tia and Nia in tow.

'Interesting that they've adopted her as their leader while Trudy's away. I wonder if they'll have some kind of top-bitch battle or something when Trudy gets back?' I think aloud.

'I bet Trudy knows whether Sienna's still with him or not,' Millie whispers, looking up from her phone.

'Do NOT ask. What does it matter?' Sam whispers. 'I'd never go back to him now, whether he was with her or not, whether he'd shat himself or not. He's not for me, he broke my heart and now I'm healing and getting better. I know I'm worth so much more than him. Their relationship doesn't interest me in the slightest. It just brings me great joy to know that he publicly shat himself.'

'That's so mature and reasonable,' Millie says.

'I am a strong independent woman,' Sam says. 'I don't need a man. But I hope this haunts him for ever.'

'Me too! We are all STRONG INDEPENDENT WOMEN!' I say and then flounder slightly and start to whisper again. 'But . . . what about Trudy's party? We're supposed to bring dates.' I try to sound casual, like it's not something I've given a second thought to, but I don't think it comes out like that.

'Well, actually, Kat, there's something I've been wanting to ask you,' Sam says, dramatically getting down on one knee next to the bed. 'Will you be my date to Trudy's party?'

'I'd LOVE to!' I gasp, leaping up to hug her.

'Now I'm jealous.' Millie sighs. 'Everyone knows that friend dates are better than romantic ones.'

'We might let you dance with us, you know?' Sam looks over to her coyly.

'Thank GOD. Nick can't dance for shit.' Millie laughs.

'Now, I think it might be time to go to sleep and have some nice dreams about Dave making a tit of himself,' Sam says, crawling back into her bed and snuggling down into the duvet with a big satisfied grin on her face.

I do the same, and as I get ready to turn the light off, I realise everything feels different today. Things don't feel so scary or so bleak. I've had the greatest day and tonight, I'm not going to touch the light switch. I don't need to. I've got my two best friends right here and everything feels pretty great.

3 Positive Things:
1. Dave shat himself in public. It's nice when karma does its thing.
2. Today might have been one of the best days of my life. Spending it with my two best friends has been magical.
3. Did I mention that Dave shat himself in public? I'm not gloating about that, though.

Monday 3rd February

8 a.m.

Sitting down to breakfast with my girls, a croissant and a black coffee because I am very chic

I didn't touch the light switch! I can't believe that I slept for the second night in a row without doing it, after over ten years.

'So you get to see Sexy Sébastien today,' Millie says, doing a little shimmy with her shoulders like some kind of embarrassing aunt.

'Oooohhhh, yessss!' Sam puts down her coffee and claps her hands delightedly at me. 'How do you feel about it?'

'I'm not really that bothered.' I sigh a little too hard, possibly giving away that I'm lying a bit because, although I'd kind of given up on the whole thing, now I'm here and we're headed into school there is of course a TINY chance of a reunion. TINY, but a chance . . . right?

But of course, I'm too busy having a great time with Sam and Millie to worry about a boy.

'I mean it's not like he's proved himself to be a conversational wizard with his messages,' I say in a reasonable manner.

'It wasn't the conversation that was a problem before, was it?' Sam slaps a long twisty pastry in her hand before taking a bite while Millie tries not to spit out the sip of coffee she's just taken.

I hope they choke.

'Look, we're having a lovely time and I'm not even BOTHERED about him. OK?' I say a little too insistently, my cheeks burning.

'OOooohkaaayyyyy.' Sam rolls her eyes at me.

'God, don't get your thong in a twist,' Millie says.

HOW DOES SHE KNOW I'M WEARING MY SECRET THONG?

9 a.m.
The school – piling out of the coach on to a playground which looks exactly like ours

The good thing is that we've managed to get a trip to Paris(ish) with our friends to learn that French schools look exactly like English schools. And now I can resume having the time of my life.

I do actually feel a bit nervous about coming face to face with the boy whose willy I treated like a game of whack-a-mole. But after this morning I'm not telling the girls that.

9.10 a.m.
French assembly

Presumably the idea is that we're all here to learn French, but they're doing the assembly in English for us, which feels slightly like it's defeating the object, no?

Everyone from our school has been seated on one side of the hall and everyone from their school is on the other side. They should be announcing the partners soon. Apparently, we're getting new ones, which is great because my last partner was rather hard work. She seemed to spend most of her time staring at Trudy and saying *'pauvre fille'* at me which I only realised after she left means 'loser'.

I clocked Sébastien as soon as we walked in here but I'm trying not to stare at him or be weird. Oh god, he's just caught me staring at him, and then I turned my head away so fast I cricked my neck.

I wonder if it's safe to sneak another peek yet? Oh shit. Yep, he's still staring at me, and he's hotter than I remember.

Now we're locked in some kind of weird eye-contact vortex and I feel so awkward. Oh god, I need to break the tension. Should I wave? But then what if I wave and he doesn't wave back? What if I wave and everyone in this whole room sees that he doesn't wave back? I'll look like I'm obsessed with him.

'Oh, look! There's Sébastien!!' Millie SHOUTS while POINTING.

'Jesus, calm down, Mum!' I say, grabbing her hand, but it's too late. He raises his hand in a wave and I raise mine in an embarrassed kind of salute. I have no idea why I didn't do a normal wave, why I instead greeted him like you would a sergeant in the army.

Wonderful, another loss for feminism. Treating the man of my affections like some kind of higher mortal already.

God. Get me out of this room so I can die of embarrassment somewhere. Why is he still staring at me? I'm too awkward for this, I feel like I'm in a staring contest. It makes me need to make a face.

Don't make a face, Kat.

Don't do it.

Why is my tongue outside of my mouth?

Why are my eyes crossed?

Why are my fingers on my head like devil horns?

Oh god. He's looking at me puzzled and I'm being weird.

I look down at the floor and remove my fingers from my head. Just going to stare at my shoes.

'What ARE you doing?' Sam asks.

'I don't know,' I mumble towards the floor.

I do now know, however, with quite some confidence, that I will not get through today without embarrassment.

9.15 a.m.

Raising my head again now I feel it's safe to look away from the floor.

'You will get a partner, and you will spend most of your time over the next three days with them,' the French version of Madame Rauche is telling everyone. I really hope my partner is in the same classes as Sam and Millie's partners. 'Tonight, we will go bowling so that you can all socialise and see French life.'

Wonderful, apparently French life involves a sport that I am DANGEROUSLY bad at. My parents banned me from playing it a while back for the safety of others.

'So, without further ado, the partners! When you hear your name, raise a hand so your partner can find you. Sébastien

Laurent and Timothy Matthews.'

Fuck. Sébastien's got #Tim. Poor him. Maybe we can bond over how creepy #Tim is, although I doubt he's as creepy for boys as he is for girls. He'll probably just tell him lots of lies about all the girls he's got off with when in reality he's repulsed them.

'Katerina Evans and Sylvie Van der Veer.' I raise my hand and look over to see the girl who's raised her hand. She's small like me, has a short pink bob, brown eyes, and looks incredibly beautiful. She waves at me, and I smile and wave back.

'Sam Francis and Therese Gillian.' A girl to the left of Sylvie puts up her hand.

'Millie Andino and Sophia Garnier.' The girl to the right of Sylvie raises her hand.

The three of us breathe a sigh of relief as it looks like our partners are all friends.

'They look like a French version of us,' Sam whispers.

'Except way cooler,' Millie says.

10.30 a.m.
French break time

So far we've been to maths which, weirdly, I think I understood more of in French than I ever do in English. Now it's break time and we're all crowded into the playground together.

I still haven't spoken to Sébastien. I haven't so much as dared to look at him since earlier. I know he's looking at me in the playground but I'm keeping my eyes firmly on the floor, my hands in my pockets and my mouth closed.

Distressingly #Tim seems to be communicating with him far more normally than I've managed to so far.

'Why are you wearing these?' asks Sylvie, staring at our three berets. 'Are you taking the piss?'

'Um no, we actually wear these all the time,' I say.

'Ah OK, I thought you were just wearing them because you were in France. Like doing the whole French beret . . . what's the word . . . stereotype!'

'Oh no. We wear these for when we do activism . . . and things,' I finish lamely. I can feel my cheeks going red again.

'Activism? What sort of activism?' asks Sylvie, looking interested.

'Feminist activism,' I say. 'I started a society at my school.'

I regret it as soon as I've said it and remember that I screwed up the Feminist Society. The memory of it makes me feel small. I do NOT want another French person calling me *perdante*. Thankfully the bell goes before anyone can say anything else and I breathe a sigh of relief.

'Oh cool, I need to hear about this over lunch, please. We are feminists too.' Sylvie smiles at me, her eyes shining, and suddenly I know we're going to get along.

1 p.m.
Lunchtime

I know I said that their school was just like ours but their lunch is much more sophisticated. Our school lunches look as if everything has been boiled within an inch of its life and then stepped on. Here there are FRESH salads. They crunch rather than squelch and they have vegetables that still look GREEN rather than having had the colour bleached out of them.

Mille, Sam and I are sitting with our new buddies and I'm vaguely aware that Sébastien is on the next table, but obviously I've barely noticed.

'This is so much better than who we were paired with in England. Do you remember, Sylvie?' Therese says.

'Urgh, she's here, though,' Sylvie says and instantly we know who she's talking about.

'Trudy?' I ask.

'Yeah, she seems to be some kind of anti-feminist? She hated us. All her minions hated us.'

'I was paired with Amelie, who seemed to be constantly scared of her,' Sophia says, 'and I'm not surprised. She's mean.'

Sophia and Therese both have similar looks going on to Sylvie. They are all dressed in black with a pop of colour here and there, except Sylvie has actual pink hair. I don't know how they get away with their piercings. Sylvie has her nose pierced, and so does Sophia, while Therese has at least five piercings in each ear. We'd never get away with that at our school. I want to ask if they've got any tattoos too, but it feels like an odd time to just interject that into the conversation when we've only just met.

'Have you seen who else is here?' Sophia asks.

'That Tim guy.' Sylvie sighs. 'I do NOT get him. He said something to me last time I did not understand.'

'The more you feel them the bigger they get?' I offer.

'Yes!' Sylvie says. 'What is this?'

'You don't want to know,' Sam says, also sighing.

'Oh god, we've got a bit of a story about him actually,' Millie says. 'At our school he's called #Tim.'

'Oh?' Sylvie says, sitting forward as I beg Millie in my head to shut up.

'Well, you see, we *were* going to spray paint #TimesUp on the school playground . . .' Millie says.

I watch Sylvie's face as Millie tells her the story of our BIG feminist failure last year, and I start to feel uneasy again at the mention of it all. But eventually her eyes crinkle and she laughs and laughs, as do the others. Then I start laughing too.

I don't think I've ever seen the funny side of it before now.

3 p.m.

A cafe in town with the girls

It turns out that Sylvie, Therese and Sophia are in a band together. They describe themselves as Riot grrrl, which I've had to secretly google, but it looks SO COOL. They've invited us to go and watch them play a gig on Wednesday night, which sounds like a fun thing to do on our last night, we just have to work out how to get past the teachers.

Tonight, of course, we're going bowling but we still have a bit of time to kill before we head off so we continue to chat away at the cafe. I feel totally sophisticated chilling in a Parisian café and like I'm living my absolute best *Emily in Paris* life right now. We really lucked out getting paired with these three. I'm not sure how good this trip will be for our French skills, though. The girls are really good at English and so far I have not uttered a word of *Français*. Oops.

Also, I STILL HAVE NOT SPOKEN TO Sébastien OR LOOKED AT HIM since earlier, even though sometimes this has meant moving my head at funny angles so as not to be in direct eye contact.

Even in Paris, the most romantic city on earth, the path to romance is paved with embarrassment.

5 p.m.
The bowling alley

Do you know what the WORST thing about bowling is? It's that everyone is BEHIND you, watching you while you bowl. This means you can't see if people are making fun of you, which when you're as bad as I am, they must be.

To make matters worse, Sébastien is on my team and I've had to resign myself to the fact that I will need to look at him, communicate with him and NOT BE WEIRD.

So far we have said 'hi' to each other and then I got butterflies and walked away as I was afraid that one of the butterflies was about to push a burp out of my mouth because, to be honest, people say butterflies, but to me it just feels like a nervous kind of wind.

5.20 p.m.

He got me one of the smaller balls to use because he said my hands are very delicate. I guess he doesn't remember our previous encounter very well?

Also, that's so NOT feminist, because actually, I'm not delicate, nor do I need a lighter ball because I'm a woman.

I will ONLY be bowling with the heavy ones from now on.

SCREW THE PATRIARCHY! I WILL SMASH IT WITH MY MASSIVE BALLS!

5.40 p.m.

That ball was really heavy. How do you know if you've given yourself a hernia?

My sporting career is over, but at least I went down fighting for what I believe in.

Heavier balls for women.

5.50 p.m.

Right, well, look . . . what just happened wasn't my fault at all, I didn't mean to nearly kill people, and no one can convict me of anything because I think I made myself clear that, after three gutter balls, I just didn't want to bowl any more, because I am RUBBISH at bowling, but people FORCED me to go up again and take my go.

I didn't want to look like I was taking it too seriously on account of the fact that I am SO BAD, so I thought, wouldn't it be funny if I really put some welly into it this time. But the ball I picked turned out to be a bit lighter than I thought it would be, and they make those finger hole-y bits so big. So, when I pulled my arm back (with quite some vigour, preparing for the throw of my life) the ball came loose and it just kind of came flying off my fingers backwards (at speed). I heard everyone scream and looked back to see that the ball had landed somewhere by the bar, skimming everyone's heads.

And now some French man is shouting at me over a tannoy system and the ENTIRE BOWLING ALLEY is staring at me.

I'll be in the toilet for the rest of this game, and the one after that. Actually, maybe just the rest of the trip.

7 p.m.

I think my face has gone back to its normal colour enough for me to step outside now, but I am still MORTIFIED. Honestly, imagine if I'd hurt someone! Imagine if my ball had KILLED SOMEONE! Standing in court pleading that I'm just quite an inept sportswoman rather than a murderer is so NOT how I imagined this trip going down.

I take a deep breath, open the door to the ladies, and see

Sébastien waiting on the other side. My stomach lurches, and my vagina kind of powers me forth.

'Are you OK?' he asks, while I try to prevent my stomach from exiting out of my mouth. 'It was funny, don't worry. I am terrible too.' He's smiling at me and his eyes are all sparkly, but all I can think about is how I need to get through this very pleasant turn of events without doing anything weird.

'I bet you've never nearly killed anyone with a bowling ball, though!' I say a bit too loudly and over enthusiastically, and he laughs politely.

Great work, Kat. Smooth.

'No,' he says, taking a step towards me. 'You seem quite . . . unique.'

Does he actually mean 'unique', or does he just mean weird? Is this the language barrier making him say 'unique' rather than 'petrifying'? He's still smiling at me and I've realised he's so close I can smell him. He smells like Coke and fries (romantic). What IS my face doing? Is that a smile? Or is it creepy? Now I'm kind of shifting my mouth around a bit. He's going to think I'm weird. Maybe I should pretend I'm chewing gum to cover it up. Yep, now I'm pretend chewing gum.

He leans towards me. Is he going to kiss me? If he kisses me, he'll realise that I'm not chewing gum. I can't kiss him now. He'll think I imagine having chewing gum in my mouth as standard. Oh gawd. He's really leaning in. I'm going to have to remove my pretend chewing gum that I'm pretend chewing from my real mouth and put my pretend chewing gum somew—

'There you are!' I hear Sylvie's voice behind him and he pulls away. THANK GOD. I think? I really ruined that moment for myself, to be honest. 'I've been looking for you everywhere. It's your turn.'

Sébastien scuttles out. I notice that Sylvie is looking deeply unimpressed, and I'm not sure if it's with Sébastien or me, but either way I don't care, I'm just glad that she ended that incredibly awkward moment for me.

'You actually WANT me to bowl again?' I ask, laughing nervously.

'We've put the bumpers up for you,' she says back, sounding quite cutting.

'Oh good. Did they put a bumper behind me to protect you guys?' I ask.

'No, just try not to kill anyone,' she says with a smile.

Right. I can do that.

Nope, can't promise a thing.

7.40 p.m.
The diner next to the bowling alley

I didn't kill anyone with my humongous balls. We all came away unscathed and have since come to the old-fashioned art-deco-style diner next door for burgers. We've been filling the girls in on the Feminist Society.

'So, we had a meeting and it turned out that there's SO much toxic masculinity in our school,' says Millie, taking a sip of her milkshake. 'So Kat got everyone to write down their experiences and then she wrote about them in her blog.'

'You have a blog?' says Sylvie, looking at me. 'That's cool.'

I smile back, a little embarrassed and afraid that she won't think I'm so cool when she hears the rest of it.

'I *had* a blog, at school,' I say.

'Why "had"?' Sylvie asks.

'Our head teacher shut it down,' I say staring at the table.

'WHY?' Sylvie, Therese and Sophia shout practically in unison, all staring at me, eyes wide.

'He got angry about the blog post I wrote. He said that it was all just boys being boys and that I was drumming up hysteria,' I say.

'NO!' says Sylvie. 'But that is oppression!'

There may sometimes be language barriers and cultural differences between people from different countries, but it seems like female oppression is something that all of us at this table understand.

'He said that I was making it up, overdramatising the situation,' I say.

'That is gaslighting.' Sophia says with authority and I'm not sure what she means.

'What is gaslighting?' Sam asks and I'm relieved I don't have to ask, I already feel like an idiot as it is.

'Saying something hasn't happened that you know has,' Therese says.

'Trying to make you believe that you imagined it,' Sylvie says.

'Oh my god,' I say as everything suddenly becomes clear. 'That's exactly what happened! He told me I'd made it out to be worse than it was and that it wasn't that bad, that I'd been overdramatic. And I started to believe him. He was trying to make me believe it wasn't true so that I'd stop. But I can't stop, because it IS happening. It IS real and I wasn't wrong. HE was.'

It feels like a weight has been lifted as it all clicks into place in my head.

'Why didn't you tell us you started thinking like that?' Sam asks.

'We would have told you it was real. We were in the meeting! We saw it all too!' Millie protests.

'I was embarrassed,' I say, feeling even more stupid that I (the queen of embarrassment) let that stop me.

'So what are you going to do?' Sylvie asks, snapping me out of my trance. 'You can't just carry on knowing that girls are being upskirted, having bottoms pinched, sent unwanted dick pics and things at school and do nothing?' Sylvie says, looking at me intensely.

'I haven't figured that out yet, but at least now I feel like I can,' I confess, feeling frustrated that I didn't trust myself, but now I know I CAN trust myself, and it's time to get back in the feminist saddle.

'You can and you will,' Sylvie says.

I look up and see her smiling at me, and for the first time in ages, I'm feeling the sparks of inspiration fly.

Back at the hostel

We all spent hours talking through ideas for bringing back the Feminist Society and now I feel a kind of restless excitement that I haven't felt for so long. It was hard to leave Sylvie and the others and come back to the hostel.

Now we're back here having a hot chocolate before bed (my second of the day – in France life is good) and it's still like we're in some kind of parallel universe or something. #Tim is again flanked by the two French girls that are staying here and they're still finding him HILARIOUS. Maybe something he's saying's got lost in translation?

'I've taken a picture of it and sent it to Nick because he thinks I'm lying,' Millie says as we stare over at it in disbelief.

'He's not funny. He's literally never made a funny joke in his life,' I say.

'I think they've misunderstood him,' Krish says coming over and leaning on the side of our table. 'They don't find me that funny, and I'm ACTUALLY funny.'

'Uh oh, watch out,' says Mille. 'Trudy's glaring over at us and I don't know why.'

'Oh, apparently one of your exchange partners caught Trudy in the toilets of the diner earlier and asked why she was so horrible to people,' Krish says.

'It's a valid question.' I shrug.

'Yeah, she didn't think so, and now she's angry with everyone.'

'When is she not?' Sam asks. 'It must be EXHAUSTING being her, to be fair.'

Sam waves over at Trudy which prompts her to stand up from her seat and start marching towards us.

'Just because you're popular in Paris doesn't change that you three are losers at home,' she says.

'Oh, but we're not?' Millie says, smiling at her. 'We're just too cool to care about you.'

'Lesbians,' Trudy grunts and storms off with Amelie following behind.

We all roll our eyes at her, not even bothering to take the bait this time.

'Do you ever want to just sneak into her room and try that trick where you put someone's hand in a bowl of water while they sleep and they wet themselves?' Krish says, and we all fall about laughing.

As Krish walks away again, I stare after him, smiling and thinking, really he's not so bad.

11 p.m.
Back in the room

I think Millie and Sam have gone straight to sleep but I'm still pumped from our conversation with the girls. Weirdly I'm thinking more about that than about the fact that I completely missed my chance to kiss Sébastien because I was being weird. Who fake-chews gum?

292

I go on Instagram just to check and see that I've got two messages.

The first one is from Sébastien! OH MY GOD. Should I wake the girls? Or leave it?

'Gig on Wednesday?'

I presume he means am I going to Sylvie's gig. I'm going to try and play it cool. I start writing but slightly lose my cool.

'I am yeah, are you? Shall we hang out? Shall we go together?'

Might delete the last bit actually. Might just settle on . . .

'I am yeah. You?'

Yeah, that's better. Maybe I should put a kiss, to make up for earlier. So he knows that I WANT a kiss.

OK I'll do that.

He replies almost instantly.

'Cool.'

No kiss back. Right. Stupid Kat. Always taking it too far!

The second message is from Sylvie. Which makes me smile.

'I had the nicest time tonight. This is for you, my feminist friend.'

I click on the link below the message and it takes me to a song called 'Rebel Girl' by Bikini Kill, so I fish around on the floor for my headphones and click play when I've found them.

It's not my usual thing but it's pretty cool. Angry. Fierce. Like Sylvie. Like I want to be.

I put the headphones down and snuggle up in my duvet with a smile on my face. I knew Paris would be good, I just didn't realise how good. It's not until I'm almost asleep that I remember about the light switch and even then I don't bother moving to touch it.

3 Positive Things:
1. I didn't actually kill anyone with the bowling ball.
2. Trudy's less popular here (hahaha) but I am obviously not taking joy in that because I am bigger than that (hahahahahahahahahahaha).
3. Sylvie is really cool and I've already learned so many things from her. I can't wait to see her band.

Tuesday 4ᵗʰ February

7 a.m.
The hostel room

I've been awake since six reading about Riot grrrl and listening to different bands. All angry and fierce and exciting, like nothing I've ever heard before, and some of the lyrics could have come straight from the inside of my head. I'm exhausted now, though, and Millie and Sam keep trying to drag the duvet off me and get me out of bed and into those disgusting showers. I keep pulling it back over me.

10 a.m.
Break time

Sylvie and I have been talking about Riot grrrl in the playground for the whole of break time. There are so many bands out there that I still have to learn about and listen to. She says she's going to make me a playlist.

I'm so pleased Sylvie's my partner, I feel like I've learned so much from her (even if I've STILL barely said a French word since we got here) and she's super cool. She seems to have so much faith in me and thinks I can get the Feminist Society back up and running when I get home. That's way more faith than I have in myself. But, somehow, I think her confidence is rubbing off on me.

10 p.m.

The hostel

I can't believe that tomorrow's our last day. I don't ever want to go home, back to the school where our head teacher oppresses and gaslights us, where everything has the cloud of GCSEs looming over it. It's so much fun and so inspiring being here and hanging out with Sylvie. I don't want to go. I don't even need to touch the light switch here. In Paris everything just seems easier.

3 Positive Things:

1. Everything in France is wonderful and I never want to go home.

2. I have made a new friend who is a feminist genius and oracle.

3. This is the fourth night in a row that I haven't touched the light switch and nothing bad has happened. Instead good things keep happening and I feel more positive than I have done in ages. Maybe it's over? Maybe I've finally cracked it?

Wednesday 5ᵗʰ February

7 a.m.

I literally bounced out of bed this morning full of excitement about what the day might hold. I was singing and dancing around trying to make the girls get up until Millie threw her hairbrush at me, hitting me in the tit.

Rude.

12 p.m.

A classroom

In a lesson, for a subject, but I haven't managed to work out which one. Oops.

So I don't know what subject this is and I'm trying to work it out, but there's currently a picture of a petrol station and a fire station on the board. Is this a class about arson?

12.05 p.m.

School is even more boring when you have no idea what's happening. It's hard not to let your mind wander.

At least I can spend some time thinking about how to bring back the Feminist Society. Without getting expelled.

1 p.m.
The dining hall

We're all sitting at a table together. Trudy and her hideous partner, the grand Madeline, who seems to be dressed head to toe in a mixture of faux fur and labels (very Trudy) are down the other end of the table.

'So everyone's coming to the gig tonight?' Sylvie asks, glancing over to check the teachers can't hear us. Apparently Krish has a plan to help us all sneak out without them noticing.

'Urgh, at that dirty little venue? I don't think so,' says Madeline.

'Fair enough, I don't think we'll miss you if you don't come,' says Sophia.

'They'll still come,' Therese whispers over to me.

I am laughing when I feel someone's breath on my neck and a low voice says in my ear, 'Looking forward to our date tonight.'

I look up with a start to see Sébastien walking past.

It takes me by surprise a bit and I nearly knock my glass of water over. I wonder if he was trying to be sexy? I don't remember the last time I cleaned out my ears, though, so I'd rather he hadn't tried to be sexy quite so near all that wax. But also . . . oh my god, it's a DATE? A DATE!

I AM GOING ON A DATE.

It's just, I always thought that if I was going on a date, maybe I'd have been asked first?

3 p.m.
History

It's fine. It's fine! It's good.

Just gotta not slap him in the dick this time.

How hard can it be?

7.30 p.m.
The hostel room

I've never eaten dinner so fast in my entire life. The three of us wolfed it down, and then snuck straight back to our room pretending to be exhausted so we could get ready for the gig.

'Do you think dates with French boys are the same as dates with English boys?' Millie asks, curling my hair in a haphazard and frankly dangerous way with her straighteners.

'I don't know, I've never been on a date with an English boy either,' I say. 'SHIT, THIS IS MY FIRST DATE EVER!' I turn to both of the girls, eyes wide, stomach fully about to lurch out of me.

'Stay calm, just breeeeeathe. We'll all be there so you've nothing to worry about,' Sam says coming in from the toilet. She seems to be walking a bit funny.

'You look kinda weird. Are you constipated, babe?' Millie asks her.

'I'm, umm . . .' Sam says looking sheepish, 'I'm wearing some of those hold-y-in pants.'

She attempts to sit down on the bed but can't bend herself so instead just lies, stiff as a board.

'Why? For what EARTHLY purpose?' says Millie as the two of us abandon my hair and go over to her.

'Do you hate your internal organs and want to crush them?' I ask.

'I found them in Mum's room and I thought, maybe I'd give them a try. I'm not sure why. I feel kinda stupid about it now.' She puts a pillow over her head.

'It's OK,' I say, soothing her with a hand on her shoulder. 'The patriarchy did this. They make you feel like your actual body isn't good enough with their adverts, in the hope that you will feel like you have to spend lots of time and money trying to achieve an unobtainable and unrealistic body shape. But you don't. YOU KNOW THAT!' I say.

'I know, I know. I just . . . haven't felt great about myself since Dave. I guess my confidence took a hit,' Sam says from behind her pillow.

'But your body is perfect and so are YOU,' Millie says, prising the pillow away from Sam.

'Besides,' says Sam, 'they are *really* uncomfortable.' She attempts to sit up but falls back down again. 'I feel like I've got trapped wind.'

'OK, let's get you out of these bad boys,' says Millie as we each take a leg and start pulling.

'Wait, are you wearing normal knickers under there or are we about to get a full vulva flash?' I ask, as they start loosening.

'Would that cheer you up? Like Baubo?' says Sam.

'NO!' Millie and I both shout, and we're laughing and laughing and pulling and pulling until . . .

THHWACK!

'OUCH!' I shout as her hold-y-in pants slap me in the face like an elastic band.

I'm thrilled to see that she's wearing knickers under there but not thrilled that her and Millie are laughing at me.

'Your gusset SLAPPED me!'

'SORRY! But you should see your face!' Sam laughs.

'Oh my god, you've actually got the imprint of a gusset on your face.' Millie is hysterical.

I grab a mirror. She's right. There's a big red mark, the size and shape of a gusset. ON MY FOREHEAD.

I'm about to go on my first ever date with a gusset on my face.

8.10 p.m.
Waiting in our room for further instructions

Krish sent a message to the WhatsApp group. He's going to keep the teachers busy while we all sneak out. He's made friends with the receptionist, a cute guy called Pierre, who's also offered to try and make sure the teachers don't have any urge to go and check on our rooms. He'll let us know when it's time to move.

Krish: THE CUCKOO IS IN THE NEST.

Krish: FLY. BE FREE.

Krish: OPERATION GET THE FUCK OUT NOW!!!!

Krish: Meet me out the front in two minutes. The teachers are on their third bottle of wine, they've no idea what day of the week it even is.

We open our door and peer out at the same time as all the others in the corridor do. Even Trudy's there, though she looks livid about it. Guess she just can't bear to miss out on the fun.

A line of us all tiptoe along the hallway, down the stairs and out the back door. We gather outside and wait for Krish to appear, then we all run down the road, freeeeeeeeeeeee, to the only bar in town.

8.30 p.m.
The bar

I clock Sébastien across the bar as soon as I walk in and take a moment to remind myself that he's here because we're on a DATE. Albeit a date with everyone else in my year, but we're here *together*.

I see his face break into a smile as he spots me, and I feel like I might throw up. He looks very handsome, wearing a grey T-shirt and black jeans, hair flopped over his forehead and his eyes locked with mine. I suddenly feel way too nervous to even go over there. I'd actually quite like to find Sylvie and wish her luck, but I guess I should go and see him. He is my DATE after all. Oh god, he's coming over.

It's weird because before, when I fancied Hot/Shit Josh, it was as if my vagina was in charge, constantly dragging me towards him to embarrass myself. Now looking at Sébastien I wonder if she's having a nap? He's super hot and yet . . .

'Hey,' he says, casually leaning down to kiss me on the cheek while I feel sick, awkward, my palms sweating. Is fancying someone supposed to make you feel like you've got a tropical disease?

'Hey,' I say twitching my head as his lips are about to make contact so they land in my eye.

I stumble back, blinking furiously, trying to make sure my eye make-up's intact. Sébastien looks a bit grossed out, it's probably the first time he's tasted eyeball. I'm not sure if I should apologise or he should apologise.

'Hey!' Sylvie pops up behind him, and I am SO RELIEVED to see her, with my remaining good eye.

'Hey!' I say, feeling my face stretch into a beam while I blink my eye back to normality.

Sylvie's sparkling. She's got glitter highlighting her cheeks, everything about her shines and I can't stop looking at her. Her clothes, her make-up, her hair – all of it is so fierce.

'We're on in fifteen minutes so I have to go, but I'm so pleased you're here!' She grabs me into a hug and I buzz with excitement. I can hardly take my eyes off her as she walks away.

8.40 p.m.

Sébastien and I are hanging out by the side of the stage, waiting for the band to start. We reached a kind of awkward silence some time ago after a few bits of small talk about drinks and looking nice and I'm now desperately racking my brains for something to talk to him about. He does look very handsome, but even IRL we seem to have NOTHING to talk about.

'Do you like reading?' I ask hopefully.

'No.'

'TV? Film?'

'Not really.'

'What do you do in your spare time?'

'Sport.'

'Oh right. What about when you're not doing sport?'

'Gym.'

We have literally NOTHING in common.

I feel my eyes glaze over a bit and I just want Sylvie to come back so we can hang out. It doesn't help that the girls keep looking over at us expectantly. I feel so lame right now.

'Hey!' Sébastien says suddenly, startling me, as he turns and puts his hand on my cheek.

I look up at him, making eye contact and wondering why I feel so out of place in a moment that I've wanted for so long.

Why doesn't this feel like I imagined it would? He's moving his hand over my face, stroking my cheek softly, and all I feel is disjointed and impatient. I've had dreams about this moment, and now it's happening, all I want is . . . not this. I think he's going to kiss me. His face is coming towards me so I hope he's going to kiss me because the only other option would be a headbutt, and that would be awful.

He leans in and just as his face starts to blur in front of me, making me go cross-eyed, I shut my eyes. He kisses me really gently on the lips and then a bit harder, but I don't really feel . . . anything. I don't know what I'm supposed to feel, I guess? I thought maybe at least a tingle in the pants or something?

And now he seems to be repeatedly pummelling my lips with his tongue. What's he doing? Oh right, yeah . . . HIS TONGUE IS IN MY MOUTH. To be honest it wasn't clear what was happening then at all. I thought maybe he just liked licking me, like a cat? I thought this stuff was supposed to come naturally, but this feels about as natural as a PE class. His tongue seems to be giving it quite some welly now, but he's just sort of swirling it around in there. It's like he's checking all my teeth one by one. I feel like I'm at the dentist. And now there's a bit of his dribble trickling down my chin. Is it polite to wipe it off?

I open my eyes, even though he's still doing some kind of deep dive of my gums, and make eye contact with Sam, I'm throwing her a kind of 'help me' expression with my eyes, but all she does is start laughing, which then draws Millie's attention to the hideousness. They're both laughing at me and my mouth has now closed up into a kind of cat's bumhole shape in horror.

HOW DO I GET THIS MAN OFF MY FACE?

Some minutes later

Finally!

He seems quite proud of himself.

I AM DYING. THAT WAS TERRIBLE.

'Gosh, just got to pop to the loo!' I say cheerily, grabbing Millie and Sam as I go.

'OK, *mon amour*! Don't be long!' he says.

I may be quite some time.

8.45 p.m.
The toilets

'Oh my god, that was SO BAD,' I say, clutching the sink.

'It looked TERRIFYING!' Millie says.

'Please keep him away from me. I know I slapped his penis but that was an ACCIDENT and I think we're even now.'

'Do you not remember him being a bad kisser before?' Sam asks.

'No! But I guess the whole memory from before is a blur.'

We can hear the sound of the band starting up outside.

'Come on, let's go and watch,' Sam says.

'Good plan,' I say.

8.50 p.m.
By the stage

There's such a huge crowd gathered by the stage when we get out of the toilet that I start to feel a bit worried that I might not be able to see properly.

'Come on! Let's go to the front!' I say, weaving my way through the crowd just as the lights on the stage come up, making it seem bigger than it is, more like Wembley than a tiny stage in a dive bar. And then the girls come out, Sylvie first, to whoops and cheers, and I join in the noise watching her sparkle under the lights.

She looks completely composed as she picks up her guitar, the glitter on her face really shimmering. It seems to be the most natural thing in the world to her to be watched by this many people. She starts to play and the moment she opens her mouth to sing, I'm completely lost.

9 p.m.

Sylvie's voice is mesmerising, and the band are amazing. Like, seriously good. I can't take my eyes off her as she dances and shines. I can see Sam and Millie dancing like lunatics next to me, but I don't want to miss any of it by dancing. I feel like I'm in a trance.

9.30 p.m.

'That was unbelievable!' I say to Sylvie when she appears from backstage, and I launch over the girls to give her a hug.

'Ahh, thank you!' she says, as we pull away from each other. She's sweaty from being on stage and we stand smiling at each other.

'Guys, we have to go! Pierre says one of the teachers is getting suss!' I hear Krish shouting from behind us. It takes me a while to process what he's actually saying. I have to go?

'You have to go?' Sylvie asks, reading my mind. 'But I've just got off stage?'

'I know,' I say, looking at the floor.

I don't want to leave, not now. When I leave that's it. We're going home tomorrow, this is the last time I'll see Sylvie, my last evening in Paris(ish), and I want to soak every second of it up.

'I have something for you, but it's backstage. Will you come?' she asks and I feel relieved.

'Sure!' I say, pleased to be following her away from the crowd, away from where I can see Sébastien and his lizard tongue looking for me, to somewhere we can be alone. Just us.

9.35 p.m.

It turns out that backstage is actually just a cold corridor. But as Sylvie leans into a guitar case and pulls out a tissue paper package, tied with string, there's nowhere else I want to be.

'Open it,' she says handing me the parcel, her eyes on me.

I tug on the string feeling clumsy and try to detach it without ripping things, but in the end my shaking fingers win and I end up having to tear the paper to get through. I see a small bit of black felt and break into the paper even further, pulling out the softest, most chic beret I've ever seen. Across the front, stitched in perfect pink, is the word: Feminist.

'Oh my god,' I say turning it over in my hands, my fingers brushing over the soft wool. 'Sylvie, that's . . . it's beautiful!'

I stare at it unable to take in how perfect it is. How *me* it is. I lean in to give her a squeeze and we stand hugging. I don't want to let go of this person who gets me so effortlessly. I'm going to miss her so much that it's hard for me to fathom that we've only been together a few days, and that there was even a time before we knew each other.

Sylvie pulls away and the two of us lock eyes. It feels like there's something tying us together, something stopping us from breaking apart or looking away. My French exchange partner has become my French BFF.

She leans forward and I think she's about to give me a kiss on the cheek to say goodbye and send me on my way because we can't stand here for ever no matter how much it feels like time's stopped. But she doesn't go for my cheek, she keeps moving towards me and I don't want her to stop. I want to keep breathing in her smell, the perfume and sweat and hairspray. Her lips graze mine and my mouth responds immediately. It doesn't tense up the way it did with Sébastien. I'm kissing her without thought or analysis. We're locking tongues and her hand's stroking my cheek, giving me a buzz in the pit of my stomach. I don't want this to end and that in itself is massively confusing.

I pull away and look at her, she's smiling and I'm smiling but I feel like I've torn in two. One bit of me wants to go back in, to carry on the kiss and the other wants to run. As far and as fast as possible.

'Kat! We have to go!' Millie and Sam's heads appear round the door and I jump away from Sylvie.

'I have to go,' I say, looking up at her, and then Millie and Sam are in our tiny space, hugging Sylvie goodbye and dragging me away and I'm feeling simultaneously numb and confused.

10 p.m.
Back at Hell Hostel

We all snuck back into the hostel with Pierre's help and now I'm trying to pay attention to what the girls are talking about as we're all getting into bed, but I can't focus. I don't know why I haven't told them about the kiss. I tell them everything, and I want to tell them, but I feel like I'm still working it out myself. I JUST KISSED A GIRL. And it was the best kiss I've ever had.

I mean, I have only ever kissed a boy once before, and it turns out he's one of the worst kissers on the planet, so I don't have much to compare it with, and I'm not sure if there's one certain way you're supposed to feel when you kiss someone, but I know the kiss with Sylvie was WAY better than the kiss with Sébastien.

But what does that mean? That kiss? And that I enjoyed that kiss? I didn't expect it, had never imagined it happening, but now I think I want it to happen again and I feel blindsided.

I didn't even realise I thought about Sylvie like that. I just wanted to hang out with her a lot, and now I'm here wanting to hold on to the kiss and the feelings from it. If I tell the girls . . . I don't know . . . it feels like it might break the spell, and the warm tingling feeling that hits me whenever I remember it. And they'll have questions. Questions about my sexuality that I've never even contemplated asking myself before.

This morning, when I woke up, I was pretty confident that I knew my sexuality, so confident that I've barely ever thought about it. Even when we left here just a few hours ago that was still the case. I've never even thought about women in that way before. Now I'm not sure what to think. Am I a lesbian? Am I bi? How do I know? Is there some kind of person in charge I can ask? I suddenly feel overwhelmed with the confusion and I want to escape. I don't know the answers to these questions, and they're questions about me.

I feel confused and lost, and I want to go back to a time when I did know. I want to concentrate on this conversation the girls are having about Dave shitting himself on the football pitch and stop my head from running in circles.

I really want to go back to how things were before tonight when they felt much simpler.

My phone beeps and I see it's a message from Sylvie and I

get an excited feeling in my tummy. I catch myself. Is this real? Am I really feeling something for her? Did Sylvie kiss me? Or did I initiate it? Is Sylvie a lesbian? Or maybe she's never kissed a girl before either?

I don't want to open the message in front of the girls. I want to be alone.

I miss home and for the first time all trip I just want to be in my room now, in my bed, where I know everything, everything's familiar and nothing's changed.

10.10 p.m.

I mean, WTF. I have literally only been kissed like once before in my life and now I have been kissed TWICE IN ONE NIGHT. I look down at my phone and decide to open the message. They're so engrossed in Dave's shitty situation they won't notice anyway.

Sylvie: I hope it was ok that I kissed you? Because I didn't know. But I thought you're going, so . . . 🙊

I don't know what to reply. Part of me wants to reply saying 'I LOVED IT! OF COURSE IT WAS!' and the other part of me wants to run away.

Me: I liked it. I just didn't expect it.

Sylvie: I didn't know if you liked girls?

312

Me: I don't know either. You're the first girl I've kissed.

Sylvie: Confused?

Me: A bit. I'm sorry xxx

Sylvie: xxx

'Earth to Kat?' Millie's waving at me. 'Who are you messaging?'

'Oh, um, no one. Just my parents,' I say. 'Think I'm gonna go and clean my make-up off!'

I head out to the bathroom.

10.30 p.m.
In the bathroom

I stare at myself in the mirror trying to work out who this person is who looks exactly the same as before but now feels completely different.

I'm not actually different, though. Am I?

Am I a lesbian?

But I definitely fancy guys?

So am I bi, then?

I've never fancied a woman before? Why Sylvie? Why now?

When I went out it was to go on a date with Sébastien, who I've been fantasising about since for ever, and then I kissed him and I felt nothing but when Sylvie kissed me . . .

313

11 p.m.

When I eventually come back to the room the girls are both asleep and the lights are out. As I climb into bed, I touch the light switch gratefully, craving something familiar, something to stop my head from feeling like it's spinning out of control. I lie there thinking about what happened, reliving how nice it felt, how amazing she looked, trying to get my head round the fact that we're leaving tomorrow and I will probably never see her again.

3 Positive Things:
1. *Way*
2. *Too*
3. *Confused*

Thursday 6th February

8 a.m.

I wake up to Millie and Sam standing at the end of the bed, gently shaking me awake.

'Um, Kat?' Millie looks worried, and I sit up.

'What's up?'

'There's something you need to see,' Sam says as she hands over her phone to me displaying a WhatsApp from Trudy to Krish's group from last night. I sit up, rubbing my eyes, trying to work out what's going on, but the moment I focus on it my blood runs cold.

It's a picture of me and Sylvie, from last night, kissing. Trudy must have been there and taken it? But how did I not notice her?

And not only that. Next Millie gently hands me her phone which is displaying Instagram. It's been posted on the **@FittyorPity** account. Underneath, the caption reads, 'A Kat that likes the pussy.'

I look at Sam and Millie and wonder if I'm still asleep, if this is a nightmare I can wake up from. I don't know what to say.

'I-I thought that account had been deleted?' I stammer.

'We all did. I guess they just deactivated it for a while. Probably started it again when the Feminist Society was shut down,' Sam says as the two of them come and sit either side of me.

I feel tears begin to run down my face and my throat starts to close up.

'Why didn't you tell us?' Millie asks gently as I choke on the tears.

'I didn't know how I felt about it,' I say. 'It just happened last night, and I didn't even know what to tell you. I just felt so confused about it.'

'Oh, Kat,' Sam says and puts her arm around me.

'So she kissed you?' Millie asks. I can't believe I'm having to talk about this now when I haven't even got my head around it. I can't believe everyone's seen this.

'Yeah, but I liked it, I think,' I say, feeling like my head might explode.

'Well, that's a good thing, no?' Sam says.

'I don't know. I'm confused. What does it mean? What does it make me?'

'It makes you YOU,' Millie says, putting an arm around me too.

'It being broadcast to the whole school SO isn't what you need while you're still working it out, though. This is so unfair, I'm sorry,' Sam says. 'Fucking Trudy . . .'

I stare at them both in amazement, because neither of them seems to be shocked by it AT ALL, or to have looked at me any differently. The only thing they're worried about is that I'm upset and that I've been outed to the whole school when I'm not even sure if there's anything to be outed about.

'Oh god, what if Freddie sees it?' I ask, my head in my hands. But really that's one of the last things I have to worry about right now. The whole world knows that I kissed a girl before I've even really registered it and before I even know how I feel, and all thanks to Trudy.

'So what if he does?' Sam says. 'He won't care.'

'God, I want to get out of here,' I say, suddenly feeling so exposed and dreading the thought of a day on a coach with a load of people who now know that I may or may not be confused about my sexuality, not to mention being cooped up with the person who sent it to everyone (Trudy), who I'm sure is revelling in this whole thing.

'Don't worry, we're with you all day,' Sam says. 'And if anyone says anything, we will DESTROY them.'

'We've got you,' says Millie, and I want to believe that's enough, but right now this feels like the absolute end of the world.

'Why don't you head for a shower?' says Sam. 'We'll sneak some breakfast back to the room and that way you don't have to see everyone yet.'

'Thanks,' I say, grabbing my towel and heading out the door.

8.05 a.m.
The corridor

As soon as I shut the door to the room and I'm outside in the corridor, I know I've made a terrible mistake. I feel slightly dizzy, as if I'm on a boat. Everything seems to be moving around me and I just have to try and get to the end of it. I feel hot and clammy. I try to move faster but my legs feel like marshmallows. I imagine that behind each door are people talking about me, whispering, laughing at me, gossiping. I hear a door click and Krish's friend Tom comes out of his room, smirking at me. I try to scuttle past, but just at that moment Trudy opens her door. It's like one of those haunted house rides, with danger popping out of every door.

'HERE SHE IS!' she's shouting into the corridor. 'I knew it! LESBIAN!'

Her words and laughter bounce around my brain like an echo. I start running down the corridor, but it's rocking and I can barely see through the blur of my tears. I vaguely hear Sam and Millie coming out of our room but I'm in too deep to stop. I can't breathe. Every bit of air gets caught in my throat and I keep running and running until I reach the shower room.

8.10 a.m.
The shower room

I lock one of the cubicle doors and crouch down close to the grimy floor. I don't care. I just need to regain my balance and my breath. I feel like I'm going to be sick.

'Kat? KAT!' Sam's calling and I can hear Millie opening the stall doors, looking for me.

'Kat!' Millie knocks on the door and I reach up to let her in.

I sink back down, trying to count my breaths as the two of them settle either side of me.

318

'What can we do, Kat?' Sam's asking but I can't say anything. I feel like something's restricting my airway. I just keep trying to count like Sarah taught me to.

8.30 a.m.

We're still on the floor of the shower, crouched down amongst all the hair and toenail clippings, and not for the first time I think about how amazing my friends are and how lucky I am to have them. A true friend really is someone who would crouch in this filth for you.

It's been so long since I last had a panic attack, and I hate feeling like it's happening again.

I'm going backwards and it's all outside of my control.

10.30 a.m.
The coach

I'm sitting hiding in the corner on the back seat with the girls but I still feel like everyone's staring at me.

I feel bad because Sylvie's sent me messages this morning, but I just can't answer them. I'm overwhelmed and confused. It felt so different last night, it felt good when it was us but now everyone's talking about it and staring at me, and I just want to be alone.

My phone beeps from under me and I dread another message from Sylvie that someone else might see, and then I feel bad, because I shouldn't feel like that about her.

Matt: Hey you ok? Xxx

I just stare at his message. Matt . . . how am I going to talk to him about this? I don't know what to say, so I put my phone away instead.

I'm suddenly filled with rage that my friends are finding out that I kissed a girl from Instagram rather than from me. And worse than that, that it's made me feel upset about something that was so nice. I feel like I've had something major taken away from me.

I know I shouldn't but I open the **@FittyorPity** Instagram account again and click on the picture of me and Sylvie. I can't help myself.

It's had two hundred and fifty likes, and comments, really gross comments that I try not to look at. But can't help but see one of them – 'fancy a 3some ladies?' I feel embarrassed and violated.

My breath starts to catch again so I begin counting in my head to try and keep things steady.

One . . . two . . . three . . . four . . . five . . .

4 p.m.
The sofa with Bea

I was so relieved to get home and find no one was here and

then I realised that Freddie would be with Issy, probably taking care of her because her dad's left. And I should have been there for Millie, making sure she was OK about going home after everything with her parents, but instead I've been uselessly and selfishly lying on the sofa staring blankly at the TV.

I'm just trying not to think because every time I do, I feel my throat start to prickle and the dizziness comes.

6 p.m.
At dinner

'Well? Tell us everything about Paris!' Mum shouts across the table.

'Yeah, it was OK,' I say, trying to avoid Freddie's gaze.

Freddie's been staring at me since he came in five minutes ago and I know that he will definitely have seen the picture, but I don't think either of us want to talk about it.

'Just OK?' Mum asks. I see her exchange a look with Dad.

'Everything all right, love?' Dad says, and I can feel them both stare at me. I don't like them watching me. I knew I should have stayed in my room.

'Just a bit tired,' I say.

'Fair enough! You've had a long journey,' Dad says as he and Mum share another concerned look and I realise I'm going to have to pick myself up a bit or they'll keep asking questions.

Yet more people asking questions that I don't know the answers to.

7.30 p.m.
Sitting in the bath

I've been in here for so long that my fingers have wrinkled to little prunes and the bath water's gone cold. I don't remember when I started crying and I don't even really know why I'm crying, all I know is that that I'd like to stop feeling like this.

I've always felt quite unsure about a lot of stuff about myself but the one thing I've never questioned is my sexuality. I just thought that if I was anything other than straight, I would know about it and I would have figured it out by now. Now I feel like I haven't got any idea about it at all and Trudy and **@FittyorPity** have made that feel like it's a bad thing.

9 p.m.
In bed

Bea's curled up peacefully at the bottom of the bed and I don't have the energy to move anywhere. It's nice being back in my own bed. It's safe and warm and there's no one else here which is the key thing.

I haven't looked at my phone for hours and I probably should have to check that Millie's OK, but I'm so tired that I keep forgetting to check. I take a look and see a few messages.

Three Queens
Sam, Millie, Me

322

Sam: How's home, Millie?

Millie: It's actually really relaxing. We've been watching films and hanging out with Mum and everything feels way less tense in here for the first time in ages.

Sam: YAY! I'm so pleased.

Millie: Kat, how you doing?

Sam: Yeah, you OK, Kat?

Millie: Kat?

Matt: Are you back? Are you OK?

Matt: Can we hang out? We can talk? You don't have to talk about it if you don't want to, but it might help?

Matt: Kat, I'm worried about you.

Sylvie: Did you get home OK?

Sylvie: I saw the photo that got posted, I'm sorry that that happened, and I hope you're OK. I'm really sorry because I feel like it was my fault and I shouldn't have kissed you.

I feel bad ignoring everyone's message – apart from Sébastien's, which I will obviously NEVER reply to – but I just can't right now. I really want to reply to Sylvie, but I just don't know what to say. Every time I try to write out a response my chest tightens. I just need some time to work it out.

10.30 p.m.

Even worse than anything that's happened with me today, than that photo and all those comments being out there, is the knowledge that @**FittyorPity**'s back, and that this time they can say and do whatever they like, because Mr Clarke has silenced us. I'm not allowed to blog, we're not allowed to have meetings, and if I push it Mr Clarke's made it perfectly clear that there will be repercussions. I can't get myself expelled right before my GCSEs.

So what, are we just supposed to sit and take it?

I turn the light off and touch the switch three times, hoping this might make this feeling of helplessness go away. It seems like months ago that I was in France, on a high and proud of myself because I didn't have to touch it any more. And now I'm at square one again. @**FittyorPity**'s back, and everything feels utterly, utterly hopeless.

Sunday 9th February

10 p.m.
In bed

I spent most of the weekend in bed. I told Mum and Dad I was sick so that I didn't have to go to school or therapy on Friday. I didn't really want to see anyone, so I turned my phone off. The girls eventually came round with Matt today and dragged me kicking and screaming out of my pit and I'm so pleased they did. I'd been wallowing because of @**FittyorPity**. I'd allowed them and Trudy to get to me when I know deep down that they're pathetic.

Matt said no one cares about the kiss, all anyone he's spoken to has mentioned is the fact that I had my privacy invaded. He pointed out quite rightly that the only people making a big deal out of it are the worst, most detestable people: Trudy and whoever @**FittyorPity** is.

We had a chat about how I felt about the kiss, though and he was really helpful and pointed out that I can kiss and like whoever I want. I don't need to label myself, I don't need to make a big decision about it if I'm not sure about anything. I guess I hadn't thought of it like that, especially as I didn't have time to really think about it before the whole school knew.

Matt and the girls helped me compose a message to Sylvie because I felt really bad that I hadn't replied. Obviously when she replied she was totally cool about it all. I should have known she would be.

So now I'm just angry that I felt so bad for so long. That I've succumbed to **@FittyorPity** and Trudy and let them make me feel ashamed. Tomorrow I'm going to go into school with my head held high. Even though I'm dreading it.

I loved the kiss. I don't know what that means but I do know that no one should have to feel bad about themselves for kissing someone.

Monday 10th February

8 a.m.

I can't think of anything I'd like to do less than go into school today. So I'm walking really slowly with Millie and Sam shuffling me along.

'No shame, remember!' Millie's saying.

'Exactly, and what is there to be ashamed about anyway? Some loser Instagram account correctly thinking your life is more interesting than theirs?' Sam's adding.

'They've probably never kissed anyone at all. That's why they're so interested,' Millie points out.

This morning Freddie told me to fuck off when I asked him to hurry up in the bathroom so at least that felt like a normal Monday morning.

'We just have to get it over with and then you'll be fine!' Sam says.

'It's like ripping off a wax strip,' Millie concludes.

I don't think I can take any more of their positive cheering on and, to be honest, I'm starting to fill with rage the more I think about it all. So I pick up my feet and start marching. All I did was kiss someone and enjoy it. I would never allow myself to be period-shamed, so I won't allow myself to be kiss-shamed either, THANK YOU VERY MUCH. No matter what happens, and what people say to me, I'm READY.

After all that, no one has actually said anything except for a couple of jeers from the boys in Year Ten who we think are behind @**FittyorPity** anyway, and they were WEAK. And when I think about all those people that liked it, they're people that follow @**FittyorPity**. You have to be a bit of a prick to follow an account like that, don't you?

But this positive outlook might be about to change. Sam, Millie and I are heading down the corridor to see Matt and Nick and I can see Trudy approaching us head on with The Bitches.

'Oh Christ.' I steel myself and then remember, it's just Trudy. The same girl who's taunted me my whole life. This is no different and it seems to be only her that cares.

'How's your girlfriend, lesbian?' she shouts with Sienna smirking next to her and The Bitches behind them, spinelessly sniggering.

'You know, Trudy, maybe you wouldn't be so interested in Kat's life if you had your own?' Sam says, giving Sienna full eye contact as she talks.

'I guess some people are just trying to distract everyone from the fact that their boyfriend shat himself . . . in public.' Millie chimes in and I feel relieved that they've got this and they won't let Trudy make me feel bad. Not this time.

As if things weren't going badly enough for the plight of feminism in this school, Trudy has just made things ten MILLION times worse. She's AUDITIONING for a date to her party. Objectifying men, pissing all over the work we did to try and stop objectification in this school. And WORSE than that, Mr Clarke's letting her hold her sexist auditions in the drama studio tomorrow lunch time. On school property! During school time!

'How are we supposed to stop people in this school from objectifying each other if it's literally EVERYWHERE and approved by the teachers.' I sigh. I so wish I'd known she was doing this earlier. I'd have had way more to say for myself.

'And this reads like something straight from the @FittyorPity account,' Sam says, jabbing at the flyer in her hand and starting to read from it. 'Looks-wise must be at least a 9, don't bother if you're an 8 and a half. There will be a topless parade.'

'A TOPLESS PARADE?' Millie and I squeak at almost the same time as I try to push back thoughts of all the times I objectified Jack Gyllenhaal cleaning a toilet, because THIS IS DIFFERENT.

What's next? A teacher-sanctioned wet T-shirt contest in the assembly hall? FFS.

Tuesday 11th February

12.30 p.m.
Watching the line for Trudy's auditions

Feminism has been betrayed today. This is an absolute atrocity.
I have so many questions.

1. How come when we wanted to hold meetings for the Feminist
Society did we have to do it in the smallest and most depressing
room in the school and when Trudy wants to hold auditions for
someone to be her date for her party, something that has NOTHING
TO DO WITH THE SCHOOL and is NO GOOD FOR SOCIETY OR
TEACHING MORALS, she gets to do it in the drama room?

2. Why is this line so long? I was expecting #Tim to be in it, but
no one else.

3. Obviously #Tim is at the front though. Not a question – just
an observation, sorry.

4. Pretty sure some of these boys don't even go here?

5. Has she hired people to make the audition line look more
padded out? It's the only explanation I can think of. I know some
of them don't go here because they look about twenty and I
think I saw one of them on *The X Factor* auditions last year.

'God this is such a sad, sad state of affairs,' Sam says, shaking her head.

'And a disgraceful misuse of the drama block,' Millie says with sorrow.

We're sitting on the bench opposite the drama block WATCHING THE WORLD BURN.

'God, look at Sienna, following Trudy around like that,' I say.

'I still think she's hiding something,' Millie says.

'I'm surprised that the other Bitches have taken it lying down, to be honest. Amelie and Tiffany have worked for YEARS to get to where they are in the hierarchy. And now they're bumped down by someone who's been here two minutes. It's pretty weird,' I say. 'But then again, she relished the **@FittyorPity** account and she tried to bump me off the trampoline. So she's definitely #TrudyTwo.'

'I'm just pleased I'm over everything with her and Dave now. I felt like I was losing my mind there. Right before we went to Paris I was feeling the lowest I've ever felt. I'm pretty happy to be feeling better than that, you know?'

'I think I know,' I say, sighing and putting my arm around her.

We sit in silence, looking around the playground filled with male models and at what a mess it all is. Definitely not perving on any of them . . . or their six packs.

Thursday 13th February

2 p.m.
Walking to PE

We're walking down the stairs on our way to PE and I'm questioning why I (an intelligent person) would have to attempt trampolining again, knowing full well that I am terrible at it. School is a disgrace.

'OW! What the FUCK!' I hear a girl a few steps below us scream – I look around and a group of Year Ten boys – the ones we think are behind @**FittyorPity** – are laughing to themselves as they turn and run off down the stairs away from her.

I head down to ask if she's OK but everyone's getting in my way. I can see her and her friend have stopped where they are on the step, with people just brushing past as if nothing's happened, when something clearly has happened, something that's really upset her too.

'Are you OK?' I ask when we finally get to them, surprised that no teachers have even stopped.

'What did he do?' Sam asks.

'He grabbed my boob,' she says through tears. 'I feel stupid but it really hurt!'

'That's not stupid, that's assault. He assaulted you! You need to tell one of the teachers.' I try to calm my rage and be as gentle as possible.

'They do it all the time. They think it's funny. One of them was taking a picture as well,' her friend says.

'What? How is violating someone funny?' Millie says.

'Jesus, does no one know about consent?' Sam asks.

'What's your name?' I ask.

'Elsie, and I'm Emily,' her friend replies for her.

'They just think it's a silly game. They call it banter. And say it's harmless,' Elsie says.

'It's sexual assault, not banter. Elsie, you shouldn't have to accept being assaulted in the corridor at school.' I'm feeling shocked.

'We have to go,' says Elsie, looking at the floor. 'We don't want to make a big deal out of it. Then it'll get even worse because they'll start shouting that we're frigid in the halls.'

I stand stuck to the spot with rage as they head up the stairs. How is this allowed to happen? How am I party to this being allowed to happen? Something NEEDS to change. And it needs to change now.

4 p.m.
In my room

I run straight up to my room when I get in. I need space so I can think about things properly. There must be SOMETHING I can do about this. It can't carry on.

I find myself on the **@FittyorPity** Instagram account to see if they've posted a pic. And there it is, proof that it's who we always expected. A picture of Elsie appears, looking embarrassed and shocked. It's horrible but looking at this doesn't solve anything. I'm just adding to the problem by being another person looking at a picture of someone humiliated, objectified and assaulted, rather than doing something about it. At least now I know for sure who's responsible.

But what's the point in knowing if I can't do anything about it? I could go to Mr Clarke with this, but the picture only shows her shock after the event, it doesn't prove what happened. And he's already shut me down once, why would this time be any different? Except that this time I know for sure that I can't let him confuse me or make me think it's nothing and I'm overreacting. I know that this time I believe myself, and we *all* saw what we saw this afternoon. *This time* I won't doubt myself, not even for a second.

Without the Feminist Society, or the blog, we have even less chance to speak up than we did before, though. How are we going to get people to listen to us?

I need to find some inspiration, so I open my messages with Sylvie and scroll through until I find the song she sent me. The sound of Riot grrrl fills my room, all the anger and injustice I'm feeling reverberates around the walls and I remember the talks we had. How inspired and full of hope I'd been in France when we talked about the Feminist Society.

The beret that I've been avoiding catches my eye and I pick it up, its soft fabric reminding me of the night I kissed Sylvie and bringing back happy memories rather than the shame that @**FittyorPity** tried to make me feel.

I position it on my head, and I stand in front of the mirror looking at my reflection. I'm stronger than **@FittyorPity**, we all are, and we're going to beat them.

4.30 p.m.
Lying on the floor with Bea, still racking my brains

Just because the problem's inside school doesn't mean that that's the only way we can solve it. We may not be allowed to hold Feminist Society meetings in the school, but no one can control what we do outside of school. Can they?

I kick myself for not thinking of it sooner and jump up feeling the first bit of real inspiration I've had for days. We don't need the school's help (which we're very clearly never going to get anyway). We can do it outside of school, together. I'll start my own blog and send it to everyone from the meetings. I can include the blog Mr Clarke took down as well, so everyone can see it, and Mum can finally read it. No one can stop me or take it down because it's MINE.

MY OWN BLOG, OUR OWN FEMINIST SOCIETY! We can still do this! We can change what's happening! I'm fired up and fuelled by the anger of the past week and everything **@FittyorPity** tried to make me feel.

I snap a picture of myself in my beret and send it to Sylvie.

Me: Plotting a feminist revolution in my beret x

Sylvie: YES! Tell me about it? X

11 p.m.

I've spent the evening telling Sylvie and the girls about my plan to revive the Feminist Society and set up a blog. I've even written my first post which I'll publish tomorrow.

The blog's a call to action, an invitation to everyone to join us for the first meeting of the new Feminist Society on Saturday at Scoops (before Trudy's party). And that's when I'll unveil PHASE TWO of the big plan. *Taps nose*.

The girls are helping me contact the other people from the Feminist Society and Sam's making flyers that we can give to people around school discreetly – not that Mr Clarke can stop us now. Not now it's outside of school time and property.

The Feminist Society will no longer be held back or told what to do. We can achieve exactly what we need to.

3 Positive Things:

1. The Feminist Society's back! And stronger than ever!
*2. We're going to stand up to @**FittyorPity** and we're going to make sure that nothing like this ever happens again.*
*3. The story of Feminist Society vs @**FittyorPity** will become the stuff of legend, and toxic masculinity shall NEVER enter our school premises again, even long after we've gone. And they will erect a statue of me upon the playing field . . . I may have gone too far.*

friday 14th february

FEMINISTS, LISTEN UP!
THE FEMINIST SOCIETY'S BACK
BANNED FROM SCHOOL BUT STILL GOING STRONG

Assault, groping and upskirting aren't banter, and
we're going to do something about it. It's not boys
being boys, and we're going to fix the problem –
with or without the head teacher's help.

JOIN US TO JOIN IN!
SCOOPS SATURDAY 2PM
EVERYONE WELCOME

8 a.m.
The kitchen

Mum and Dad fall silent as I walk into the kitchen and I think I've caught them talking about the blog. I told Mum I was working on something big yesterday and then sent her the link this morning. It seemed like the best way to show them.

I know they'll be supportive. Also now I KNOW Mr Clarke was wrong and I need to carry on fighting to stop the toxic masculinity in school.

'Morning . . .' I say tentatively.

'We just read your blog,' Mum says.

'Why didn't you tell us what was going on?' Dad asks, sounding concerned.

'We would have done something!' Mum says.

I was worried about this but I'm just going to be honest with them.

'When Mr Clarke shut down the Feminist Society he said I was overdramatising things, that it wasn't that bad. That I'd exaggerated how bad things were with the groping and the upskirting. And the way he talked to me and told me I was just playing a game made me feel stupid. Like I was wrong.' I see fury on their faces. 'I felt embarrassed about it. But now I *know he* was wrong and I shouldn't have listened to him or let him get in my head.'

'That little weasel!' Mum looks like she's about to start vibrating with rage and Dad's put his coffee down with a thump.

'That's gaslighting!' Dad exclaims.

'We need you to tell us everything,' Mum says firmly.

I feel like I've got things under control, I just need to tell them the plan and I know they'll feel the same too.

8.10 a.m.

I've finished filling them in on everything that happened at the meeting, the blog and Mr Clarke shutting it down. And I've told them the whole plan for the new Feminist Society, even the top secret bits.

338

'I'm furious that Mr Clarke talked to you like that, but I'm also so impressed with the way you've carried on fighting it. And your plan's great,' Mum's saying.

'I just don't understand how he thinks that it's OK to talk to students like that when they're raising such serious concerns,' Dad says, looking thoughtful.

'I have to go,' I say, taking another look at the kitchen clock. 'I need to hand out flyers for tomorrow with the girls before school.'

I grab my things together and start heading for the door.

'Kitty Kat?' Dad calls, using the silly name I hate, and I turn to look at him. 'We're proud of you.'

8.20 a.m.
Walking to school

We're armed with flyers to hand out at the school gates and now that we know who's in **@FittyorPity** we can avoid them too, so when we do eventually start PHASE TWO they won't know what's hit them.

11 a.m.
History

The blog's had over three hundred likes, people are reposting it everywhere and we've run out of flyers. I can barely focus because I keep thinking about PHASE TWO of the plan, and how I'm going to tell everyone tomorrow.

4 p.m.
Sarah's office

'So, Kat, it's been a while since our last session. Fill me in. How are things?'

Oh dear god, I have a LOT to tell her . . .

4.10 p.m.

'Well, your friends are completely right. You don't owe anyone an explanation of your sexuality. However, entitled they might feel to it.' I've just finished telling Sarah about my unexpected trip to Paris and my even more unexpected kiss. 'You know, you don't have to fit into a box that someone else created. You're an individual.'

And that is so true.

4.30 p.m.

'I'm just so angry and I can't help feeling like I've let people down. Elsie wouldn't have been groped on Thursday if I'd sorted things out properly. I've known what's been happening in school now for over a month – it's time to do something about it.' We've been talking about the Feminist Society and the plans for the meeting tomorrow.

'That's a lot to hold, you can't take responsibility for Elsie being groped. That responsibility lies with the boys who did it,

340

and your headteacher for the way he's refused to deal with the situation. And they should face the appropriate consequences. You need to remember this isn't just on your shoulders, Kat. It's not your problem to deal with alone. This is a problem that you have to face with others. There are so many of you with this collective anger and you're going to use it for good,' Sarah says. 'Protest is strongest when it's done together. And it sounds like you've got a huge group supporting and lifting each other up. Exactly the way it should be. I'm just so sorry that it's gone this far without anyone stepping in and that you've been let down by the system so badly.'

Sarah's right, and tomorrow we can do this together.

6 p.m.
My room

'I would obviously never slut-shame my own mother but does the WHOLE street really need to see her and Derek at it? Why can't they just draw the blinds?' Matt says, staring out of my window across the street.

'Maybe they don't realise people can see? They're not even "at it", they're having a cuddle while they watch TV. Also, had she not have opened her legs you wouldn't exist,' I point out. 'Let her have a bit of fun.'

'How would you feel if the whole street was watching YOUR mum practically shagging a man across his coffee table?' Matt throws his arms up dramatically and I roll my eyes at him. If he thinks what they're doing is shagging I would question his virginity after all.

'My mum would never shag a man on a coffee table because Dad's got bad knees,' I say.

'Right, but Mrs Chivers across the road is watching.'

'Mrs Chivers watches everything because she doesn't have a TV, now PLEASE can we get back to talking about the meeting tomorrow? I need your help!' I say.

'You're fine! You know EXACTLY what you're doing!'

'But what if no one comes?' I ask because let's face it, I've been burned by this before.

'I'm definitely going, and Si and the girls and Nick, so there will at least be all of us. Jane is coming. She said so on your post. Aimee messaged earlier and said they were coming. And I bet people in your year and from the other years will come, they're all just scared because of Trudy's rant earlier about it being the same day as her party. People will come, you'll see.'

I want him to be right but I can't stop imagining sitting at the really long table in Scoops by myself for an hour while families queue up waiting for the table and Mrs Coop, the angry old lady who runs Scoops, tries to move me on with her broom.

'If anything, Mrs Coop is going to be waggling her broom at you in anger because you've filled her coffee shop with the *youth* who she says don't buy anything.' Matt says reading my mind. 'And FYI if she does that, I'm going to pretend I don't know you because she's been giving me a free cookie every time I go in since I was three and I am NOT losing my free cookie.'

'Wow,' I say, eyeballing him. 'It really is every MAN for himself, isn't it? What happened to allyship? What happened to supporting the feminist cause? You're willing to give up our friendship all for a free cookie.'

'It's double chocolate.' He shrugs.

God, I hadn't thought about Mrs Coop getting angry before. She's much less mobile than she used to be these days, but she's been known to chase people out with a broom when they've annoyed her or done something she deems indecent. This used to extend to holding hands but she's had to move with the times.

Shit, now I'm worrying about that as well.

I wonder if there will ever be a day when I don't worry about anything? If, like, there could just be one, SINGLE day when I don't at some point feel like the world is going to end.

My phone beeps.

Sylvie: How are you feeling about the big meeting tomorrow?

> **Me:** Excited, nervous. I'm trying to talk to Matt about it but he keeps getting distracted because his mum's shagging the neighbour.

Sylvie: What is shagging, please?

3 Positive Things:

1. Tomorrow is the rebirth of the Feminist Society.

2. This time tomorrow we'll be at Trudy's much talked about party. (How can a party seem so SINISTER? I guess it's because the person throwing it is a monster. Attendance is almost compulsory and yet treated with distain. I for one, though, can't wait to sit with my friends having a giggle at it all.)

3. I taught a French person what the word 'shagging' means – doing wonders for international relations every day.

Saturday 15th February

10 a.m.

I barely slept last night for worrying about the Feminist Society reunion today. About who might come or might not come. And whether we'll manage to achieve everything. I keep reminding myself what Sarah said, though. Loads of people have been affected by this, and we're all in it together.

2 p.m.
Scoops

There were already TEN people here when we arrived (TEN!), but the place was empty apart from that, so when old Mrs Coop swings by to tell me that I should have booked before throwing a party at her cafe I point out to her that the place is EMPTY apart from us, and she doesn't get her broom out. Thank god.

We sit at the big, long table and hope that we can all fit round it. If not, there are extra tables nearby, but right now we keep adding more and more chairs round the table as more people arrive.

There are about thirty of us around the crowded table when Mrs Coop approaches with her order pad.

'Each one of you better order something, or you can get out,' she says.

Is it any wonder that business is clearly booming for her on a Saturday? She really is the hostess with the mostest (anger).

2.10 p.m.

Thanks to Mrs Coop's insistence on taking all of our orders one by one and writing each down in full, painstakingly, while repeatedly having to ask us to speak up and say our orders again, we've lost the first ten minutes of the meeting to ordering.

'So now that we're ready, it came to our attention . . .' I try to speak loudly so that everyone can hear, but it's terrifying with this many eyes on me, and I'm stumbling a bit over my words and resisting the urge to curl up in the corner. 'It came to our attention that after Mr Clarke banned us from doing any more Feminist Society meetings, things haven't got better at the school. In fact, things have definitely got much worse now that Year Ten boys are going round groping girls on a whim. Year Ten boys who we suspect are responsible for **@Fittyorpity**. We know that the issue may extend outside of this collective of boys as well and our worry is that younger boys will see this behaviour and look up to or imitate it.'

Everyone is nodding and there's now a second row of seats around the table. I feel like I'm in an auditorium. I clear my throat and try to ignore the amount of people and just carry on talking. Aímee smiles at me, spurring me on to keep talking.

'With this in mind, as Mr Clarke has decided to silence us, we need to take drastic action. I'm proposing that we protest.'

346

There's a murmur of excitement around the table and I swallow the seemingly huge amount of excess saliva in my mouth before carrying on. 'On Monday morning we show that we won't be silenced, with a protest. As the first bell goes, we'll just sit down in the playground and refuse to go to class or move until Mr Clarke agrees to do something about the issue. He needs to hold the boys behind @**FittyorPity** accountable and to make changes to prevent groping on school grounds and increase safety.'

There's excited chatter and I can barely bring myself to look around but when I do everyone's smiling and nodding.

'I love this!' says Jane. 'We should contact the school board as well. Tell them what we're doing on Monday morning before we do it. We need them on our side so that they can force him to agree to putting firmer rules and punishments in place regarding the sexual harassment and abuse happening in our school, along with any slut-shaming or body-shaming.'

'Great idea,' I say, 'and then no more @**FittyorPity**!'

There are general murmurs of agreement around the table and everyone looks as eager as I am to get planning.

Mr Coop arrives with a tray full of hot chocolates. He takes one look at us all and tuts.

'Bloody women's libbers,' he's muttering to himself while putting the tray of drinks on the table. 'Men can't do anything any more without women telling us off for being sexist. I'd hand out your drinks but you'd only say I didn't think you were capable of picking them up yourselves,' he says with more than a hint of bitterness.

Mrs Coop comes up behind him, smiling for the first time, possibly ever.

'You should have said what this meeting was for, my loves. These drinks are on the house!' She puts down another tray of milkshakes and teas. I bloody knew that somewhere in there Mrs Coop was actually a good egg. I KNEW IT!

'Aww thanks, Mrs Coop!' Millie says as Mrs Coop puts a giant double chocolate cookie in front of Matt and ruffles his hair.

'Good boy,' she says, winking at him.

There are lots of other mutterings of 'Thanks, Mrs Coop,' around the table and Matt's beaming up at her like some kind of angelic toddler.

'Maybe we could tell the local paper?' Aimee suggests.

'Great idea . . .' I say.

Looking at Aimee reminds me about our first conversation and how I need to make sure that whatever we do from here on out, we're including everyone. It's not feminism if it's not intersectional.

'My dad works for the paper!' a girl across the table says before introducing herself. 'I'm Stacey!'

'Yes! This is great!' I say writing everything down so I can keep track of who's doing what.

Millie, Sam and I look at each other as a buzz fills Scoops, and I think we're actually going to do it. My heart lifts as I see how much support there is around this table. Even Mrs Coop of Scoops looks proud to be in on it all.

5 p.m.
Getting ready in Millie's bedroom

Sylvie: So what's the plan?

> **Me:** On Monday when we get to school and the bell rings for lessons we all sit in the playground (it better not be raining) and we stay there until we've made an impact. We're inviting the media and there's no time before that for *him* to find out about it and stop us.

Sylvie: YESS!! I love this! This is proper, old-school activism. I'm so proud.

> **Me:** I'll be wearing my beret, of course.

Sylvie: 🙂

'What's she smiling about?' Sam asks Millie, pointing to me.

'Sylvie, she's texting Sylvie,' Millie says, looking over my shoulder.

'OOOOooohh! How's that going?' Sam asks.

'It's nice, we're just friends, I like talking to her,' I say, still smiling.

7.30 p.m.
The Den

We're standing outside The Den staring up at it with pretty much the same expression we had on our faces on the first day back at school.

'Remind me again why we're here?' I ask.

'Because we thought about not coming and got massive FOMO,' Sam reminds me. 'It looks grim. We just need to go in and SEE it, make sure that we were able to be part of this hideousness, for the memories. Then we can go home, or at least somewhere where we won't catch syphilis from the walls.'

There are birthday banners all over the outside of The Den. It's been Trudyfied. I wouldn't be surprised if when we walk in Trudy's sitting on a throne on stage wearing a crown.

7.33 p.m.

Trudy's sitting on a throne on stage wearing a crown with (shock horror) one of the boys from **@FittyorPity** sitting next to her, also wearing a crown – yet more proof, if I ever needed it, that she's the one that sent them the picture. Apparently, we're supposed to go up on to the stage and deliver her our gifts and birthday wishes. Like the wise men visiting the baby fucking Jesus.

There are two problems with this:

1. We have not brought her gifts (I owe her nothing).
2. We do not wish her a happy birthday. We are merely here to see what goes down.

But nobody else appears to be doing this either. The only other people up on the stage with her are The Bitches and Sienna . . . I wonder when we'll stop counting her as separate and just accept that The Bitches have multiplied.

Looking around I can see that the no-drinking rule has been flouted and drinks have been spiked with vodka all over the place. Also, I think the bar staff are struggling to work out who's eighteen and who isn't. Oops!

The floor's sticky, it's sweaty in here, it smells, the music's too loud, and the lights are blinding me and making me feel dizzy. I know I sound like an old woman but actually this is my idea of HELL.

Every time we walk past someone who was at Scoops this afternoon, though, I get a 'hi' or a smile, sometimes a fist bump and I feel like there's a sense of togetherness for Monday that even Trudy can't crush.

'Drinks?' Matt asks.

'Yes!' Nick says, clearly pleased that he decided not to drive tonight.

'Many,' Sam says.

As we all head to the bar I spot Dave amongst all his football buddies. Obviously, the whole school has had a laugh at him shitting himself and then got over it and now he's just back to being one of the lads with a funny story to tell. I see him glancing over at us and hope he's not even THINKING about looking at Sam.

I honestly feel like everyone shamed me more when I

dropped my menstrual cup at Josh's feet last year. How is period-shaming still a thing when shit-shaming doesn't seem to be? I got over it much quicker than everyone else because I know a menstrual cup is nothing to be ashamed of, but WHY did everyone else consider it more shameful than Dave ACTUALLY SHITTING HIMSELF?

Because he's a man.

Patriarchy.

Monday can't come soon enough.

8.30 p.m.
Still in strobe hell

'I need the loo.' Millie says.

The three of us traipse over to the toilet and start the difficult task of weeing without touching ANYTHING. There's so much graffiti on this wall you could make a book out of it. Someone called Simon apparently has herpes and no one is to sleep with him. Poor Simon, it sounds sore. Also, do they mean like genital herpes or just cold sores? Because loads of people have the second one. So *shrug*.

We're all concentrating so hard on not touching anything that we're peeing in total silence.

I hear the main toilet door open but I'm absolutely NOT going to be hurrying when I'm in this perilous squat position. Whoever it is has to wait.

'Did you hear Amelie said she found out more about Sienna?

Like, she KNOWS her secret and she said she's going to bust her tonight.' I recognise Tia's voice outside.

Oh, this is VERY INTERESTING. I wonder who she's talking to. I can hear all three of us have stopped peeing so the other girls must be listening too. I don't want to make any noise in case it draws attention to us, though, so I'm still in my squat, straining to hear.

'What did she say it was?' I hear Nia's voice.

'She just said 'All will be revealed',' Tia replies.

'God, I hope so. Who does she think she is anyway? We've worked for years to be Trudy's Bitches and she just comes in and gets an automatic pass to the front of the queue?'

'I know, right? Amelie has been loyal for YEARS, well, apart from that thing with Josh last year, BUT to just push her aside like that? CRIMINAL.'

'I'm perfect now,' Tia says as I hear them start walking to the door (I hope that's where they're going anyway, because I cannot hold this position for much longer.)

We stay completely still until they've left and then the three of us resume peeing at once. We hurry to finish and come out of the cubicles at the same time and stare at each other.

'The most informative wee I've ever had,' Mille says.

'I wonder what they mean about Sienna?' Sam asks. 'What's her big secret?'

'I fear we might have to hang out here for a while longer to find out,' Mille says, looking pained.

We find Matt and Si by the bar with some of the guys from Sixth Form and tell them everything we heard.

'Ooooh, I NEED to know what the secret is!' Matt's beside himself with the promise of some kind of excitement.

'I knew she was fishy. When do you think we'll find out?' Si asks, chewing on a cocktail stick from the bar like he's watched too many cowboy films.

'I think now!' Sam points over to the stage where Amelie's appeared, swaying and looking slightly worse for wear.

'YESSS!' Matt shuffles forward with Si to get a better view.

Amelie's unsteadily grabbing a microphone from the side of the stage while Trudy clocks her from her throne, looking furious. I imagine that microphone had been set up for some kind of speech about how great she is and how her parents bought her a pony and how she will attach the poor thing to a carriage and make it pull her around like the queen she isn't.

'EVERYONE!' Amelie slurs into the mic. 'EVERYONE! MUSIC! OFF!'

Everyone turns their attention to her as the music stops. We're all waiting expectantly, but poor Amelie is taking a little while to compose herself.

'As Trudy's oldest and BEST friend, I wanted to wish her a special happy birthday.' She gestures at Trudy who does the most awkward smile I've ever seen. 'And as this is allllllll about

354

Trudy, I wanted to take the opportunity to introduce you all properly to her newest friend, Sienna.' She gestures towards where Sienna is standing on the stage and Sienna does a little wave, looking confused.

'Sienna is a liar!' Amelie shouts as Sienna's face falls.

The whole room gasps and there's a low rumble of chatter while Sienna stands frozen, looking horrified on stage. Trudy's jaw drops. The rest of her face remains stony, while her mouth resembles a train tunnel. This is the most expression I've ever seen from her. I look over at Dave whose attention has been grabbed just like everyone else's.

'When Sienna joined the school we were all given the impression that she was EXPELLED from her last school for a small incident involving the police that her parents were covering up. There were rumours of a fire. THAT IS A LIE. Sienna had to leave her last school because she was SUCH A LOSER that she was bullied EVERY DAY until it got so bad that she told her parents she couldn't cope any more. That's the truth of it. She's not some bad-ass, super-cool rebel. She's just a sad, friendless, liar who couldn't cope and had to run away.'

Trudy's still completely frozen to the spot, which is probably a good thing because otherwise someone would probably have to tear her off Sienna. Instead, Sienna's free to run off the stage and out of the room, looking utterly crushed while everyone watches on.

'Jesus,' Sam says, I think feeling the same as me, that we're sorry we waited for this and willed this to happen.

'Poor Sienna,' I say.

'Never thought I'd say this, but I agree. Poor Sienna,' Sam says. 'I know she's behaved really badly, but that's rough. What's Amelie DOING announcing it like that? And being bullied's terrible, but not lame. I knew Amelie was pretty bad, but finding out something like that and sharing it like THIS? Awful.'

'I guess jealousy makes people twisted.' Millie sighs.

'Should we follow her? Check she's OK? I know what she did to you was shitty, Sam, but I just feel like she's probably in a bad place . . .' I say.

'Let's go.' Sam nods.

Si and Matt are still standing with their mouths open and Nick just doesn't know where to look. They'll be processing for a while I guess.

8.50 p.m.
The toilets

As we enter the toilet we hear crying that stops abruptly when the door shuts behind us. There's only one stall closed so we gather round.

'Sienna, are you OK?' Sam shouts, knocking on the stall door gently. 'That was pretty brutal. We're worried about you.'

There's silence apart from a few sniffs behind the door.

'You can ignore us but we'll just stay here until you come out,' Sam says.

356

'We just want to know you're OK,' Millie says.

We stand staring at each other, not sure what to do. I feel bad that I judged someone I knew nothing about but then I also know that she didn't behave in the best way. This is one of those really confusing times where I can't work out if I've done something wrong or not, and sometimes it's actually a grey area. I really wish things were a bit clearer cut than that.

'Where's your brother?' Millie asks. 'Shall we go and get him?'

'NO!' Sienna shouts. 'He told me not to embarrass him.'

'That's not very nice,' Sam says, looking at me and Millie. We're all relieved that we've had some communication, at least. 'When did he say that?'

'When I started at school. He said he didn't want people to know what happened and he helped me make up the rumour. He thought it would stop me getting bullied again and told me to keep my head down and make sure no one ever found out the truth.'

'That's pretty awful,' I say. 'I'm sorry.'

'Why don't you come out?' Sam offers and I can hear Sienna shuffling behind the door.

'Why are you being so nice to me? I've been terrible to you.' Sienna sniffs wearily. 'Why do you even care if I'm OK or not?'

'Because no one deserves what just happened out there,' Sam says. 'And it sounds like you've had a pretty bad time of it too.'

'It hasn't been great,' Sienna finally agrees after a long

pause, but she still sounds unsure.

'You can always talk to us about it, you know?' Millie offers.

'Yeah, might feel better to talk about it, especially now someone else has told a version of your story for you without your consent.' I say.

We can hear Sienna blowing her nose behind the door, but apart from that there's silence. Maybe she's trying to work out if she can trust us. I'd probably have trouble trusting people too after what she's been through.

'I was at a private girls' school before, but I never really fit in,' she finally starts. 'The other girls in my year just didn't like me. At first, they'd say I didn't belong because I wasn't from around there, and that I was too ugly to be their friend and then as I got older they'd write things like "ugly" and "slut" on my locker. It got worse when I started seeing a guy from the boys' school down the road called Steve in secret. The girls in my year found out and were furious because one of them – a girl called Clara – fancied him. They didn't understand why he'd want to be with me rather than Clara. The bullying got worse and worse. Once, in class, Clara's friends cut my hair when I was too busy paying attention to notice. It was algebra and I love algebra, so I didn't realise what they'd done till I left. Everyone was laughing at the big gap in the back of my hair. They spread rumours that I wet the bed and stuff like that so that Steve eventually broke up with me because he couldn't work out why they'd lie so much. But even after Steve broke up with me, he didn't want Clara, which made her even angrier and made the bullying worse. Eventually it all got too much, and I couldn't take it any more. I had no escape from them, so I begged my parents to let me come home and go to a different school.'

'That's awful, I'm sorry. Is that why you became friends with Trudy? Because you didn't want her to bully you?' Sam asks.

Good thinking, Sam. That's pretty genius.

'I just thought, you know, if you can't beat 'em join 'em. So I did. And before I knew it, I was one of them. But I was still really scared. So I thought if I had a boyfriend it would help make sure I stayed on top.' She takes a big gasp of air. 'I'm really sorry, Sam. I knew Dave liked me and I just went for it. I was so awful to you. Then I dumped him because of what happened, because I can't be a loser again. I can't. I'm so sorry.'

I can hear her doing the kind of crying that won't stop for a while and I can't help but feel really bad for her. I know she behaved appallingly but I guess it's more complicated than that. People aren't just all good or all bad. Being human doesn't seem to be as straightforward as I used to think it was. It sounds like she had such a hard time that I wouldn't blame her for wanting to make sure that nothing like that ever happened again, even if she did go about it in completely the wrong way.

'Why don't you come out? Talk to us properly and let us help?' Sam suggests.

I'm so proud of Sam right now. Considering this is the girl that literally destroyed her relationship, she's amazing.

'Why would you be nice to me? I ruined your relationship! I

stole your boyfriend and then dumped him!' Sienna says between gasps, crying.

'You didn't steal him, you can't steal a person, they're not property, he walked willingly. You saved me, if anything. It's better for me to know the man he is now. He could have done the same thing in a few years' time, and it would have been worse. Anyway, there were two people involved, not just you, and if he was the right man for me, he wouldn't have left so easily.'

I hear the lock turn and the door swings back to reveal Sienna, looking somehow smaller. Mascara tracks run down her face, and I want to give her a hug, which is certainly something I have never felt towards her before.

'I'm sorry,' she says, still crying. 'I don't want to be this person any more. I don't want to be part of The Bitches, I just wanted to survive secondary school, get my GCSEs and then get away from everyone.'

'I get that,' Sam says. 'You've had a rough time. You don't have to be friends with Trudy. We can make sure she doesn't do anything shitty, and there's not long left until exams. We're here if you want to talk.'

'Thank you, but right now I think I just want to go home,' Sienna says. 'There's a door round the back that Trudy made her parents come in so that no one saw them. I'll just sneak out of there.'

'OK,' Sam says and gives her a hug.

'Thank you. You're so nice, I'm sorry I was such a cow. I'll be there at the sit-in with you on Monday,' Sienna says, before she gathers herself together and heads out.

I never thought in a million years that I'd feel sorry for Sienna. But I've always known what an amazing woman my friend is.

10 p.m.
OWNING the dancefloor

After all the drama, Trudy and The Bitches are nowhere to be seen, thusly the atmosphere at this party has got considerably better. The DJ's playing some One Direction and we're having the greatest time dancing and being silly. Even Matt seems to have forgotten about the filth.

'Why is Dave staring at you?' Millie asks Sam as we're twirling around while Si and Matt do some kind of *Dirty Dancing*-style tango situation through us all.

'No idea, not interested,' Sam says, dancing away, barely stopping to answer.

'Shit, I think he might be coming over.' I watch as he starts weaving his way towards us.

'Urgh, why?' Sam asks. 'If he's coming over here to ruin my fun, I don't want to know.'

Sam, Millie and I carry on dancing but as Dave gets closer Matt and Si stop dancing.

'Oh no. I don't think so,' Si says with his hand on his hip.

'The fucking AUDACITY.' Matt gasps.

I can see Dave looks nervous because he's wiping his palms

on his jeans, and he should be . . . he should be petrified.

'Hey, Sam,' he says, trying to get her attention, but Sam doesn't stop dancing. 'Sam? Can I talk to you?'

'I don't think she wants to?' I suggest more gently than I intended. I really need to be fiercer.

'I need to say sorry,' Dave shouts over to her, despite her not stopping. 'I treated you badly, I was a shitty boyfriend and an even shittier person and I'm sorry.'

'No worries,' Sam says but still carries on dancing.

Millie and I are trying to keep dancing too but I feel like I'm witnessing a thing of greatness right now. She didn't even stoop so low as to comment on the shitty thing. I'm itching to make a comment about it. I'm so proud of her. Matt and Si are also watching this masterclass in class and grace.

'Can we be friends? Or maybe go for coffee next week?'

'No thanks,' she says, still not looking at him.

He stares over at her with sad puppy eyes, and Millie and I nod at each other. She's been clear enough and very kind about it in the circumstances.

'I think it's probably best if you head,' I say. 'I don't think she wants to talk.'

Dave looks at me and then sighs.

'OK, but look,' he shouts over my head to Sam, 'I really mean it, I'm sorry about Sienna. I can't explain it, I just . . . I messed up. I got scared that maybe I was just going to be in one relationship for ever, and I think the commitment got to me and I couldn't take it. I screwed up really badly and I hurt you.

I'm really sorry. I wasn't thinking straight.'

'It's fine,' Sam says, finally stopping dancing. 'I'm over it. It hurt, but I'm done now. I just want to hang out with my friends. Please?'

'OK. But if you ever want to talk or anything, just, text? I'm sorry.' Dave turns and leaves looking really sad and Millie, Sam, Matt, Si and I go back to dancing just as BTS comes on. 💚

12 p.m.
In bed – snug as a burrito

3 Positive Things:
1. Sam
2. Millie
3. Me

Sunday 16th February

9 a.m.
In bed, FaceTiming with my girls

I'm wrapped up in bed with Bea, a cup of tea and the girls on FaceTime, debriefing from last night's party.

'One of Nick's friends said that after we left Trudy had a total diva strop and smashed up her throne,' Millie says. 'And then one of the bouncers carried her off kicking and screaming like she was a toddler. They heard her parents telling her she was grounded until she got a hold on her rage blackouts.'

We all giggle for a little bit at the thought of Trudy being scooped up by the bouncer.

'You were amazing last night, Sam,' I say, staring with admiration at my friend.

'A hero,' Millie adds.

'Nah, I feel really bad for Sienna.'

'It sounds terrible, what happened at her last school,' I say, taking a sip of my tea. 'I guess she wasn't the second coming of Satan after all, just someone trying to get by after having a hard time.'

'The worst. I always think we're so lucky to have each other, you know?' Millie says.

'Always,' I say.

'And nothing's gonna change that,' Sam says. 'Anyway, I think Sienna did me a favour, at least Dave and I had broken up before he publicly shat himself.'

9 p.m.

On the sofa

Preparing for tomorrow, the day that I will make a stand for feminism. Hopefully. As long as people show up. Oh god.

We're watching a film about the Suffragettes that Dad thought might help me to feel ready for tomorrow. Me and the girls all 'grammed about the protest, and so have the other people who were at the meeting. I've got over five hundred likes on my post which is pretty cool, I just hope all of those people come and sit down with us.

'See, Kat! This'll be you tomorrow!' Dad says, gesturing at the telly.

'Will you be joining in, Freddie?' Mum asks pointedly.

'Um . . . sure . . . I mean . . . Issy's going to, so I guess if she does then it'll look weird if I don't,' he says. I like how he makes it sound like it's just a convenience thing, or an act of duty to his girlfriend, so that I don't feel too much like he actually cares.

Watching this film makes me feel excited for tomorrow, that we at last get to stand up – or, in our case, sit down – for what we believe in, and smash the patriarchy (with our bums).

3 Positive Things:

1. I am spurred on by the Suffragettes movie.

*2. We will take down @**FittyorPity**, Mr Clarke and the entire patriarchy (or at least two of those things)*

3. TOMORROW IS THE DAY!

Monday 17th february

Sitting at my dressing table

I am a brave and intrepid feminist, making my voice heard, and ensuring that, at the very least, no girl ever gets her boobs grabbed at our school without consequences again.

> **FEMINIST SOCIETY FOREVER**
> Sam, Millie, Me

> **Sam:** My sister sent me an image of this pin from the Amsterdam Museum that's a vagina riding a horse with a sword and crossbow. I feel like it should be our new WhatsApp group pic.

> **Me:** YESSS, SAM!!!!

> **Millie:** YESSSSS!!!

> **Message:** WhatsApp Group picture changed by Sam.

8.15 a.m.
My room

I place my feminist beret on my head and take a snap for Sylvie. I feel strong, somehow taller than usual and ready to fight for what's right.

Me: I'm ready to go!

Sylvie: You look ready to take on the world. I'm so proud of you! X

Me: 😊 I wouldn't feel nearly this strong without you x

I know that things with Sylvie have confused me and made me question the one thing I thought I always knew about myself – my sexuality, which I still have absolutely no firm answer on, by the way – but I also wouldn't change meeting her for the world.

I straighten my beret and head downstairs to wait for Millie and Sam's arrival.

8.45 a.m.
The playground

Sam, Millie and I are back in the spot where we accidentally wrote #Tim on the playground last term, waiting for the bell to go to signal the start of form room and the time to sit down for feminism and equality.

I feel a bit bad that we haven't included Miss Mills in our plans, but I also think it's probably for the best. The last thing I want is for her to get in trouble again.

I can see the others that were at the meeting dotted around the playground and there do seem to be more people than usual hanging about. Sam's made a fresh banner that she's concealing in her bag.

The good thing is that Mr Clarke can't know about it yet anyway, because I haven't been summoned to his beige office for a discussion about how hysterical I am. *Eyeroll*

'Guys,' Sam says, 'I was going to tell you about this later, you know, after we smashed the patriarchy and everything. But I don't think I can hold it in any longer. I found out this morning, I got the scholarship, for art camp. I'm in!'

'WHHHHATTTT!' Millie and I scream at almost the same time.

'SAM!' I exclaim as the three of us jump up and down.

This has to be a good omen for today.

We're unstoppable.

8.49 a.m.

Here we go, any minute now. The three of us are either going to be sitting down on our own or sitting down with other people joining us. Small mercies, it is freezing cold but not raining, and Sam and Millie are MASSIVELY jealous of my beret.

I see Trudy and The Bitches striding towards us, scowling. Unsurprisingly they're not with Sienna. I hope she's OK.

'I can't believe you actually think anyone will take you seriously?' Trudy says, sneering at me. 'And that hat? Please!'

'If that's true, Trudy, why are there so many people here?' Sam asks.

'And why are you so het up about it anyway? If you don't care, just walk away,' I say. I'm ignoring her comment about my beret because I know it's fabulous.

Trudy makes a huffing noise and is about to stomp off when Sienna appears, walking past her towards us.

'Err, what do you think you're doing showing your face after everything you've done?' Trudy shouts at her.

'Hey!' Sam says to Sienna as she comes and stands with us.

'Hey!' Sienna says, ignoring Trudy.

'You can't just ignore me. You RUINED my sixteenth!' Trudy shouts as everyone ignores her. 'STOP IGNORING ME!'

'Trudy, *I* didn't ruin your party. *I* wasn't the one that lost their shit, *I* wasn't the one that treated everyone like dirt so that they barely wanted to be there in the first place,' Sienna says with a strength that I'm in awe of.

'You're FINISHED!' Trudy rages. 'We don't want you in The Bitches any more. And you're not exactly going to be friends with these guys. You STOLE Sam's boyfriend!'

'Actually, I think she probably did me a favour, you know?' Sam says, shrugging.

'Fucking lesbian feminists,' Trudy mutters under her breath as she stomps off, prompting the four of us to burst into hysterics.

Apparently on Saturday night Amelie got in BIG trouble with Trudy for detracting the focus of the party away from her, so now Amelie's trailing at the back, far behind Tia and Nia, looking at the ground. I don't think what Amelie did was great, but not for the same reasons as Trudy. I will never understand why anyone would want to be a member of The Bitches. They all deserve each other.

'You OK?' Sam asks Sienna, squeezing her hand.

'Yeah. I'm sorry again about everything. And you too, Millie, Kat,' Sienna says, unable to look at us.

'Ah, you're OK,' Millie says.

'Yeah, it sounds like you've had a crappy time,' I say.

RIIIIIINNNNNG RIIIIIIIINNNNGGGGG

I feel adrenaline hit me. This is it. The moment of truth.

We immediately sit down and Sam pulls a long banner out of her bag and unrolls it. It reads 'STOP TOXIC MASCULINITY NOW'.

'Sam, that's amazing!' I say, taking in all the beautiful paintings of Michelle Obama, Emeline Pankhurst and Malala.

'Thanks!' Sam says as she looks at the banner, smiling.

Just as we're getting as comfortable as it's possible to be on cold concrete, Comedy Krish arrives by my side and plops himself down on the ground next to me. He pulls a sign out of his bag that reads 'Groping's gross'. I stare at him as he looks straight ahead, trying to ignore me. Eventually he turns to face me, a big smile on his face.

'What, like you thought I wouldn't join in and support you?' he says.

We smile at each other and I start to realise that friends and allies really can pop up from the most unexpected places.

I take a look around the playground. It's packed. There are hundreds of people sitting down, right from Year Sevens all the way to Year Elevens. All of them just sitting there with us, protesting toxic masculinity, assault and upskirting. Some of them are holding up small placards. Just across from us are

Aimee and their friends, smiling, and supported by everyone sitting in this playground with them. I want to make sure that no one feels excluded, and that everyone knows that feminism's here for them. I don't want anyone to question whether or not they can be part of this like Aimee did. No one should be excluded from equality. I check to make sure that no one's looking unsure if they should be here or not.

Some people walking past ask why we're all sitting down, and as they find out, most of them sit down too. Which fills me with joy, and I'm choosing to believe that it's not just because they want to skip classes.

9 a.m.
FREEZING COLD

'Who are those people?' Millie points towards the gate as a group of people with cameras and phones held out advance towards us.

'Hey, Kat,' Jane shouts over at me. 'The press are here!'

'They're all press?' I ask.

'Yes! The *Post*, the *Evening News*, *News at Ten*, the *Telegraph*, *The Times* and the *Mail*. I went regional and national, I hope that was OK? But as soon as I started telling people what we were doing and what had happened so far, they saw the story. I think they thought a school head teacher ignoring girls saying that they were being groped and harassed was quite bad. Just like we did.'

I feel bad for not appreciating Jane at first. We're on the same team and I've learned a lot from her. And the amount of press she's got here RULES.

'ARE ALL THOSE PRESS?' Matt comes over with Nick to sit with us.

'Apparently so!' I say.

'Who's going to talk to them?' Nick asks.

'Kat, of course!' Jane says.

I stare directly at Jane, then at Matt and then back to Jane. I just thought a grown-up would do that? Someone capable? But I guess I DID organise this so maybe it's time to start believing *I'm* someone capable.

I'm distracted by more commotion. There's a far-off chanting coming from the alleyway by the back of the playground that's getting closer and closer. We're all straining to hear it at first and then it starts to become clearer.

Someone is chanting 'Safe education for our kids'. With a megaphone!

Finally, I see who it is as a huge group headed by my mum and dad come striding through the school gates. Behind them are Millie's parents, Sam's parents, Matt's mum with Dishy Derek, and a whole load of other parents that I recognise from my year and the other years. There are LOADS of them. How have they managed this? Shouldn't they be at work?

'Oh.'

'My.'

'Feminist.'

'Christ,' Sam, Millie, Matt and I say staring at the parents.

I feel such a rush of love and appreciation for my parents and all the others. Something about them joining us makes it feel so special. And there's the magic again – the magic that we shouldn't need, but it's here and it's how we'll beat this.

I wave over at them, and Dad gives me a little salute, his eyes glimmering mischievously.

Then out of the corner of my eye I see Mr Clarke rushing out of the main block. He looks red-faced and flustered as the cameras by the gate switch from filming us to filming him.

'WHAT ON EARTH DO YOU THINK YOU'RE DOING? GET TO CLASS!' he shouts above the noise, before rushing over to try and stop the cameras filming him. He's putting his hand out but there are too many of them.

Mum, Dad and the group of parents who've been slowly marching in our direction finally reach me and now Dad's handing me the megaphone he's been shouting into. He gives me a look and I stand and take it from him, trying to keep a steady hand, realising what I have to do. I see my friends smiling up at me, and I take a deep breath and hold my head up.

'We're not going to class until you agree to protect us from toxic masculinity,' I start, shocked by the confidence in my voice, spurred on by the faces of parents and friends around me, all nodding encouragingly. The cameras have moved back away from Mr Clarke and I know they're filming me now. I feel like I'm having an out-of-body experience and everything's a bit blurry and shaky, but I need to carry on. I know what I'm doing.

I've got this.

'Young people at this school are subject to a culture of toxic masculinity. They're being period shamed, slut shamed, groped in the hallways and judged for the way they look. They're having their photos taken against their will and posted online; then they're laughed at, outed, or rated one to ten on their attractiveness. The people that are doing this feel empowered to punch down and make a joke of other people to take their confidence away and keep them oppressed. They feel empowered to behave like this because the school is doing nothing. In fact, the school has blamed US, and tried to silence US.' I take another breath, feeling my fury rise, and try to keep my voice steady despite all the anger we've kept in for so long finally being released. 'We're not going to class until you agree to do something about it. Until you acknowledge the problem. Acknowledge that this school has a problem and agree to sit down with the school board and come up with a plan to ensure an equal and safe education for all young people at this school. If something happens, if someone gets groped or harassed or has photos posted of them online against their will, they should be able to report it, and know that there will be consequences. It's important. No one should feel they have to put up with behaviour like this or that they're unsafe at school, and no one should feel they're dealing with it alone. You have the power to do something about it and that needs to start now.'

And then I stop, and sit down again, my hands shaking. Clapping and cheers erupting all around me.

9.20 a.m.

Mr Clarke's storming back into the main block, trying to escape the cameras and parents shouting questions at him.

'What do you think he'll do?' Sam asks, moving aside to make room for the parents who've come to sit with us.

'Probably barricade himself in there and pretend nothing's happening like usual,' I say.

'He can't really do that,' says Millie's mum.

'It's true, if nothing else the parents are coming down on him now,' says Millie's dad, and I look over at Millie, realising that this is the first time her parents have been together in the same place since the separation.

'How did you both manage to get the time to come?' Millie asks as Issy and Freddie come over to sit with us too.

'Some things are more important than work, and when you have two daughters at a school that isn't taking them and their safety seriously, that gets priority over everything else. Even big lawsuits,' Millie's dad says.

'We're always here for our girls. Nothing changes that,' her mum says, and I see Millie and Issy share a smile.

'Excuse me, could we have a quick word?' I look up to see one of the journalists holding out a microphone. I guess I'm not going to get out of that one. I stand and head over to the others with her.

As I walk with her, I look out across the sea of people sitting all around the playground. There must be hundreds of people here.

At the side of the playground I see Miss Mills, who smiles at me and does a big thumbs up.

'We've got the school board on the phone,' the journalist's saying, pointing to someone chatting away on the phone. 'They said that they'd been assured there was no such problem when they tried to investigate before and they'd like to talk to you to find out more. Would you be able to talk to them after we've taken some pictures of you?'

Yes! I knew we could get the school board onside. They won't let it go with this much press behind it. For the first time I feel like I've made a real change, like things at this school won't go back to how they were before. And that's down to all of us, and the Feminist Society.

As the photographers take pictures of me, and I get ready to tell the school board everything, I feel very aware of my feminist beret. It feels perfect for these pictures, because for the first time I feel one hundred per cent sure that that's exactly what I am.

3 Positive Things:
1. We've done it, all of us in this playground together, we've started something, and now we can't be stopped.
2. I am finally one hundred per cent sure that I am a feminist.
3. I am not one hundred per cent sure of my sexuality, but I am OK with that. I will be whoever I am.

A Note on feminism

Feminism should always be about inclusivity. It's about equality, about supporting each other, lifting each other up and being an ally to those in need. There should be no space for hatred or intolerance in feminism. Kat would never accept it, and neither should you.

A Note on mental health

If you're struggling with some of the same things as Kat does, there's always someone to listen to you. No matter what you feel, you're never alone. Below are some people you can contact, anytime.

Samaritans
Confidential and emotional support for people who are experiencing feelings of distress and despair.
Call free on **116 123** to speak to a Samaritan or go to **www.samaritans.org**
Lines are open 24/7 and 365 days a year.

Mind
Offers advice and confidential support to anyone experiencing a mental health problem.
Call on **0300 123 3393** or find them at **www.mind.org.uk**
Helplines are open 9am–6pm on weekdays except for bank holidays.

Shout UK

Shout is a free, confidential, 24/7 text messaging support service for anyone who is struggling to cope.

Text **SHOUT** to **85258** or find them at **https://giveusashout.org**

Text any time for free, to talk with a trained volunteer who'll help you feel calmer.

Acknowledgements

I've learned a lot since writing the first book and that's mostly down to the people who read it and the amazing schools I visited. A huge thank you goes to the pupils and amazing librarians at Conyers, Framwell Gate, Cramlington Learning Village, Lancaster Girls' Grammar and The Green School. With you in the world, we're all headed for a better time.

This book wouldn't have been possible without the support and hard work of a huge amount of people. First thanks go to my brilliant editor Sarah Lambert who has always believed in and championed me and Kat, and Lily Morgan, for bringing my scrambled thoughts together in such an expert way. And a big thanks to Naomi Greenwood for getting me over the final hurdle and being an excellent editor for the 2021 stretch – you are a hero!

Thank you to the dream team at Hachette Children's Group who I am so grateful to work with: Emily Thomas, Hannah Bradridge, Beth McWilliams, Ruth Girmatsion, Michelle Brackenborough, Ruth Alltimes and Hilary Murray Hill. And to my wonderful agent Chloe Seager and all at Madeline Milburn. (Sorry for phoning you crying so often.) And Alice Sutherland-Hawes the original supporter and champion of me and Kat.

Thank you to my own Millies and Sams: Anna Fritz, Sarah Lavery-Clarke, Maria Farren, and Carolyn Roper, Abi Nightingale (always my best vagina), James Goodill, Victoria Goodall,

Victoria Daniels, Debora Robertson, Liz Vater, and Jo Adams. And to Mum, Dad, Jo, Paul, James, Viktor, Emma and Max.

Thank you to Lis Tribe (your belief in me will never be forgotten!), Stoke Newington Bookshop for the best party ever, and Tsam, Martha and Emma at Waterstones Newcastle (I'm coming back ASAP).

Thanks to H – my very own Sarah.

And finally, thank you to my new family, Angus and Nick. Thank you for your cups of tea, your reassuring paws, the laughter, and most of all thank you for loving me.

I am so very lucky. X